I'd Give Anything

A Novel

Marisa de los Santos

HARPER LARGE PRINT

An Imprint of HarperCollins*Publishers*

I'D GIVE ANYTHING. Copyright © 2020 by Marisa de los Santos. All rights reserved. Printed in the United States of America. No part of this book may be used or reproduced in any manner whatsoever without written permission except in the case of brief quotations embodied in critical articles and reviews. For information, address HarperCollins Publishers, 195 Broadway, New York, NY 10007.

HarperCollins books may be purchased for educational, business, or sales promotional use. For information, please e-mail the Special Markets Department at SPsales@harpercollins.com.

FIRST HARPER LARGE PRINT EDITION

ISBN: 978-0-06-284452-1

Library of Congress Cataloging-in-Publication Data is available upon request.

20 21 22 23 24 LSC 10 9 8 7 6 5 4 3 2 1

I'd Give Anything

LARGE
PRINT

For my friend
Dawn Manley,
who gives me joy and infinite kindness and Twizzlers
and who helps put all the pieces together

I'd Give Anything

Chapter One

June 30, 1997

You know those times when the person you are and the person you want to be are exactly—down to your smallest fingernail moon and flimsiest eyelash and your left knee and the part in your hair—the same person? (That fingernail moon is actually called a lunula, by the way, a fact I just learned but that I'm sure I'll still remember years from now when I'm wherever I am reading this journal because how could anyone forget a word like that, so pale and curved like a shell on a beach?)

Tonight was one of those times, and it's interesting because it could have easily turned out to be an ordinary night (although, for us, even ordinary is kind of great). We

go to the quarry a lot. We sit under pretty
skies a lot, not just at the quarry but other
places, too. The champagne was new, a first,
but I can't swear that it was the champagne
that actually tipped things from ordinary
to everything-in-the-right-place, all-of-us-
exactly-who-we-want-to-be splendid. I love the
word "splendid."

It was dark. Serious dark. Just an edge
of moon, like a little silver smile tipped
sideways; the sky sugared with stars. The
woods on the far bank weren't really woods but
just a big black ruffle, and the woods on our
side clanged with peepers or bugs or I don't
know what else, not deafeningly like in real
summer, but in that edge-of-spring way. In a
more minor, sleepier key.

We were all there: Kirsten, CJ, Gray, me.
The fantastic four. The *forever* four.

And Trev, too, a little ways away, sitting
with his back against a pine tree, smoking,
just a moving pinprick of orange and an outline
I'd know anywhere. I hate it when he smokes
because I really need him to live forever and
not get cancer, but if I ever told him to stop,
I'd sound like our mom, which is obviously

the worst, most traitorous thing I could do. Tonight, though, I didn't even want to. Trev just being there, his long, slow exhales, the smell of cigarette in the crisp air mixing with the other smells—dirt, pine needles, the metal smell of water—was comforting. Like Trevor was God, watching over us.

We sat on the ground, and even though I forgot and left the blanket back in the car, I swear the dirt under us wasn't hard at all. Gray leaning against a rock, me leaning against Gray, my back, his chest, long, scrawny me, and dense, strong, wide Gray. We passed around the bottle Trev stole from our mom's wine collection (and if I know Trevor, he'd tried to snag the most expensive one just to spite her), and divided among five, it didn't go far, but oh my God, *champagne*. Gold and silver at the same time, sharp and ice-cold and burning. Kirsten said to sip, but I said, "Screw that," and gulped and felt the sizzle light a path from my throat to my feet.

No wonder people drink champagne at celebrations. And here we were, my friends and I, with nothing to celebrate except for everything.

We talked the way we do: blizzards of words, everyone laughing and interrupting, followed by small silences, like soap bubbles floating. CJ told one of his long, random, fact-packed stories, which started with how some kids stole his shorts out of his gym locker (again) and tacked them up on the science bulletin board (again), and ended—by some CJ logic—in a mini-lecture about water-resistant lotus plant leaves, and it was the easiest thing in the world to be the way we were: just voices, gleams of teeth, eyes, Kirsten's white sweatshirt, her weird caw of a laugh cracking the overhanging quiet. And, it hit me so hard how, oh my God, I love these people, and all at once, I realized we had to do something to honor the, I don't know, *completeness* of everything. The everything of everything, as if two hours could contain every single good, pure, fun, gorgeous thing the world had to offer.

I gave the back of Gray's hand a hard kiss and disentangled and stood up.

"Okay, we're jumping!" I said.

"Hell, no," drawled Kirsten.

"Hell, yes," I said. "It's already been decided."

"Not by me," said Kirsten.

"Not by me, either," I said. "I'm just the messenger. It's been *decided*."

Gray laughed, and, oh, but my boy's laugh is better than champagne. It's like a cross between a guitar strum and hot toast with butter and honey. "Too cold," he said.

Even though it was a little chilly for a June night, I said, "It's *summer*!"

"Too dark, too," said Kirsten, shuddering. "How do we know for sure that the water's even down there? Maybe someone moved it. Maybe it's full of sharks."

"You never know! CJ," I said, pointing at him, "you jump with me."

"It's not like I'm terrified or anything," said CJ, scooting backward away from me. "It's not like I have a primal fear of dark water. Or of jumping into the void. I mean it's the same water as always, right?"

"Of course it's not," I scoffed. "The whole point is that it's different! The whole point is jumping into the void."

"You," said Gray, shaking his head and reaching for me. "Come back and sit with me, crazy Zinny."

But I was already taking off my clothes, stripping down to my bra and underwear.

"It'll be magnificent, dumbasses," I told them. I love the word "magnificent."

I walked to the edge, to the same spot we'd all jumped from—even, once and only once, CJ, under duress and holding his nose, his eyes squeezed shut—in the daylight. I closed my eyes for a few seconds and held out my arms, the cool air making all the hair on them rise. Standing there, I could feel not only the air, but also the stars in the sky, the entire Milky Way swirling on my skin and blazing down my spine and fizzing like champagne through my veins.

I tossed back my head and sang, "O, holy night, the stars were brightly shining," even though I can't really sing and it was nowhere near Christmas.

The bugs went still. They actually did.

And then I heard Trevor say, "Wait, Zin," and there he was, my brother, grinning like a devil in his boxers and his T-shirt, in his splendor and magnificence. And we locked our hands together, Trev and I, and we jumped.

Chapter Two

GINNY

Here's what I learned on that Thursday afternoon in the produce section of Devonshire Market: sometimes, your hands can be wiser than you are; sometimes, they can sit there on the ends of your arms just like always, and comprehend truths that your mind hasn't yet comprehended. Truths like: Ginny Beale, life as you know it just ended.

I don't recommend it: having life as you know it end in Devonshire Market. Particularly not in Devonshire Market on a busy autumn afternoon when you're wearing a brand-new cream-colored Patagonia fleece and holding two tomatoes, one in each hand. The tomatoes were heirlooms, the left one a piebald purple and jade, the right one striped like a palm-size watermelon, both prizefighter-battered and lumpily picturesque in a way that screamed eight dollars a pound. And if life as you know it *must* end like this—Devonshire Market, fleece, heirlooms—be sure you're not engaged in conversation (*the* conversation, the one that ends life as you know it) with a man dangling an actual woven, double-handled marketing basket from the crook of his arm like Little Red Riding Hood.

That's what everyone called it (and by "everyone" I mean, of course, we who possessed the willingness to buy tomatoes priced at eight dollars a pound): Devonshire Market, no *the*, and if that sounds vaguely British to you ("at university," "in hospital"), I'm pretty sure it was meant to. The market was not located in a town named Devonshire; there was no town named that within a thousand-mile radius, possibly within ten thousand, possibly within the entire New World. Instead, the market was, as Jeb, the son of the owner once told me, named after clotted cream, the kind that comes in a jar.

The man was Dirk Holofcener-Sharf, the husband of my husband Harris's coworker and my sort-of friend Elise Holofcener-Sharf. Dirk had a long, melancholy face like an old-time crooner, wore white bucks without socks, and was either brilliant or a social maladroit, depending on who you asked, reputations that seemed to derive mainly from the socklessness, but also from the fact that Dirk wrote film reviews for the local paper and displayed a marked unwillingness—or an inability, depending on who you asked—to make small talk.

To me, Dirk just seemed shy. On the rare occasions when I'd seen him at cocktail or dinner parties, he was always aslant, propped up against something—a wall, a tree, a piece of furniture—his face telegraphing a naked, if unlikely, combination of boredom and trepidation, a "how did I get here and when can I leave?" look. Unlikely to some people, I guess I mean, but not to me. I recognized that expression, having scrupulously kept it off my own face on similar occasions for most of two decades. Every time I saw Dirk like that, I would wish he and I could give each other a sign, a secret code word deposited directly into each other's mind, maybe, a glimpse of matching cryptic tattoos, or our two hands lifted, colored light beams visible only to us shooting from our palms to meet across the party, anything to say, "We come from the same planet, and one day, we will go back."

So when I saw him, just feet away from me in the produce section, I felt a rush of kindred-spirit spirit, and I paused for a few seconds to observe. Dirk held his phone to his ear with one hand and appraised tomatillos with the other, lifting each one, first to his nose, then to eye level, rotating it gently, fingering the papery husk, placing it either back onto the pile or into his basket. Once, twice, again. It was a ceremony, a dance. Then, as I watched, the dance halted. Dirk's hand froze, arrested mid-pirouette, his mouth forming words I couldn't hear. Slowly, Dirk took his phone from his ear, gazed at it mournfully, shook his head, slipped the phone into his jacket pocket, looked up, and saw me.

And in one white-hot instant, the world went raw and primitive. Dirk changed from a sad-eyed man with a marketing basket to a frightened animal. Flared nostrils; wide, panic-twitchy eyes; stark neck cords; lips pulling back from his teeth. If a creature standing on two legs to begin with could be said to rear, Dirk reared. Dirk was the horse, and I was the rattlesnake, right there in Devonshire Market. And, yes, I am exaggerating, but not nearly as much as you might think.

I said, "Dirk, are you all right?"

If he had turned around and run out the door with his basket full of tomatillos and who knew what other unpaid-for items, it would have surprised me less than what he did do, which was to take two halting steps toward me and blurt out, "I'm so sorry about Harris."

I said, "Look, can I get you a glass of water or something?"

Dirk squeezed his eyes shut, took the same hand that

had been so gently touching the tomatillos, and used it to slap himself on the forehead, repeatedly.

"Shit," he said. "Shit, shit."

"Hey," I said. "Stop that."

He stopped and opened his blue eyes, and I waited to see what disconcerting thing Dirk Holofcener-Sharf would do next in the middle of Devonshire Market.

He sighed. "You don't know. About Harris."

"Oh, I'm sure I do," I said, because if there was one thing I did know, it was everything about Harris.

"He was fired, Ginny," said Dirk.

The statement was so obviously incorrect, so clearly a product of Dirk's sudden cardiac event or bout of brain fever or whatever I'd just witnessed, that my heart didn't so much as flutter.

"And I should not be the one to tell you this, but since I already blew that, I think you should know: there seems to be some kind of scandal happening."

Scandal.

I smiled at Dirk. "You're saying that my husband, Harris, was fired from his job because of a scandal?"

"Yes," said Dirk, nodding. "I'm sorry you had to find out like this."

I laughed. "Dirk, honey, have you met Harris?"

Dirk blinked. "Well, yeah. You know I have."

"So you know that he is the embodiment of everything scandal is not. He's the opposite of scandal. He is competence, reliability, upstandingness, if that's a word."

"I don't think it is."

"If it weren't a word before, it just now needed to be invented to describe my husband. To be used in a description of my husband, I guess I mean, since upstandingness is a noun, not an adjective."

I wasn't babbling. On the contrary, my brain was in such a state of imperturbability that I could make fine grammatical distinctions without skipping a beat. Also, in the face of Dirk's wildly inaccurate information and misplaced sympathy, which, kindred spiritedness notwithstanding, were starting to annoy me, I felt the need to be extra-correct, if correctness is something that can have degrees.

Dirk's shoulders drooped. "Okay. I'm sorry I told you he got fired. I just found out and saw you and got flustered."

Dirk doubling down on his misinformation doubled my annoyance.

"Listen. Whatever you think you found out? You didn't," I explained, slowly, patiently. "Because I have been married to Harris McCue for sixteen years, and *Harris* is the *opposite* of fired. Is, was, will always be."

"Okay," said Dirk, drooping. "Fine. You're probably right. I'll see you later."

Just before he turned away, I said, "You know, Dirk, you might want to rethink the marketing basket."

It was a cheap, mean-girl shot, but right then, my annoyance at Dirk was so great that not only did I shoot, but his subsequent wince and the hurt in his eyes rolled off me like water droplets off a lotus leaf.

But then, Dirk said, "Really? Is it weird? It just seemed—practical," and his tone as he stared down at the basket was so doleful that I felt instantly terrible: cruel and petty and two inches high.

I sighed. "I'm sorry. It *is* practical and very environmentally friendly. I absolutely should not have said that."

"No," said Dirk, smiling a heartbreak of a smile at me. "I'm bad at knowing what's weird. I have a broken weird meter, I think. So thanks."

He left then, turned and shuffled out of Produce and toward the shining glass display cases of Cheese, dropping unhappy glances at his basket every few steps.

I watched until Dirk was out of sight, and only then did I look down and notice my hands. While the rest of me had been busy being cool and unruffled, my hands had been and were still undergoing what I can only describe as a miniature seismic event. I barely recognized them: racked with tremors, rigid as talons, gripping the tomatoes so hard that my nails dug in, and with wonder and horror, as I stared, I watched my right thumbnail pop clean through the fragile flesh, a puncture wound that bled a rivulet of pinkish juice down my hand to stain my new, cream-colored cuff.

Somehow, I pried my fingers from the bruised fruit, abandoning it and my shopping cart, got myself to my car, and called Harris.

He answered the phone like this: "Oh."

"Oh?"

"I meant hi. Hi. Hello."

I shut my eyes.

"I just had the oddest conversation with Elise's husband at the market," I said.

Nothing from Harris. Not even breathing. It was as if that one sentence had opened a sinkhole of silence between us, and as it yawned wider, I could almost see life as we knew it tumbling in. Our mailbox. Our flagstone retaining wall. Our rose plants and firepit. The whole set of jadeite dishes Harris's mother had given us as a wedding gift—milky green plates Frisbeeing into the void. Our books opening, birdlike. Harris's precious green ceramic egg-shaped grill plummeting like a bomb. And then Avery, Avery, Avery, swan-diving, toes pointed, chestnut ponytail flying.

Avery? No. Oh no. Hell, no. Never, ever, ever Avery. My hands stopped shaking at the thought. Whatever Harris had done, no matter how scandalous, it would not touch a hair on Avery's head.

Then, Harris said—and I know that there can be degrees of empty because his was the emptiest voice I had ever heard—Harris said, "It wasn't an affair."

It was only later that night that I wondered what else they'd known, those canny hands of mine. About the girl, eighteen years old? About the months of emails and texts, thick and furious and all skirting the edge, the very, very thin edge of sordid? Did they know the exact shade of blond? The depth of my husband's flattered foolishness? The precise angle and rate at which he fell from grace? I wondered if my hands held inside them, even then, as I sat inside the fogging windows of my car in the parking lot of Devonshire Market, the word that Harris and I would never use but that his boss had sicced on Harris just that morning and would again, his boss and probably everyone else we knew, a long, thin, hissing snake of a word: *obsession.*

Her name was Cressida Wall, a striking name for anyone, but particularly for a high school senior, although I didn't know when I heard her name that Cressida

Wall was still in high school, since it wasn't until later in our conversation that Harris coughed up her age. Until that point, he had called her "a woman from work." I didn't even immediately absorb how striking a name Cressida Wall was because the noteworthiness of the name paled in comparison to the noteworthiness of Harris's tone when he spoke it to me for the first time. As we sat in our yard, at one end of the long teak dining table that we'd bought last summer, each ensconced in our own beautiful black-and-white rattan French bistro chair, my forty-five-year-old pharmaceutical company vice president husband said, "I was having a business lunch at the Vedge Table with this woman from work when Dale Pinckney spotted us and misconstrued what he was seeing." He paused. "Her name is Cressida Wall."

Just like that. All by itself. Present tense. Not casually folded into the first sentence, "This woman from work, Cressida Wall," but delivered in the form of an announcement. Except that announcements are meant for the people listening, and when Harris said the girl's name, his gaze went shuttered and inward; his voice turned private and deliberate. He sat there in our yard, with our southern magnolia and almost-bare sugar maple (the few unraked leaves like red handprints on the grass) and the raised flower beds full of loam (once chocolaty, now chalky) and the rows of hydrangeas (faded to magenta and rust) along the fence, sat there with all those carefully tended pieces of our life—our life and Avery's life—bearing witness, and he didn't so much speak the syllables of the girl's name as light each one like a candle: Cres, Sid, Ah, Wall.

"Dale Pinckney is an idiot," I said.

Harris looked down at his big square hands, which were pressed together, prayer-fashion, on the tabletop. "He thought we were holding hands across the table."

When Harris said this, he shifted his hands so that the fingers interlocked.

Oh, Harris, for the love of God.

"But he was wrong," I prompted.

Harris looked at me, as if he'd forgotten I was there.

"Oh. Well, yes. I mean no. We were holding hands, I guess, but—"

"Momentarily?"

"Yes. Momentarily. At the moment that Dale saw us."

"Like an encouraging squeeze," I supplied.

Harris nodded, uncertainly.

"Because she works for you, right? And she's been doing a good job."

Harris's eyes lit up. "Ah, yeah, a hell of a job! Cressida has been doing great work, really exceptional work.

She's gifted in a way that you just don't see very often, with a real instinct for marketing. Normally, we don't keep interns on after the summer ends, but she is so remarkable that I took a special interest."

Really, Harris, did you? Because I never would've guessed.

"You mentored her," I said, encouragingly. "That's so like you."

Harris smiled down at his interlocked hands.

It was only then that I realized what he'd said.

"Did you say 'intern'?" I asked. My heart broke into a gallop. Silently, I told my hands that if they began shaking again, I would have them surgically removed at the first opportunity.

Harris's smile switched off, and his eyes met mine.

"You're saying that this Wall person is a college student? Because it seems to me that you just called her a woman."

Always prone to dry-mouth, particularly in times of stress, Harris swallowed. "Our interns must be at least eighteen," he said.

"So you called her a woman because, being over eighteen, she is technically an adult?"

"Cressida *is* an adult!" When he said this, Harris's voice got louder; his cheeks reddened.

"An adult who is actually a college kid," I said.

Harris's face had always been the sort that changes color quickly, like a mood ring. It was one of the many reasons he was a terrible liar and poker player. Now, in an instant, he paled.

"A high school senior," he said. "But old for her grade."

I dropped my face into my hands. "Oh, Harris."

"We usually hire college kids, but we made an exception."

"Let me guess," I said, from inside my hands. "Because she was so exceptional."

"She was."

I slapped my hands down on the table. "Our daughter is fifteen years old."

Harris winced, as if I'd hit him instead of the table.

"I know," he said.

"Oh God, she might even know this girl."

"Ginny."

"Please tell me she doesn't go to Lucretia Mott. Just tell me that."

"Jesus, of course not. You think I would do that?"

"Do what, Harris? What thing did you do with this girl that you would, of course, never have done were she a student at our daughter's school?"

"Nothing," he said. "I did nothing with this girl."

"Could you manage to keep the regret out of your tone when you say that? Could you do me that courtesy?"

"Nothing happened, Ginny."

"Well, since you were *fired*, Harris, sacked, kicked to the curb, clearly *something* happened."

"You don't have to be mean, you know," said Harris.

Because I couldn't trust my newly untrustworthy hands not to grab him by the throat, I got up from my chair and took a walk around the yard.

It was November. Everything was cut back, tied up, put away, spent. The Adirondack chairs stacked in the storage shed with the hanging pots and their wrought-iron hooks. The gazebo bird feeder we'd bought at an Amish store in Lancaster and the two blue blown-glass teardrop hummingbird feeders, all carefully wrapped and stowed in the basement. Little marble birdbath empty of water. Bushes and trees and planters empty of blooms. But under the limestone-colored sky, there was grace in my sleeping garden. Harmony. Quietude. I tried to let it embrace me the way it sometimes did in the early mornings when I sat out there with my coffee and my dogs and watched the apricot light fill the tree branches. Now, peace didn't really come, but something else did—or began to—shyly sending out a few delicate tendrils: tenderness, not so much for my husband as for the garden, the unsuspecting burlap-covered rose plants and dormant flower beds, the fence with its hopeful row of shiny copper fence post caps, the whole life we'd made. The twin tornadoes that had earlier begun to rage inside my head and stomach slowed their writhing.

I walked back to the table where Harris sat, his hands fidgeting, his big shoulders bowed, his square jaw shifting in the manner of a child who is trying not to cry. I sat down.

"It wasn't an affair," he said, without looking up. "I wouldn't do that, especially not with a woman of that age."

"Just tell me," I said.

"I let it get too personal. I won't deny that. I got overly invested I guess you could say. And I knew how it could look to other people if they found out. So I tried to keep that from happening. I did some very stupid things."

"Just," I said.

I stopped to take a deep breath, in through the nose, out through the mouth, a cleansing breath I guess it was, although nothing really felt cleaner afterward.

"Tell me."

We were a full thirty minutes into—which turned out to be approximately two-thirds of the way through—

the conversation that followed before I understood that Harris had not gotten fired because of the thing (the nothing) that had happened with Cressida Wall, eighteen years old. Instead, his boss, Paul Jones, had fired him because of the "very stupid things" he had done to try to hide the nothing that had happened with Cressida, to try to keep the meddling and misconstruing Dale Pinckney from reporting the momentary hand-squeeze he had witnessed in the Vedge Table, a chase you'd think Harris might have cut to more quickly, particularly since the "very stupid things" were not only stupid but also, possibly, illegal. But for the first thirty minutes, all I heard about was Cressida.

He said this:

"To be honest, I forget Cressida's age most of the time, and maybe that's irresponsible, but, in my own defense, I'm not the only one in the office that happens to. I couldn't be. Cressida is more mature and self-possessed than women twice her age. And smart, insightful. She would start talking, and you'd just think, 'Wow, that makes so much sense.' Not, 'That makes so much sense for a high school student,' but for anyone. And her face; it has adult bone structure, undeniably adult. And her eyes. Her eyes, too."

And this:

"HR read our emails, as part of their investigation. They seemed surprised that I hadn't deleted them, but why should I have? They're mine. And, hell, you can read the emails, Ginny. There's nothing inappropriate, not a single sentence that crosses a line. I'll grant that the sheer number looks bad. We sent each other a lot of emails, sometimes in the middle of the night, as Paul pointed out. But they were completely innocent. And it wasn't like I was flooding her inbox. She answered all of them. Every single one. You can check."

And also, this:

"Paul tried to paint it as if I'd pursued her, but I didn't. If anything, *she* chose *me*."

Half an hour of this: my trying to ignore the impossible-to-ignore notes of pride in his voice, Harris's enthusiasm for the girl leaking out from the tight container I tried to make hold our conversation. Whenever I saw an opening, I mentally jumped in with edits to his story, replacing words, adding modifiers or dependent clauses, the grammar of ambiguity: "innocent" became "professional," "investigation" became "routine inquiry," "wrote each other a lot of emails" became "corresponded fairly frequently," "in the middle of the night" became "after typical business hours."

I couldn't do a thing with the part about her bone structure and her eyes, except to cut him off before he went below the neck.

"So the HR department did its due diligence by Dale's ridiculous accusation and found nothing, since there was obviously nothing to find," I said. "And still Paul fired you to—what? Nip rumors in the bud? That sounds sketchy to me. I think we should consult a lawyer."

Harris flushed and shook his head.

"When Dale approached me and threatened to go to Paul, I panicked."

"Rattled," I said. "You got rattled, as anyone might. Because his take on the matter was so far off the mark."

"Yes, that's right. And on an impulse, just completely off the cuff, I offered to give him a bit of information."

My mouth took a page from Harris's book and went dry.

"Nothing really earth-shattering, but something that was still, at that time, insider information. About a new chemotherapy drug."

I flinched first at the word *chemotherapy* and then, retroactively, *insider*.

"Unreleased," I said. "As yet unreleased information."

As if the information were an extra track on a Beyoncé record, as if my husband hadn't been prepared to silence his accuser with the offer of making money off the suffering of cancer patients.

Then, I said, "Oh, Harris."

When his eyes met mine, they were full of tears. "I'm sorry, Ginny. Not for my relationship with Cressida because that was—"

"Professional. Aboveboard. As HR's inquiry bore out."

"But I was worried how it would look. There are so many people who are ready to believe the worst. I was concerned that Paul would force this productive relationship we'd built, this beneficial mentor-mentee type of relationship, to end just because of the way it might look to suspicious minds. He might even have fired Cressida."

Yes, I wanted to manage this mischief with a vengeance, to piece together a narrative, with a shiny pieced-together Harris at its center, that would bring my daughter the least amount of pain. And I needed Harris to believe in that narrative. But, oh my Lord, there are limits, and when Harris said what he'd just said, I snapped. I jumped up, knocking my beautiful café chair onto our beautiful Bermuda grass lawn.

"Do you hear yourself, Harris?"

If I live to be a hundred, I might be able to forgive Harris the look of utter blankness that followed my outburst, the look that said, "I do hear myself, and I have no idea what you're upset about," but probably not. Almost definitely not.

"You did this thing that got you fired, that could even get you thrown in jail, that could send the rosebushes and the plates from your mother and your cherished green egg all catapulting into a giant black screaming hole, all to protect that girl? To *keep her with you?*"

Harris was an intelligent man. He had never been stupid, but he'd also never been quick. Now, I watched my words work their way first through Harris's usual slow, steady collection of cogs and wheels (no doubt slowed down further by my gratuitous plummeting plates, et cetera imagery) and then crack through the mantle of his breathless fixation on Cressida before hitting his consciousness. His eyes woke up. His jaw dropped a centimeter. Fever pink flooded his cheeks.

"I just meant—"

I reached out and gripped his jacket sleeve.

"Listen to me. Let. Go. Of. Cressida."

"But I never—"

I yanked at his sleeve.

"Okay. Fine. You never. We'll go with that. But what did or didn't happen doesn't matter. *She* doesn't matter. And by that I mean, the girl, what you did, all of it just stopped being material. Just stopped *being*. Do you understand that?"

"I don't know what you mean."

"I mean Avery."

"What? You know I would never hurt Avery."

Suddenly, I felt tired, weary to my bone marrow and the tiny veins in my eyes. My hair felt tired. I let go of Harris's sleeve, righted my chair, sat, and leaned my tired cheek against my tired palm.

"Maybe you wouldn't. But you did." I turned my free hand in a weary circle in the air. "This world. We made it for her and let her be safe inside it."

"She's still safe. This has nothing to do with her."

I wanted to wind myself up in burlap and sleep alongside the rosebushes.

"She's a teenager in the age of social media, in a town where everyone knows everything," I said.

I watched Harris absorb this. His eyes filled with tears, again; the tears spilled over. This man who had spent a lifetime keeping his emotions stowed away, hidden from almost everyone, especially himself, had suddenly experienced every one of them in the course of a day that wasn't even over yet. Harris crying. Harris crying knocked the meanness right out of me. Still, I had to finish explaining, to make him understand what was at stake.

"But even if she didn't know what other people thought," I said, gently, "or even if she were the single fifteen-year-old in the history of the universe who didn't care what people thought, she would still have to reckon with you."

"Me." It wasn't a question. Harris wiped his face with the backs of both hands. I waited. "Because I did something dishonest, offering Dale the unreleased information. And I'm not who she thought I was."

Oh, my friend. The dishonesty is the least of it. For Avery, compared to the eighteen-year-old girl, the dishonesty will weigh exactly nothing.

Harris stared out into the yard, through which twilight had wound like a cat, smudging its edges, turning everything to shades of gray: blue smoke and dove and charcoal and ash. I looked, too, and Harris and I sat there together, our faces turned in the same direction and egg-pale in the dim light. *If only we could turn back the clock,* I thought and shivered. I tugged my jacket sleeves over my hands and tried to will late summer into the yard, fireflies like glitter in the hydrangeas, fragrance of rose and honeysuckle tingeing the evening air with the sweetest kind of ache.

"Maybe I'll put in a pond," said Harris, quietly. "A little one. Back in that blank spot between the two biggest trees. Put some of those big goldfish in it. And some underwater ferns or whatever they eat."

I searched for the word and found it, clear and pretty, a single syllable, amber like a drop of honey.

"*Koi,*" I said.

I imagined that Harris was imagining it, too: the impossible brightness, the ribbony swimming, the whole pond shining like a newly minted penny dropped into our yard.

As if there were forgiveness in sunlight glancing off the backs of fish, hope in the color orange, magic in a pretty word. As if the addition of one more beautiful thing to our beautiful lives could save us.

Chapter Three

March 20, 1997

This is how I'll tell this story to our children, mine and Gray's: "Your mother fell in love with your father on the first day of spring."

Beautiful. Beautiful, right?

Although, I have to say I also like the phrase "vernal equinox," since it seems to connect our love with the orbit of the Earth, which strikes me as totally accurate. Picture the exact center of the sun directly above where we sat on that stone wall that runs like a seam through Brandywine Creek State Park, stitching wild meadow to green grass field. Picture that sun's clean spring light catching in our eyelashes and hair and goldening all our edges. If I just invented the word "goldening," it's because I needed it. Maybe that's how all words are invented: something new to the universe happens, and you have to christen it.

I fell in love in broad daylight. I fell in love in a crowd of people, with kites adorning the sky over our heads. One kite was shaped like a monarch butterfly, black and pumpkin-orange winging through the blue. One kite had rainbow streamers. One was diamond shaped and yellow with a crisscross and little red ponytail bows all down the tail, exactly like a kite in a picture book. I'll tell our kids that, how the sky was full of pretty things held there by wind, how the sky was blue-iris blue.

CJ sat on the other side of Gray. Kirsten sat on the other side of me. Gray and I were in the middle, where we belonged.

I remember everything. I remember the exact moment.

In one hand, I held a thermos lid of hot chocolate. In my other hand, I held my long hair, twisted, to keep it from blowing into my face while I drank. My hands were cold.

"My hands are getting frostbite," I said.

"Hardly," said CJ. "It's forty-eight degrees out."

Kirsten leaned forward to glare across me and Gray at CJ.

"You can't know that. You think that if you say 'forty-eight' instead of 'fifty,' we'll all think you know. But you don't."

"You don't know it's not forty-eight," observed CJ.

"What about wind chill? Does that forty-eight include wind chill?"

"Wind chill is crap."

"Wind chill is not crap," said Kirsten. "Every person who has ever been in wind knows that."

"Wind chill is based on human perception, which varies, obviously. There is no universally accepted standard of measurement. It's crap."

"Do you have gloves?" said Gray.

"In my pockets," I said.

Gray reached over, put his hand over mine, the one holding my hank of hair. Gray held on to my hair, wound it once around his hand, and I looked at his face. I'd seen that face

a million times. I'd never seen that face
before. I didn't stop looking at him as I
slid my hand out from under his and wrangled
my right glove from my pocket. I didn't stop
looking when he reached out and with enormous
carefulness, took my cup of hot chocolate. I
did stop when I put my gloves on because my
hands were suddenly confused and fumbling, and
I couldn't find my thumbholes. But by then it
had already happened.

It wasn't the fact that he did something
nice for me. Because in the two and a half
years we four had been friends, ever since
the start of ninth grade, Gray had always
done nice things, done them just like he did
with my hair: automatically. It wasn't even
that he touched my hand, because he had to
have done that before. All I know is that
there it was: love. Love in the sunlight, in
the colors of the kites, in Gray's deep-set
brown eyes, in the fuzziness of my gloves,
and shining right out of Gray's hands as
they reached toward me, first one, then the
other. And more than anywhere else, inside
of me, like I was made of it. Love right
down to my mitochondria.

I didn't say it out loud or ask Gray if he
felt it, too. I just said, "Thanks, Gray," and
his name was a sweetness in my mouth, and I took
back my hot chocolate and my twist of hair.

That night, though, I got out my craft box
and made boats out of heavy, shiny paper,
shades of blue and purple. I made tiny
white origami swans, folding and creasing
as perfectly as I had ever done anything,
and I made little white snowflakes with my
smallest, sharpest scissors. Then the next
night, I threaded them onto fishing line:
swan, flake, swan, flake, swan, flake, with
knots in between and a knot at the end, until
I had eight strings full of paper birds and
snow. And then, last night, I got a long piece
of grosgrain ribbon and cut holes all along
it and then looped each piece of fishing line
through, one through each hole, so that when
I stood up from my desk chair and held up the
long ribbon by its ends, the eight strings
dangled and danced and made a kind of swan/
flake curtain, all white.

Maybe an hour before sunrise, I put the
swans and boats and a roll of duct tape into
a cardboard box and sneaked out my back door

and drove to Gray's house. When I got out of
my car, I stood for a minute in the cold air,
looking at the house and imagining Gray inside
it, inside his room, inside his bed, and the
thought of him—out of all the people in the
world—tucked into his own personal space of
sleep, that Gray-shaped alcove in the universe
that was a secret from everyone but him, made
me feel so protective, like I'd kill anyone
who ever tried to hurt him.

Then, I went to the back of the house and
found the big kitchen window that overlooks
his backyard. I stood on the sill and taped
the ribbon to the top of the window frame.
When I jumped down and looked, even in the
dark, the swans and snowflakes twirled and
gleamed. I placed the boats, one by one, in
the pond Gray's dad had made in the backyard.
They looked brave and quiet floating there.
I didn't see any, but I hoped there were fish
flickering just under the surface, gazing up
with their round eyes, wondering.

He will probably guess that I did it.
Someday soon, I'll probably tell him. I'm
almost positive he's going to love me back. But
right now, sitting here at my window writing

this, with the sky turning flamingo-colored over my yard, all that matters is that I gave him something beautiful.

Maybe he's awake. Maybe he's seeing it right now.

March 24, 1997

Today, I opened my locker, and there, riding atop the slick ocean of my AP Bio book, was one of the boats I'd made, a purple one, a little misshapen from getting wet in the pond and then drying out, but still looking basically like a boat. And inside were two cutout figures, like paper dolls, a boy one with crayoned dark brown hair and eyes and a girl one with light brown hair and eyes. They weren't great works of art or anything, but it didn't matter. They were us. They were holding hands.

April 21, 1997

We talk every night. The next morning, I remember sentences from the night before and play them over and over inside my head. I tell myself I will never forget them, and I haven't yet, but if we are going to be together forever—which we are—I figure I should write them down for safekeeping. That way, when I get old, Gray and I can sit on a porch swing or something and read them and reach back and gather up the sound of our voices, soft in the dark. Gray's voice is low and deep and dove-gray like his name and feathered around the edges. Catch that and hold on: the dark room, our voices the only thing in the entire universe.

Here are some things we said. We have never said any of these things to anyone else.

This:

Gray: "I thought I'd get used to missing my mom. But she died nine years ago and it turns out there are always new things I want her to be here for, so I miss her in new ways all the time. Like you. Just this week, I missed her in six different ways, just because of you."

Gray: "You're the only person I know who is never afraid of anything."

Me: "But I am. I'm afraid of being ordinary."

Gray: "Never gonna happen."

Me: "It might."

Gray: "Nope. No way."

Me: "What if you help? What if every time I start to be ordinary, you pull me back. Do you think you can do that?"

Gray: "You won't need me to. But if you do, it'll be easy. I'll just remind you that you're Zinny Beale, love of my life."

This:

Me: "For me, personally, I think the only right thing to do is put new things into the world. Things no one has ever thought of before. Like writing and art. I feel like there are all these unmade things inside my head, waiting for me to let them loose into the world. A whole galaxy of unmade things, so bright it hurts."

This:

Gray: "I love my dad. But it's like he doesn't know me. I feel like he sees me in snapshots: on the football field, being a good student. But he doesn't see the big-picture me. I know this sounds weird, but I think I see myself that way, too. Like I'm an outside person watching me do things. Except when I'm with you. Then, I'm on the inside."

Chapter Four

GINNY

When my brother, Trevor, and I needed to escape our house, which was often, we would wait until our mother was in bed, sneak out the back door, and ride our bikes to the Quaker burial ground. I don't exactly know why we'd chosen that spot; I don't even remember deciding on it. It seemed to me that as soon as Trevor headed for it, that first time, in the serpentine way he liked to ride and that I liked to imitate, I knew where he was going. We had both been on field trips there to see the graves of the local abolitionist hero and of the signer of the Constitution, and to stand on the wide brown floorboards in the square, restrained space of the Friends Meeting House to hear about the Underground Railroad. So maybe it was the association with freedom that drew us, although I'm relieved to say that self-absorbed and aggrieved as we were, even we didn't put our suffering on par with that of actual enslaved people.

What I mostly remember about the place is how *ours* it was. The headstones small and rectangular, like molars, rising just above the grass line; the oaks and maples, huge and breathing all around; the imperturbable Meeting House standing quietly by. Trevor and I would sprawl on the grass where the graves were gathered like friends and look up at the sky or into the thick crochet-work of branches. We didn't always talk. Often, we would just lie there, letting our anger dissipate into the trees or be carried away by the looping whine of a distant siren. We listened to the city, which was all around but felt far away, all the while knowing that if we did want to talk, in that place, we could say anything, voice thoughts we would never have spoken anywhere else and that we would never, in the outside world, mention again. Later, in high school, when I was assigned the book *A Separate Peace*, the title sent my mind straight to that graveyard. It was our island, our snow globe, our tiny piece of peace. After Trevor had his final apocalyptic fight with our mother and left our house, I never went back there. That little bit of preciousness got lost along with everything else—the tiniest, innermost grief in my Russian nesting doll of grief—and I believed I would spend the rest of my life missing it.

And then, six months ago, on a very early May morning, not long after we'd gotten Dobbsy and Walt, I discovered the dog park. I'd known it was there, of course, a big green splotch in the middle of a woodsy city park not a mile from our house, but I discovered it all the same. When I stepped out of my car and stood on the dewy grass, under a sky of pink and gas-flame blue and floating gold, surrounded by a snowfall-quality hush, I felt like Henry Hudson, blinking at the dazzle of the bay. I recognized where I was: in a completely new world and also home. On that first day, a Tuesday, there were just two other early risers, a very short, not-thin woman and a very tall, thin man. Mag and Daniel. Owners of Dinah the Lab and Mose the golden, respectively. Within a week of mornings, we were friends, our dogs were friends, and the dog park was my new—*our* new, although probably they'd never had an old one—Quaker burial ground.

Which is maybe why, fewer than forty-eight hours after Harris knocked the legs out from under our family life, when Daniel smiled and said, "Hey, we missed you yesterday morning," I blurted out, "Harris got fired," and I put my hands over my face and started to cry, audibly. So audibly that, in an instant,

Dobbsy and Walt were loping across the grass—and if you think that tiny short-legged dogs can't lope, you're wrong—to rest their front paws on my shins, one dog per shin, and Mag's muscular arm was gripping my quaking shoulders.

"Ugh," said Mag. "Fired?"

"Spectacularly," I said, bitterly. "A big, splashy fireworks firing. With a scandal and attempted bribery and God knows what else."

"Shit," said Mag.

"And there was a thing," I wailed, "with a girl!"

"Shit again," said Mag.

"Not sex. At least, not sex *yet*, but a thing, a fixation-type thing, and she was way too young." Even there, in the dog park, I wasn't ready to say just how young.

Still crying, I dropped my hands from my face, wiped them on my jeans, and looked bleakly from Mag to Daniel.

"And I have to tell Avery."

"Aw, shit, shit, shit," said Mag.

Daniel didn't say a word but walked over to me on his very long legs, bent down, picked up Walt, and put him into my arms. Walt stared at me with the kindest concern I'd ever seen on anyone's face and then began to rub the side of his head against my cheek. Standing there with the warm weight of Walt, with his silky fur buffing my skin and his adorable skull bumping against my cheekbone, I felt the anger and shame and sadness seep away, just a little. I sighed and sat down cross-legged on the prickly fall grass so that Dobbsy and Walt could settle into the nest my legs made. After a few seconds, Daniel sat, too, a fairly complicated procedure, like a music stand folding up, and then Mag plopped down between us.

"If Harris got into some kind of compromising situation with a girl, when he is married to gorgeous, funny you, he's colossally dumb, as damn dumb as dirt," said Mag. "Right, Daniel?"

"As damn dumb as *damn* dirt," agreed Daniel.

I laughed and rubbed my eyes. "Thanks."

I thought for a moment and then said, "Is it weird that that's not the worst part? The betrayal?"

There was a silence before Daniel said, "Well, no. It makes sense that telling Avery would be the worst part. Georgia is only twelve, not a teenager yet, but if I screwed up like that, especially if her friends found out—and you know I'm not even married, so she wouldn't have to come to terms with the adultery stuff—well, it would be . . ." He made a face like a person who had just witnessed something horrible, like a murder or a train wreck, but then caught my eye and said, "Not—that bad?"

"Nice catch," I said.

He gave me a rueful half smile. "I'm sorry. Tween angst is new territory for me. I guess I'm pretty spooked by it. I'm sure it'll be okay."

"No, you were right. It'll be awful."

"Okay, but is the betrayal the *second* worst thing?" asked Mag, eyeing me.

I considered again and shook my head.

"Third?" asked Mag. "Because Sara and I have only been married a couple of years, but if she had a thing with a girl at work? It would definitely be top three. Hell, it would be number one, but, then, we don't have kids."

I sighed and began to count on my fingers. "One, telling Avery. Two, worrying about worrying for the next who knows how many years about how it might be affecting her. Like, if she doesn't date in high school or college, is that because she can't trust men? Or if she never gets married, is that because she doesn't think marriage ever works out? Or if she does get married but decides not to ever have kids, is that because her father let her down so profoundly? These are just a few examples."

"Worrying about worrying," said Mag, with awe. "I don't think I knew people did that."

"Pre-worrying," I said. "Laying the groundwork for other worrying. One of my specialties."

"Three?" said Daniel.

I lifted a third finger. "Pity. The pitying looks I'll get. I hate and despise pitying looks, even when they're sincere."

"Yeah, I know the feeling," said Daniel, nodding.

I remembered then that his wife had died two and a half years earlier.

"Oh God, of course you know."

Reflexively, I scooped up Walt and handed him to Daniel, who, reflexively, kissed the top of my dog's head, right at the spot where his hair parted in the middle.

"So—fourth?" said Mag. "The betrayal is fourth?"

"I don't know," I said. "Maybe? I did ask him to sleep, for the foreseeable future, in this little guest suite we have that's over the garage, which I guess means I'm upset about the cheating or the potential cheating or the flirtation or obsession or dalliance or whatever it was, right?"

"Well, that's an interesting question," said Mag, scratching her head.

"Dalliance," said Daniel. "I like it. I mean, I don't like that he dallied, obviously, but since you'll need a word to call this, uh, turn of events, that seems like a good choice."

"Thanks. I just thought of it. Here's the thing. More than once over the years, and this started not that long after we were married, I've thought that my marriage wouldn't last forever."

"Oh," said Mag. "Wow."

"I can't believe I just said that," I said.

"Why?" said Daniel. He looked truly puzzled, a line appearing between his dark, straight eyebrows.

"You're right. I can absolutely believe I just said that."

"You should say what you want," said Daniel.

"Well, in that case."

"Uh-oh," said Mag, laughing. "Here we go!"

"It hasn't been so much an active desire for our marriage to end as it's been a failure of my imagination to envision us being together forever. Maybe it *should* have been an active desire for it to end, but we had Avery not long after we got married, and she never slept, ever, and, for years, I was so tired all the time."

"Too tired to want your marriage to end," said Mag. "That's tired."

"How old were you when you got married?" asked Daniel.

"Twenty-three."

"Shotgun wedding?" Mag asked.

Daniel winced. "Sheesh. Do people still call it that?"

"Yep," said Mag.

"I guess what I mean is do people still call it that when they're talking to a person who might have actually had what might technically qualify as that kind of wedding? Especially when that person is in kind of a shaky emotional state?"

"Nope," said Mag. "Sorry."

"It's okay," I said. "My mother didn't threaten anyone with a shotgun, but possibly only because she didn't have to. The pregnancy just kind of decided it for us. Or something. It's all a bit of a blur. We'd been dating since I was nineteen, dating in this day-to-day kind of way. Not really a cumulative way, if that makes sense. For instance, until I found out I was pregnant, I never thought I'd marry him. Not *actively* thought anyway."

"I'm sensing a certain lack of urgency in your relationship with Harris," said Daniel, deadpan.

I laughed. "I think that's what I used to like about it, actually."

"Calm seas," said Mag. "There are worse things."

"Avery was a terrible sleeper, always. No naps, except by accident or out of sheer screaming exhaustion. God-awful night sleeping, wake-ups every two hours. She still struggles with insomnia, which is painful to watch. Anyway, I honestly think that Harris and I spent so many years so sleep deprived that we didn't notice just how lacking in luster our lackluster marriage was."

"And now I guess you're noticing," said Mag. "Which, if you don't mind my saying, is maybe not the worst thing to happen."

"Maybe not. But what the hell, Harris? Calm seas! Calm seas was the whole point of Harris. That's what I wanted for Avery. Stability. A home she could have faith in."

"Sounds reasonable to me," said Daniel, with a weariness that made me want to hand him another dog, even though he still had his hands full of Walt and Mose had come back from his adventuring to rest his butter-yellow chin on Daniel's knee.

"It does, doesn't it? And Ave's insomnia, it makes her fragile. Anxious, even in the daytime. And you know what else? If my marriage is going to end, I do want it to be out of urgency on my part. Or even Harris's. I want it to be a decision, and this feels random, like a meteor striking. I hate it."

"I can see how you would," said Daniel.

I remembered Harris from the night before, placing his shaving cream, toothbrush, razor into his leather Dopp kit with a slow care so characteristic that it hurt my heart. Before that, he had slid a suit, dress shirt, and tie into his hang-up bag, even though he had no place in the world to wear them.

"We will figure out what to do," I'd told him.

"Do?" he'd said, filling that tiny word with an ocean of hopelessness.

"I'll find a therapist for you." I'd said it mostly because it was the one thing I could think of to offer. Later, I realized I hadn't said "for us."

"Thank you," he'd told me.

Before he left, his shoulders bent under the weight of his bags, he'd said, "Nothing happened. It really didn't. You can read our emails, my and Cressida's. You should. I looked back over them, read every single one. Nothing, nothing wrong. Not a wrong word in the entire batch."

Now, I looked at my friends and said, "I just want to declare this right now, with you two and these four good dogs as witnesses: I won't let Avery's life fall apart."

"That's the spirit," said Mag.

Daniel could have said that if his daughter had survived her mother's dying at the age of thirty-four, mine could surely survive her father's dalliance. He could have said that sometimes families and worlds, no matter how careful everyone is, no matter how much love, fall apart and there's not a thing you—or all of modern medicine—can do to stop it.

Instead, he said, "You? Are you kidding? Of course you won't."

That afternoon I went to visit my mother. Before I'd even sidestepped the ramp and walked up the front steps to my mother's door—the door of the house Trevor and I had grown up in—I heard the opera: incandescent, full-throated sorrow turning the air on the pillared porch deep blue and reverberant. I didn't recognize the singer. I didn't know what opera the aria was from, a fact that would have elicited icy scorn from my mother. I didn't understand a word of Italian. But the grief in the woman's song was unmistakable, the indigo hopelessness, the unbearable, irretrievable loss.

Although I had possessed a key to that house for thirty years, I knew how my mother hated to be caught off guard. As I always did, I rang the bell, and I heard the single bright chime of it get caught by the music like a tossed marble landing in an open hand. Before the chime had fully faded, Agnes opened the door.

In her dark jeans, immaculate white shirt, and vermillion Tod's loafers, Agnes looked more like a well-heeled young society matron than a nurse/caretaker for a wheelchair-bound cancer patient. But I knew that inside those perfectly creased sleeves were some mighty biceps, ready to transfer my mother from wheelchair to velvet armchair or mahogany dining chair or backyard Adirondack chair whenever it was required, which was often, since my mother found the wheelchair, with its black, breathable fabric and aluminum tubing, unsightly and insisted on spending as little time in it as possible. I also knew that, after Agnes had arrived at her house on the first day in fuchsia scrubs and white clogs, my mother had purchased her entire outfit. The white shirt was one of three. After two wearings, my mother would send one shirt out to be cleaned and pressed—or rather would send Agnes to have it sent out to be cleaned and pressed—and Agnes would come to work in a fresh one.

Agnes smiled at me, but I could see the frustration in her eyes. She was as efficient and patient as anyone I had ever met, but my mother was not an easy person to care for. In fact, if she had been an easy person ever, in any way, even for a day, I had never witnessed it.

"She's in the sunroom with her tea and cookies," said Agnes.

"Lemon snaps from Rolf's?"

"Well, it *is* Wednesday," said Agnes.

Rolf's Bakery's lemon snaps on Mondays and Wednesdays. Devonshire Market's currant scones on Tuesdays and Thursdays. Cesarini's mini cannolis on Fridays and Saturdays. Each bakery had a small string-tied box marked with my mother's name ready for Agnes to pick up on the designated days. Sundays were a day of tea-sweets rest, just as God had commanded.

Agnes was too professional to roll her eyes at a patient's behavior, but the way she said *Wednesday* suggested that she was *thinking* of rolling her eyes. She gave me a tiny private smile. I gave her one back.

"You are an angel and a saint and the world's best sport," I told Agnes, not for the first time.

"I wouldn't go that far," said Agnes. "She gives me the extras to take home for my boyfriend. She may be singlehandedly keeping our relationship afloat."

"Wouldn't be the first time Cesarini's cannolis saved the day. Maybe I should try that."

"You?" said Agnes, startled. "Does your day need saving?"

With a small pang of annoyance, I recognized that particular brand of startle. It said: "You of the perfect life are worrying about something?" I also recognized that, since I was the one who had carefully cultivated the myth of my family's perfect life, my pang of annoyance, however small, was pure hypocrisy.

"Hey, you never know," I said, breezily. "I should probably keep some cannolis in my back pocket, just in case."

"That sounds messy," said Agnes, with a shudder and a grin.

Oh honey, I thought, *you have no idea.*

My mother sat in her delicate Duncan Phyfe lyre-back chair at her delicate little round Duncan Phyfe table in her beautiful stone-floor sunroom with sunlight misting through the long windows and opera swirling around her. A china plate of Rolf's lemon snaps arranged on a plate before her. Two cookies on a second, smaller plate, one cookie broken exactly in half, both otherwise untouched. A plate smaller still bearing three slices of lemon, so thin as to be translucent. An even thinner china teacup, a wisp of a teacup, on a matching saucer. A flute-narrow crystal vase eliciting one white lily. My mother as she'd forever been, Adela Beale at her quintessence: ramrod straight and hard as nails and surrounded by deliberate and delicate beauty. But, although I had seen her two days before, her frailness stunned me like a blow to the solar plexus. I could never get used to it, that my mother—all fierce, force, incisiveness, mercilessness—should, in the end, fade. I'd expected fireworks. Clouds parting and a bodily ascent. I'd expected her to go on for-ever.

"Virginia. Come sit."

Her voice was as sharp as always. Her eyes were lasers. I sat down in the chair opposite my mother. She leaned toward me an inch or two, her gaze flickering over my face.

"What's happened?" she said.

As little as she had ever seemed to discern—or bother to notice—my other emotions or states of being, my mother had an eagle eye for trouble. For two full seconds, I considered saying, "Happened? I don't know what you mean. Everything is fine." But I knew it would be no use. And then there was also the fact that telling her was my whole reason for coming. The story came out in a single, long, sad, sordid stream of words.

"Harris was fired. He developed a relationship with an intern, a young one. I don't know how far it went. Possibly, he was obsessed with her. I'd say it's even likely. A lower level employee at his company saw them holding hands across a table at a restaurant. In an attempt to keep him quiet, Harris offered him inside information on a new drug that's about to launch, something big. The employee went to Harris's boss. The boss fired him."

It never paid to try to give my mother anything but the unvarnished truth. I'd tried many times, mostly when I was between the ages of eight and eighteen, and it always somehow came back to bite me. In this instance, I wasn't even tempted. I needed to tell her the true story, even if it would be the last time I ever told it to anyone.

Nothing. Not a hitch in her breathing or a narrowing of her eyes. Once, in high school, I'd asked my brainy friend CJ what the coldest liquid on Earth was so I could say that it ran in her veins.

"Liquid helium," he'd said. "Which doesn't exist in nature. It has to be made in a lab, but most scientists settle for cooling things off with liquid nitrogen instead because liquid helium is stupid expensive. It's like the Rolls-Royce of lab-cooled gases."

"Only the best and fridgidest for Adela," I'd said.

"When she looks at you, her eyeballs alone could give you the kind of frostbite that makes your nose turn black and fall off," my friend Kirsten had said, shuddering.

Now, my mother said, "How young?"

"Eighteen. A high school senior."

Her face was immovable, a frozen lake.

"Lucretia Mott?"

"No. St. Michael's."

"Name?"

"Cressida Wall."

"What do her parents do? St. Michael's isn't exactly cheap."

"I don't know. I guess I can ask Harris."

"Don't bother. I can find out myself. Does Avery know?"

"Not yet. But she will." My chest felt tight just thinking about this.

"Of course she will. Everyone in town will make sure of that."

I sat up straighter. "*I'll* make sure of it. She needs to know the truth. The bare bones of it anyway. We don't lie to our daughter."

My mother just flicked her index finger. It was the smallest gesture. Her hand didn't even rise from the table next to her plate, but somehow, with it, she managed to dismiss me, Harris, the entire concept of Truth, and the relationship Harris and I had built with our only child. She did not dismiss the child herself, because if there was one person in her world whom Adela Beale considered eternally undismissable, forever worthy of her attention, it was Avery.

"The truth. Well, I'm sure you have some semi-hysterical, psychobabble, morning-talk-show reason for that. What you tell her is your business. My concern is what others will think and what they'll aim at her. That's the story that matters most."

"I know," I said. "That's why I'm here."

"Of course that's why. Have you told anyone else? That ridiculous Kristin, for instance?"

"Kirsten's been my friend for over twenty years, which incidentally means that you know her name is not Kristin. She has an MBA from Wharton and runs her own highly successful business. When does she get to stop being ridiculous?"

"Have you told her?"

"Not yet. I haven't had time. And maybe I wasn't ready to hear her say what I know she'll say."

"Which is?"

"Finally."

"Finally your husband shows a spark of life?"

"Hey! Ouch. And anyway, you like Harris."

"I wouldn't go that far. But Harrises do serve a purpose."

"Harrises? Like he came off an assembly line? Like my husband is a Barbie?"

"They are functional without mess and drama. Until they aren't, apparently."

"He's always been a kind man. Honest and hard-working. A good father."

My mother lifted an eyebrow.

"Okay. Until he wasn't," I said. I wanted to rub my eyes, which felt tired, but few things aggravated my mother more than smudged mascara. I settled for rubbing the crescent of skin just beneath each eye.

"The eye area is like tissue paper," said my mother, "except that the crinkles stay."

"Thank you," I said. "What was I saying?"

"That, in a shocking display of sound judgment, you haven't told that ridiculous Kristin about Harris's lapse."

"Right. *Finally* you can stop playing house with Harris. *Finally* you can end this charade. *Finally* you can find a man who doesn't bore your best friend to tears. Those are the *finally*s Kirsten will mean."

"Is the Kristin portion of this conversation over?"

"Can you help?"

I knew the answer before I asked. My mother had run multiple successful political campaigns in our city, including her own. She'd turned bad guys into everymen, everymen into heroes. She'd recast drunk driving records, embezzlement, and assault as virtual virtues. In her day—a day that almost certainly hadn't ended yet, despite the physical ravages of age and illness—Adela Beale had spun this town like a top.

"This Harris nonsense is nothing," said my mother. "Nothing. Child's play."

She laughed and said, "I should probably avoid that phrase, though. In this particular instance."

I snatched up a lemon snap and bit it.

"Thanks for your compassion, Mom."

Another finger-flick jettisoned compassion and motherly concern into the stratosphere. Adela's eyes met mine, and even though I had known her forever, I had to hold back a full-body shiver.

"Are you sure you want my help?" she asked.

I hesitated.

"There is a teenaged girl involved," I reminded her.

At this, Adela lifted one penciled eyebrow.

"I know. She's my granddaughter."

In that second, when my mother said those words, I recognized where I was: standing on the vertiginous edge of solid moral ground, with the dark pit of my mother's ruthlessness gaping below me. I could leap or not. Before I could even quite consider this choice, a memory of Avery from just that morning flashed into my mind. Avery reading the sports page, furrowing her pretty brows at the plight of her beloved Sixers, her skinny fingers holding a piece of toast made the way she liked it, toasted just to goldenness with the thinnest varnish of peanut butter. And I didn't leap. It was more like what happens to those tourists who stand at the lip of the Grand Canyon for a photo, the sky wild with sunset behind them, and the ground just crumbles out from under their feet. I thought of Avery and her paper and her toast and I was falling.

"All I want is for Avery to get through her days without hearing murmurings that her father is a creep who got obsessed with a child and then resorted to bribery to cover it up," I said. "I want his name to be cleared, to have him be perceived as bumbling but well intentioned, maybe, which is exactly what he's been for almost the entire balance of his life. That's it. Nothing else. So, within those parameters, yes. I want your help."

I saw it, the spark in her eyes, the color in her hollow cheeks, the purse of her lips. I really didn't think my mother was happy that her son-in-law, husband of her only daughter, had lost his mind and his job and his moral compass because of a teenaged girl. I mean I couldn't be sure, but I didn't think so. Certainly, she was anything but happy about the pain it might cause Avery. Oh, but the woman loved a challenge. I watched it enliven her, like green and yellow springtime creeping over a barren winter landscape in a nature show. Who knew? Maybe it would even keep her alive for a while, despite her doctors' grim predictions. For a bizarre few seconds, I felt noble, like a thoughtful child who had given her poor sick mother a gift.

As I looked at her I noticed again what I'd seen the last two times we'd been together, something new about her face. Deep lines hooked around the corners of her mouth. A high clench to her shoulders. Shaky hands. It struck me that what I was seeing was pain.

"So how are you, Mom?"

"Dying," said my mother. Her lips twisted. "But I'm still having a better day than you are, I daresay."

I laughed.

"I daresay you're right," I told her.

As I prepared to get up and leave she said, "This is what happens when you marry a man you think will never surprise you."

Because this was true but was something I had never articulated to my mother or to anyone else and had barely admitted to myself, I froze for a moment, halfway out of my chair. Then, I finished standing up.

"It seemed like a good idea at the time," I said.

As soon as I said this, my mother's face committed the rare and remarkable act of softening. She shut her eyes almost as if she were blinking back tears, and I wanted to shout: "Stop!" But when she opened them again, her eyes were dry.

"Yes, I can see how it might have," she said and, with one last flick of her finger, dismissed me.

When my daughter, Avery, was born, taking a full twenty-five hours to hem and haw, crown and retreat her way into the world, she didn't cry, just radiated pale gold light and stared around with wondering fawn eyes. Later that day, in my hospital room, after Harris convinced me to let them put her into the nursery so that I could sleep after the long labor (and so that he could go home to his own bed), when the nurse took her from me, I swear—and no amount of infant brain science can change my mind about this—she turned her head to look over her shoulder and stare exactly into my eyes, and a mantle of peace fell over me. That's precisely how it was: a direct gaze and a mantle of peace. I felt visited upon; I believed we had a spirit child, a mystic, a Buddha. I fell asleep certain that her days would slip like pearls onto the string of my life, one luminosity after the next after the next, and I slept for six hours.

I woke up in my dark, quiet room, twenty-three years old, alone, bereft of my child's presence, craving her river stone tranquility and her tuft of hair. Gingerly, I sat up, shimmied myself to the edge of the bed, slid into my slippers, and found my way to the nursery, one with a big viewing window, just like in the movies. Through the glass, the rows of bassinets awash in faint lunar light from some unseen source created a landscape that struck me as solemn, lonesome, and majestic, like Stonehenge, except that even through the closed door, I could hear one baby crying, an unhinged sound, hoarse goose-calls scratching rents in the stillness. The night nurse sitting at a desk outside the nursery gave me a tired smile and, when she checked my hospital bracelet, a wry laugh.

"She's fine. I've gone in twice. Normal temperature, normal everything. Some of them just cry. Although that one seems to be trying to set a record."

"You mean"—I gestured toward the window—"that one's mine?"

The nurse nodded. "Yours," she said. "Forever and ever."

"You think it's because she misses me, right?"

"Sure," said the nurse. "Let's go with that."

It was the beginning of over fifteen years (and count-ing) of insomnia, of watching my daughter be not just awake in the middle of the night but something beyond awake, hyper-attuned, as if not only her eyes but also her entire consciousness were dilated, letting in too much world. When she was crib-bound, she would scream until I picked her up, at which point her screams would drain out of her little by little until she fell into a soap bubble–fragile sleep. When I tried to put her down, performing a kind of breath-held series of glacially slow ballet moves in which my chest remained pressed to her body long after she had made contact with the mattress, she would wait until the moment when I thought I was home free, when my hand was on the doorknob, to scream once again.

Once she could get out of bed by herself, she would come into our room and stand next to ours, edgy and trembling as a gazelle when the lions are nearby, whispering, "Mama," her middle-of-the-night name for me (the rest of the time it was "Mommy"), until I walked her back and either resettled her and left or, more often, lay down next to her, where she affixed herself to me with the tenacity of a tree toad. Until she was five years old, the wakeups occurred every two hours. At five, old enough both to read on her own and to feel ashamed of sleeping with her mother, she would come into our room just two or three times a week. On the mornings of the nights that she didn't, I would walk into her room to find all her lights burning and books everywhere, on the floor, on the bed, sometimes splayed open across her chest, or tucked under her head. Her face would be flushed, damp tendrils of dark hair sticking to her pink cheeks, as if she hadn't so much fallen into sleep as wrestled it bodily to the ground.

At fifteen, when most of her friends could sleep anytime, anywhere, and well past noon, Avery and I had
cobbled together a bedtime system that involved equal
parts science, common sense, and superstition verging
on witchcraft. A weighted blanket, a diffuser with an
array of essential oils on rotation (lavender, jasmine,
vetiver, bergamot, rose, vanilla, chamomile), meditation
apps, visualization apps, soothing music, soothing
teas, melatonin, breathing exercises, yoga poses, warm
baths, soothing bath salts, soothing books, amber light-
bulbs: Avery would try various combinations of these
elements until something worked, and then she would
use that combination again and again, until it stopped
working, which it always, eventually, did, usually because some bump in her daytime life jarred her and
caused the tricky off switch in her brain to malfunc-
tion. The bumps were mostly ordinary growing-up
issues—a fight with a friend, a big test, a bad grade,
a missed goal on the field hockey field, a boy who
decided he liked someone else—but after dark, fueled
by adrenaline and exhaustion, the bumps would grow
into mountains, into volcanoes.

But what always astonished me about Avery was
how pulled together she seemed during the day. Not
seemed, was. Funny, popular, a better than decent
athlete, a way better than decent student. Her friends

and teachers didn't know, couldn't have guessed, that the girl with the clear eyes, ringing laugh, and sheet of shining hair, the one winning debates and field hockey games and reading her papers aloud in class, was also the one who would sit in the passenger seat on our desperation nighttime drives, her eyes fixed on the windshield, her right thumbnail clenched between her teeth or the one who would still, at least once a month, sleep in our bed with me, slipping in one side while Harris, out of long habit, slipped out the other.

When I got home from my mother's house, Avery was already there, sitting at the kitchen table with her favorite snack laid out before her: a bowl of microwave popcorn, a dish of yellow mustard to dip it in, and a glass of milk. Her laptop sat open on the table as she watched what I knew without looking was an episode of *Friends,* her latest resurrected-from-the-past series. She'd watched the whole ten years' worth of episodes twice through and was starting on a third go-round. When she heard me come in, she didn't glance up but lifted a finger and announced, "I'm about to do home-work, just as soon as Chandler chokes on the gum."

She sat there, my daughter, so lovely and absorbed and eyelashy and full of grace in her soft gray sweater and red suede sneakers, her hair tucked behind her ears and pouring down her back.

"Fine, but after the choking, maybe you could put off doing homework for a few minutes," I said.

With a dramatic flourish, Avery hit pause and cast concerned eyes upon me.

"Mom, are you feeling okay?"

"Ha-ha."

"Because I thought I just heard you request that I *delay homework,* which just can't be right. Are you feverish? Or possibly febrile?"

"Feverish and febrile are the same thing."

"Really, Mom? Thank you so much for clarifying that. How about drunk?"

"Drunk is different."

"Are you it?"

"I wish."

"Blow to the head, maybe?"

I wanted her to go on and on in exactly this manner all night long. But instead I said, "Honey, I need to talk to you about something," and her playfulness vanished—instantly, like a channel switch—and was replaced by a tense, watchful stillness. I wanted to slap myself and then Harris and then Harris again, harder.

I sat down at the table and closed her laptop and told her. I had asked Harris if I could be the one to tell, which made so much sense that I couldn't even get mad

at how eagerly—like a frog snapping up a juicy fly—
he'd agreed. After some soul-searching, I had decided
to tell the truth, but with all of my darkest suspicions,
even the ones that were so close to certainties as to be
almost indistinguishable, left out.

After I'd finished, Avery shut her eyes and said, with
tenderness and sorrow, "Oh, Dad. What did you do?"

"Honey, your father's not a person who is used to
people thinking he's done anything wrong, so when it
happened, he panicked."

"By 'it happened,' you mean that someone thought
he'd done something wrong, right? Not that he actually
had. Right?"

I paused, searching for a path between facts and
what I only believed were facts, and settled on, "Dale
Pinckney jumped to the conclusion that your father
was having a sexual relationship with the woman he'd
seen him with, his intern."

Avery held up her hand, like a traffic cop.

"Sorry," I said. "Bad choice of words. I just hate the
word *affair*, always have. It's too pretty."

Avery shook her head.

"You said woman," said Avery. "It should be girl.
You said she was still in high school, so even if she was
eighteen, she was still a high school girl. If you say
woman, it sounds like you're trying to cover something

up or make it sound better than it was. So it's girl. We should just say that."

"Okay," I said. "But anyway, he wasn't. Dale Pinckney was wrong."

While I did not know this to be an absolute fact, I felt in my bones that Harris had not had sex with Cressida Wall. I couldn't quite explain why. Maybe because his demeanor bespoke longing—bottomless, desperate—but not satisfaction. I would not have gone so far as to say that he *wouldn't* have had sex with her at some point; I just didn't think he had.

"But just knowing how it appeared to Dale sent your father into a whirlpool of confusion. So he tried to convince Dale not to tell his boss. Your dad couldn't bear the thought of other people thinking what Dale thought."

Avery considered this, and then looked up at me, with light in her eyes. "Oh. Because of us. He wanted to protect us."

I remembered my conversation with Harris that first night in our yard. *He wanted to continue his relationship with Cressida,* I thought. But there was no way I could say those words to my child with her face full of hope. Besides, maybe wanting to protect us was part of Harris's motivation, deep down. Who was I to say it wasn't?

"Well, that would make sense," I said. "He would never want anything to hurt you."

Avery sat in silence, serious, blinking, thoughts flickering in her coffee-colored eyes. Then she looked at me and said, "Who is she?"

I hesitated. "It doesn't matter, does it?"

Avery sat up straighter. "You can tell me her name. What if I know her? Does she go to my school?"

"No, no, of course not."

"Please just tell me."

Even though I had spoken aloud that odd name more than once, I suddenly found it hard—physically hard—to say. *Oh, Harris, could you not have dallied with a Susie or an Anne?* My mouth was sticky, clumsy. I swallowed. "Cressida Wall."

Avery gasped, her mouth falling open. Automatically, she raised her right thumbnail, rested it on her lip, which was trembling, bit down. I knew what I was seeing: doubt swinging toward her like a wrecking ball, her faith in Harris taking a hit, bricks tumbling down.

"She's beautiful," said Avery, her voice tight and small. "Everybody thinks so."

Because I didn't know what to say, I reached out and took Avery's glossy bowed head between my hands.

"She's a senior at St. Michael's. She runs track, and she was at that debate competition last summer. I follow her on social media. She's beautiful."

"It doesn't matter, honey. Except that it probably has something to do with why Dale jumped to the wrong conclusion."

Then, she said, in that same tiny heartrending, shrink-wrapped voice, "Do you think Dad thought she was?"

I kissed the top of her head. I had never wanted to lie to anyone so much.

"Dad is kind of a distracted guy. He doesn't always notice what other people notice," I said. God knows it was true.

"Still," she said. "*Do* you?"

I lifted her hair and pulled the silken weight of it over one of her shoulders and began to braid. There was a voice I used—low, slow, cadenced, chant-like—on those car rides or when Avery would lie next to me in the middle of the night, her brain jangling with frightening thoughts. I used it now.

"When you were little, like three years old, right after we'd moved into this house, I would take you to the playground, and, oh my gosh, you loved it. It was fenced in with a gate that shut, so the kids could roam around by themselves, and you adored that freedom. You'd climb and dig in the sand and go inside the playhouse or you would lie belly-down on one of the big swings. There were so many kids, but I always knew right where you were, even when I was talking to other moms. I just knew. And then one weekend, your dad asked to take you by himself, and I didn't really want him to. Because of the way he's distracted, always in a bit of a fog. I was afraid he wouldn't keep track of you. But I didn't want to say no. So he put you in the wagon and pulled you to the playground, and after I was pretty sure you two must have gotten there, I ran over and sidled up to the playground, outside the fence, and hid behind a tree. And you know what I saw?"

Her eyes met mine. "What?"

"You climbing up the jungle gym with great big Dad climbing right behind you. I saw other parents watching him, but he didn't notice. All he noticed was you. And he ducked into the playhouse even though he barely fit through the door. It was like *Gulliver's Travels.* He even sat in the sandbox."

Avery smiled. "He probably took up the whole sandbox," she said.

"He loves you so much."

It wasn't an answer to her question about whether her father thought Cressida Wall was beautiful. I knew it, and I knew she knew it, but I set before her the one thing I recognized at that moment—at that moment and for all time—to be absolutely true about Harris McCue, the best, most basic fact of him. Avery might've gotten mad or walked out or demanded an answer to her question, but she didn't. Neither did she say, "I love him, too." But she let my sentence rest there between us, and then her teeth released her thumbnail, and she said, in the tone of someone agreeing to perform a task or do a favor, the tone of someone who has decided: "Okay."

Chapter Five

June 15, 1997

Tonight, at the Quaker burial ground, Trevor
said, "I hate her," and even though he'd said
it before and had even yelled directly at her,
in the meanest possible voice, like someone
spitting in someone's face, "I hate you!" more
times than I could count, sometimes sticking
in a "fucking" or a "bitch" or both, I never
believed he really meant it until tonight.

I was lying on my back on the grass between
two gravestones with Trevor nearby lying on
his back between two others. The humidity
and the city lights had thrown a veil over
the sky, but you could still see some stars,
white and dissolving, and I was about to say
something about how weird it was to think

that the stars were always up there, even in
the daytime, how brighter lights just trick us
into thinking they're gone, when Trevor said
it, not loud but hard and ugly, like an ax
blow: I hate her.

Right away, I imagined all those Quaker
souls in their little gauze bonnets and plain
dresses and black suits—our friends, is how I
thought of them, our guardian angels—hearing
the venom in my brother's voice. I imagined
the whisper of their skirts and coats as they
drew back from us, all their inner lights
startled and fluttering like candle flames in
a breeze.

He doesn't mean it, I wanted to tell them.

Except that I know Trev better than anyone
and I think he did.

Sitting here now, in my room, at three
in the morning, feeling like the only awake
person in the universe, I'm trying to figure
out exactly why I think he meant it, about
what made this time different. It could be
because of the place, the burial ground. I
can't remember Trevor ever saying those words
in that place before. Usually, no matter how
boiling mad we are when we sneak out of our

house, our fury spends itself on the ride
over, as we whoosh soundlessly past lines of
parked cars, past storefronts and row houses
with their awning-shaded windows like sleepy
eyes, so that by the time we're leaning our
bikes against the low wrought-iron burial-
ground fence and tugging open the gate, which
is always unlocked, we are mostly emptied of
it. We rarely bring up whatever it was that
sent us reeling out the door and instead talk
about other things—school, our friends, books,
whether or not pure good or pure evil exists,
whether or not we believe in God—or we don't
talk at all, just sit inside a loose, comfy
pocket of shared silence.

But when we do talk there, we mean what we
say. It's like an unspoken rule. Or more like
an unwritten vow, the kind you sign with *X*s
of blood. At the burial ground, we tell the
truth.

Can a person hate—truly hate, the way
people hate Nazis or slavery or war—his own
mother?

They had a fight. They always have fights,
but I guess maybe this one was especially
bad. I don't know because I wasn't there to

hear it. I usually stick around to argue in Trevor's defense when he's too mad (or drunk or stoned, which sometimes happens) to stick up for himself, but mostly just so he knows I'm where I always am, which is on his side.

But I wasn't there this time.

Tonight's fight—well, last night's now, I guess—started months ago, when we were sitting at the dinner table and Mom told Trevor that she had decided that he would live at home during his upcoming first year of college. No "I need to talk to you about something," no "You're not going to like hearing this, but." She didn't even put her silverware down or clear her damn throat. Just carved up Trevor's future the same way she cut the meat on her plate: calm, calm, calm, slice, slice, slice. I'll never forget that voice. So much like a scalpel that you can almost see eerie arctic operating room lights flashing off the blade.

Trevor said, "That's not happening."

"You will commute until you demonstrate to my satisfaction that you are responsible enough not to disgrace yourself or—more to the point—your family."

Before Trevor could jump in and totally demolish his chances of changing her mind, I said, "That's not fair!"

No one looked at me.

"It's like you've already decided he'll mess up, Mom! How can you do that? You can't! You need to give him a chance first!"

Again, not a glance. It was like one of those dreams where you may as well be trapped inside a Mason jar with the lid sealed tight.

"Like you'd ever actually stick to that," said Trevor, sneering. "So—what now? I'm supposed to beg and promise I'll behave? Grovel? Is that what you want? Because I know you can't wait to get rid of me."

"You will stay here for your freshman year, assuming you don't flunk out before it's over, at the end of which I will assess. Consider it a test," said Mom, and she went back to cutting her steak.

Then, Trevor had stood up, leaned over, and, with one giant sweep of his arm, sent her plate and water glass crashing onto the floor.

My mother had looked down at the rubble of crystal and china on the floor, made a ticking noise with her tongue, and said, "At least it wasn't the Waterford."

They'd had five different versions of the fight since then, and last night's ended with Trevor shouting that he would make her regret it, that whatever disgraceful behavior she'd expected from him at school would be nothing compared to what he'd do right here at home. Then, he ran out of the house, leaving the front door gaping like an open mouth behind him.

My mother said, "Virginia, shut the door; mosquitoes are coming in."

At about ten o'clock that night, from my bedroom window, I watched a police car glide into our driveway, with my brother in the backseat. I opened my window to listen. Trevor had gone out with his friend Eddie Rourke in Eddie's pickup truck. When the cop stopped them, Trevor was drunk and there were three stolen stop signs in the bed of Eddie's truck.

By the time I got down the stairs, Trevor was standing in a splatter of streetlight with his back to the police car, his hands jammed into the pockets of his shorts, his eyes on the ground, and Mom was shaking hands with the officer, a kid who couldn't have been much older than Trevor. After he left, Mom didn't say a word, just turned and walked—with precise, unhurried steps—down the driveway, up the stairs to the porch, and into the house. If she has ever even once cut across our lawn, I've never seen it. I stood with my heart banging and a sob welling in my chest, watching my brother staring down at the road as if he were trying to burn holes in the asphalt with his eyes.

His shoulders inside his thrift-store plaid shirt. His overgrown hair resting on the collar. The smell of lilacs from the bush in our yard infiltrating the night air. Those three things together filled me with a sudden, sad, wild loneliness, like a wolf howl.

Then, Trevor turned and saw me, and the grin that cut across his face shone in the streetlight.

"Tried to talk the guy into the lights and siren, but he wouldn't do it," he said.

For a second, I couldn't find my voice. Then, I eked out a "too bad" so flat and hoarse it got lost in the singing of the crickets.

When we went inside, I saw that the door to Mom's study was shut, and I knew she was doing what she'd done before: making a phone call that would scrub her son's latest screwup right out of existence. I knew that when she came out, she'd find Trevor, and there would be another fight, a terrible one.

Trevor hissed, "Fuck her," then climbed the stairs to his room and flopped face-first onto his bed.

My brother has been my favorite person ever since I can remember, my first friend, but all I could think about was giant objects hurtling toward each other, screams, twisted metal, the smell of burning brakes and rubber tires, smoke in the air, blood on the road.

It was the trust that broke me: all those law-abiding drivers with their belief in signs and signals and carefulness, their belief in the right-of-way, in a fair and orderly universe. It hit me: how we turn our breakable bodies over to the world for safekeeping every single day. One uprooted stop sign and all those years of growing and going to school, laughing, sledding in winter, turning pages of books, getting

haircuts, brushing teeth, learning to swim:
over, done, extinguished.

From far away downstairs, I heard the
office door open, my mother's footsteps,
regular as a metronome.

And I left. Just walked out of his room,
down the hall into my own, and I shut the door
and put on music and lay in the dark with my
churning stomach and leaking eyes and cracked
heart and tried not to throw up.

*The police put the signs back in time. No
one died. No one died. No one died.*

It was my version of praying.

I fell asleep. I must have because Trevor
was shaking me awake.

"Let's go," he whispered.

The first time Trevor and I sneaked out,
he was twelve, I was eleven, and our parents
were having the fight that would finally set
the busted pieces of their marriage on fire
and obliterate it forever. In the seven years
since then, when Trevor's asked me to go, I've
never said no.

"No," I said.

He took his hand off my shoulder. I could feel
him standing there in the dark like a statue.

Then, he whispered, "They were all four-way stops."

"What?"

"The one at Baxter and Simon's Bridge. The one down there by that old mill they turned into a restaurant. And this other one a few miles over the PA line, near a Christmas tree farm. I mean, I know people could still have gotten hurt, but right then, when I did it? I was thinking that it would be okay because all the other cars would stop. And I told the cop all the places, so he could put them back. I swear. When Eddie and I were in the car, before he stopped at Ed's house, he called the locations in on his radio."

"Oh!" I blurted out, and I sat up in bed and started sucking in air like a person who'd been drowning and finally breaks the surface of the water.

"Hey, hey," said Trevor. He rested his hand on the top of my head, just for a couple of seconds.

Later, at the burial ground, I said, "I should have known, Trev," and I counted on him to understand what I meant.

"No, you're fine," he said.

And then, he said, "All those years ago, she should've let me go with Dad."

He's said it before. Every time, it hurts the exact same amount as it did the first time, when I was eleven. Every time, I wonder how he could imagine living away from me, leaving me alone.

That's when he said he hated her.

I believe in intensity. I believe in diving into the quarry, in standing right under the waterfall. You know what I mean, right? But Trevor's fury at my mother, that constant, seething volcanic rage. I can't think it's right. She is harsh and hard and frozen as a glacier. But I look at her sometimes, when she's reading or listening to opera or arranging flowers in a vase, and I see that she is human.

Also, she is our *mother*.

"I think she's turning me into a monster, like her," said Trevor.

"That will never happen, ever," I told him.

"Maybe it already has."

"They were all four-way stops," I reminded him. "That's who you really are. The guy who wants to drive Mom crazy but doesn't want anyone to get hurt."

"Like you know," he said, but I could tell from his voice that he was smiling.

"I do," I said.

I flung my arms open on the grass.

"I know everything."

Chapter Six

GINNY

I had underestimated my friend Kirsten. "Finally!" was not the first thing she said. In fact, I don't think she uttered the word even once. When she called, and, after a couple seconds of hesitation, I steeled myself and answered, the first words out of her mouth were: "How's our girl doing with this?"

Kirsten had a longtime boyfriend named Tex and no children, but she'd called sharesies on Avery while she was still in utero, and, because we were short on blood relations (especially nonpotentially sociopathic ones) and I was long on love for Kirsten, I'd happily agreed.

"You heard."

"Not from you, which we will address at a later time, but yes."

"Well. It's been, what? Four days. So far, at school, she's overheard—and possibly was meant to overhear—three conversations. Two of them involved calling the girl in question a 'slut.' One involved her friend Alice telling their mutual friend Paigie that, just to be safe, her mom isn't allowing her to come to our house for a while because Harris is possibly a child molester."

"For a while? Because child molesters just need a little time to get all that pesky molesting out of their system?"

"Obviously, Alice's mom doesn't watch enough *Law and Order.*"

"Still, two out of three, right?" said Kirsten. "The others sound like they were blaming the girl. Slut is no joke. In our day, kids threw that word around like it was, I don't know, bitch. But nowadays, calling someone a slut will get you suspended just like that, especially at Lucretia Mott. So they are pulling out the big shame guns on this girl."

"Great. Let's pop the champagne."

"Have they talked, Avery and Harris?"

"No. I talked to her, and then I talked to him about talking to her, and he decided to let her be the one to bring it up to him. And oddly enough, I don't think she's quite figured out how to do that."

"'So, Dad, about that high school girl you were trying to seduce . . .'"

"Wait. That's what you heard?"

"I heard that something inappropriate happened between Harris and a gorgeous eighteen-year-old intern. Because no gorgeous eighteen-year-old in her right mind would sleep with Harris, I figured it was more like he was trying to seduce her in his clumsy, bumbling way and she got grossed out and turned him in."

"That is a very flattering assumption, to both me and Harris."

"Not to you. You were a gorgeous eighteen-year-old when you met Harris, and you're gorgeous twenty years later. So I can only assume you aren't in your right mind."

"Oh, okay. Thanks for explaining that."

"Is Avery sleeping?"

"Not that I've noticed. And I would notice, since she's been in bed with me every night since she found out."

"I'm sorry, Gin. Night drives?"

"Not yet. She's been very quiet, doing her homework, watching shows on her computer. Even in the middle of the night, she doesn't really say anything. The child molester incident was rough, though. I keep trying to prepare myself for a total breakdown, and then I remember that I've never figured out how to do that."

"Avery is sturdier than you think."

"I don't know about that. I hope so."

"Can I say something else?"

"There's more?"

"Hallelujah. Hal. Le. Lu. YAH!"

"Ha! There it is."

"It?"

"I was thinking you'd say 'finally,' actually, but 'hallelujah' works, too."

"Are you telling me it hasn't occurred to you that there might be a silver lining here? That this might be a wakeup call? A golden opportunity?"

"I guess I've been too busy worrying about the possibly irreparable damage to my daughter's psyche to fully absorb the perks of my husband's dalliance with a high school girl, his subsequent attempt to bribe his coworker into keeping silent, and his resulting loss of employment and income."

"Dalliance, huh? Vague. Old-fashioned. Slightly lighthearted. I think it works."

"Good."

"Hold on, though. I didn't hear about the bribery."

"Attempted bribery. It's what got him fired. Someone threatened to rat him out about the dalliance, so he offered hush money or hush stock tips or hush company secrets or something. Harris says that HR did some investigating and decided not to pursue the dalliance charges. They fired him because he betrayed the company."

"Well, it's nice to know they've got their priorities straight. You know, I'm surprised you haven't unleashed Adela on this girl. Couldn't your mom get her deported? Or at least distort facts and manipulate public opinion so that everyone thinks that Harris quit his job to free up more time for volunteering at homeless shelters?"

I wanted to confess that I had already done the unleashing, that, in fact, I had an appointment at my mother's house in half an hour to receive an update on her fact distortion and manipulation of public opinion, but I was overcome with shame.

"You're funny, Kirsten."

"Okay, but seriously, can you kick Harris out already?"

"He's sleeping in the garage guest suite, for now."

"And by 'for now,' you mean that, later, soon, he will be sleeping in one of those nice furnished apartments down the road where all the single men in town go when their wives kick them out."

"I haven't gotten that far. Reminder: Harris is a nice person. Or he's hitherto been a nice person. Your dislike of him doesn't speak well of you."

"I don't dislike Harris. I dislike that he's your husband. Strongly, strongly, strongly dislike."

"Well, that's so much better."

Her voice took on a musing note. "But you know, I'm not sure I'd say I like him, either. Liking is probably too aggressive a word for what I feel for Harris."

"Liking is too aggressive?"

"What's a word for not minding that he exists but not wanting him to be married to my brilliant, gorgeous, scintillating friend."

I sighed. "I don't think I've qualified as any of those things in a long time, since high school at least."

"Oh, Gin," said Kirsten, her voice going soft. "You still qualify. You've just kind of gone underground with the scintillating for the past, um, twenty years or so."

"You're mean. And brutally honest. And mean. But I love you, anyway."

"So it's all decided. Harris is history. Scintillating Ginny is making a comeback. And I love you, too."

Her parents divorced when Cressida was in elementary school," said my mother. "Her mother remarried and lives in Florida, of all places. Cressida visits her, but she lives with her father, Peter Wall. He was an engineer, but he has lately been on medical leave."

I was talking to my mother, talking to her, for the first time since she'd gotten sick and maybe for the first time ever in our adult lives, in her bedroom. She wasn't in bed, nor was she in pajamas, and even though she had a perfect right to be both of those things, I was relieved that she wasn't. Even so, the sight of her in an armchair next to the bed, her feet propped on a velvet tufted ottoman, with a blanket over her legs, was causing me minor internal earthquakes.

And then there was the fact that she was sounding like a wiseguy reporting on a stakeout to her mafia don.

"Mom, why are you digging up information on Cressida's family?"

"The medical leave story is possibly false. There may have been drinking involved. Or drugs. Who knows?"

A burning started up in my stomach.

"Hold on, Mom. Stop."

"The girl is bright, an A student with Ivy League-ish aspirations. Apparently, she applied early decision to Vanderbilt. She's beautiful in the manner of cheap blondes. Probably, they could afford St. Michael's when her father was employed, but now, Vanderbilt would probably be a real stretch."

"There's financial aid," I said.

"There is. Perhaps you'd like to sit down with Peter Wall and discuss his finances, maybe help him fill out the financial aid forms? Or how about a personal loan to help foot the bill for dear Cressida's tuition."

I held up my hands.

"None of this matters. Why are you even—?"

"The point is that they are in reduced circumstances," she said. "They need money."

"Who cares? This is about *Harris*!"

"Obviously it's about Harris. I suspect the girl got her father involved or perhaps it was the other way around."

"Involved in what?"

"The plan to trap Harris into giving Cressida money."

"No, no, no, no. The *plan* is for you to whisper in a few ears, tell people that Harris got confused, that he was only trying to help Cressida, that he made an honest mistake."

"Maybe it was planned from the beginning," said my mother, continuing as if I'd never spoken. "Maybe the idea evolved once it became clear that Harris's generous heart and his natural fatherly concern made him an easy mark. In any case, she flattered him, spent time alone with him, batted her eyelashes, et cetera. She began to ask for gifts, money. She gave him a woe-is-me story about her father's having been fired and vaunted her oh so admirable goal to attend a top-ranked college. It's possible that she hoped Harris would set up a fund for her."

"You're going to spread the rumor that Cressida Wall, high school girl, plotted to have sex with a forty-five-year-old man in exchange for a 529 plan?"

My mother ignored me. "When that didn't work, because Harris is a devoted family man, her father, one assumes, persuaded her to get Harris into an awkward and easily misconstrued position in order to blackmail him."

I felt sick. "What father would urge his child to throw herself at a middle-aged married man?"

"A desperate one. Mind you, he *may* not have gone so far as to persuade her to offer sex to Harris."

"May not have? Her father didn't actually do any of this, did he?"

My mother gave me a thousand-yard, dead-of-winter stare.

"And blackmail? She's eighteen years old!" I said.

"I know that kind of person, Virginia, and she will stop at nothing."

I knew that kind of person, too.

"Please tell me that you haven't shared this— narrative. It's all hypothetical at this point, correct? You haven't already launched this smear campaign."

"Your concern for the Walls is touching," replied my mother, not sounding at all touched.

"Listen to me. Stop. Cressida is a little girl, just like Avery. Leave her alone." Saying this and remembering Harris's voice when he talked about Cressida, a human child, someone's daughter, made me shudder.

To my surprise and relief, my mother said, "All right, fine. I understand, Virginia. I don't share your sentimental concern for the very people who have disrupted your life, but I understand. I'll only do the minimum of what needs to be done so that we can all sleep better at night."

I would've bet money that my mother had never lost a night's sleep over anything. "Really?"

"Yes."

"Thank you."

"Please remember, Virginia, that I do what I do for the greater good, always for the greater good. But I don't enjoy it."

I reached out and touched her hand.

"Mom. Are you okay?"

She smiled, a genuine smile. For a moment, the etched, trembling pain in her face got lost in her mischievous luminousness, and for a fraction of a second she turned her hand over and held mine. "Okay. Sometimes, I enjoy it."

"That's more like it."

She slid her hand away.

"Can we move on now?" she said.

I considered. "Soon, I think. I would like to. The problem is that I'm not sure where to move on *to*. I hate to have my marriage end this way, but I also can't imagine staying in it. But I'm afraid of what our splitting up will do to Avery. I mean, the two of them aren't even talking right now, but I'm sure that her parents' divorcing would hurt her. Maybe we should hang in there until she goes to college? But does that feel right? Natural? I don't know. I don't think so."

My mother made an impatient sound in her throat. "Fascinating issues, all. Plenty of food for thought. But what I meant is can we move on to a new topic of conversation."

I laughed. "Sure."

"I don't want a funeral."

I sat back in my chair. "You're not a big preamble person, are you? You just sail right in."

"I don't handle you with kid gloves. You should take it as a compliment."

"I do, I guess. But, wait. You don't want a funeral? You?"

"Of course not."

"What? I always pictured something huge with governors and senators and ex-governors and ex-senators and trumpets and pomp and circumstance and long eulogies and maybe some lying in state, whatever that actually means."

"Don't be ridiculous."

"Or maybe like what they did with Lincoln. Put your fancy coffin on a train for a couple of weeks, go through a hundred-something cities, stopping every few miles to let the townspeople line up to pay their respects."

"I don't want people discussing me, telling stories without me there to edit them for accuracy. I refuse to allow others to get the last word, particularly when they're just trying to garner attention for themselves."

"Ah. Controlling the narrative, even after you're gone."

"I have always lived life on my own terms."

"That's true. Sometimes, other people have also lived their lives on your terms."

My mother shrugged. "There's a little thing called free will. But many don't have the fortitude to exercise it."

I wondered if she was talking about Trevor. Or about me. But I didn't ask.

"I've written my obituary," she said. "Henry Hill has a copy. He also has my will. Trevor gets a small sum, enough so that he can't contest. Everything else goes to you and then to Avery."

"By 'then to,' you mean when I die?"

"Everyone dies, Virginia."

"I knew that, actually. But thanks for the reminder. But, Mom—"

"I know what you're going to say, and I can tell you that Trevor has never wanted to be my beneficiary in any capacity. He's disdained benefiting from my generosity, my expertise, my help since he was twelve years old. He wouldn't want my money even if I'd chosen to leave it all to him. If he were to contest my will, it would merely be to spite me."

"But it could be a last gesture of goodwill, a way of letting him know how you really feel about him."

"Oh, I think he's well aware of how I feel about him," said my mother. She gestured to the far corner of her bedroom. I turned to look.

"Your vintage Louis Vuitton suitcase? You want Trevor to have that?"

It was from the 1920s, hard-sided, in nearly perfect condition. A truly exquisite object.

"Good God, no. It's for Avery. I filled it with books I would like her to have, some valuable, others not. Things I think she would like. There's also a note from me inside. I was hoping you'd consent to allow her to open the suitcase and read the note in private. I just wanted to give her something personal to remember me by."

"Mom, that's lovely. Of course she should do that."

"Thank you. Please bring it with you when you leave today."

"Oh, but why don't I bring her by this weekend and you can give it to her yourself? Wouldn't that be better?"

Then, my mother said, in a calm, matter-of-fact tone, "I don't think I'll be here this weekend."

A shiver ran through me.

"What? Don't say that."

My mother leaned back in her chair, her hands resting lightly on its arms, her expression almost gentle.

"As I said before, I have always done things on my own terms. You know that," she said.

I leaned over and put one of my hands over one of hers. We were not people who often touched each other, but for the second time in thirty minutes, I held my mother's hand in mine. Her skin was soft, thin and loose as a silk glove.

"What are you saying?"

"I'm saying that I would like you to take this box of books and give it to Avery."

"You wouldn't do anything—rash, would you?"

"Don't be stupid," she scoffed. "I am many things, but I am never rash. I am also never desperate or despairing or whatever else you might be thinking."

I nodded. "Yes, you're never any of those. But please just remember—"

I almost said it: I love you. Because what I felt for my mother might not have been the staunch camaraderie I used to feel—mostly still did feel—for my faraway brother, Trevor, or the utter comfort of being with Kirsten or the weary but long-standing affection I'd always felt for Harris. Certainly, it bore no resemblance to my fierce, exhilarating, searing, bone-deep, sky-wide, all-in love for my daughter. But it was love all the same, love distant and fraught and inescapable.

I couldn't say it to her, though. Saying those words would be like introducing an invasive plant into our fragile little ecosystem of a relationship.

Instead, I said, "Mom, you could live a lot longer than you or anyone else expects. You never know."

My mother smiled. "When you were a girl, you used to love that phrase. *You never know.* Remember?"

My breath caught in my chest.

"You noticed that?" I said.

"You'd say it all the time, not with anxiety the way people sometimes do, but with relish."

It was something that would slip my mind for weeks, months. How, once, I had been a soaring, iridescent girl, a girl who loved the mystery of life, the potential in every moment to tip over into something else, you never knew what. How could it be that my mother, Adela Beale, had all these years held on to this truth about me?

Then, she said, "You went full tilt, didn't you? Headlong into everything. You were something to see back then."

You know when you're little and it starts to snow, and you catch flakes like tiny stars on the dark sleeve of your jacket and they are amazing, and you don't want to move or breathe?

Finally, I said, "Mom. I didn't know you saw that in me. I thought you just thought I was wild. Careless."

And then it was over. Her face went sharp again. She said with bite, "I don't miss much. Careless, yes. I noticed that. And I also noticed when you started to be careful."

"You say that like it's a bad thing."

She lifted an eyebrow.

"What can I say? People change," I said.

"Yes," she said. "Sometimes they do. Sometimes, people go through a difficult time and they change."

I flashed to the second half of my senior year in high school, my room with the blinds drawn, my body creaky as an old woman's, my heart barren as the moon.

"That's right," I said.

"But then, after a time, if they have any backbone at all, if they're not a complete invertebrate, they pull up their socks, find the part of themselves they misplaced, and take it back."

I saw what was happening: my mother, controlling as ever, wanting to end the conversation on a classic hard-as-nails, acid-tongued Adela Beale note. Another day, what she'd said would have made me furious, but I smiled.

"I was something to see. You said that," I teased.

My mother moved her hand in the manner of someone waving off a bad smell.

"That suitcase is heavy," she said. "Don't scuff the walls on your way down the stairs."

Chapter Seven

August 24, 1997

Language has a way of turning ugly in my
mother's mouth. For instance, adjectives.
She can take a perfectly decent, even
complimentary word like "vivacious," fill
it with battery acid, and hurl it at a
person, her own daughter, for instance,
like a toxic water balloon, so that by the
time it splatters all over her target, me,
for instance, the word goes from meaning
"effervescent" or "lively" to a synonym for
some rancid, nonexistent word that means
shallow, desperate, clownish, and tedious all
at the same time.

It's very clever on her part because if I
get mad or hurt and accuse her of insulting

me, she'll say that she was not aware that "vivacious" is generally considered an insult and that I must be unusually "sensitive" to pick up on such a connotation. And then—if I don't just shut my mouth and head the hell out of the room, if I let myself get sucked in, which I stupidly too often let myself get— it begins all over again with "sensitive." It would almost be better if she just called me shallow, desperate, clownish, and tedious. Oh, wait. She does that, too.

Adela's favorite words to throw at me are a whole slew of synonyms for the word "idealistic." Quixotic, starry-eyed, romantic, hopeful, optimistic. Obviously, it takes a very special kind of person—and an even more special kind of mother—to turn "hopeful" into an insult, but without raising her voice or sneering or even showing any facial expression, God forbid, whatsoever, Adela pulls it off.

And mostly, I tell her or myself or Trev or Kirsten or CJ or Gray that she's wrong. Dead, dead, dead wrong. That she's a hardboiled, soulless, cynical, embittered *wrong person.* Because when you keep your expectations lofty

and your eyes full of stars, the world rises
to meet you and glows to dazzle you, and
anyway, idealism is just plain brave. And the
beauty of the universe belongs to the brave!
It should and it must and it does. It does.

But there are moments, heart-sunk, throat-
tight moments, when I get scared that she's
right.

Tonight, Gray and I had sex.

I'd wanted it for so long. To be honest,
I'd wanted it before I fell in love with Gray,
wanted it as an experience, the way I have
always wanted to skydive. The newness. The
daring. The letting go, letting go, letting go.

But I love Gray. So I wanted it like that
and also differently. Specifically. Gray and
the barbershop powder scent of his neck and
the way the tendons move in his hands and his
torso like a statue come to life. And his low
laugh. And how certain he is when he throws a
football or a rock across water or anything.

I wanted him so much. Wanted him sharply
like pain and constantly like a drawn-
out ache. Feverishly and also with slow
concentration and calm certainty. From a
distance and also so close up I couldn't tell

whose body was whose. All summer long, I
wanted him like that.

Remember that myth about Tantalus? How the
water receded before he could drink? How the
fruit hung just out of his reach? Until all he
could think about was coolness slipping down
his throat, his teeth sinking into tart flesh,
juice on his tongue. Tantalized is what I was,
all summer long.

"I want you, too," my sweet Gray would say,
his breathing heavy. "I just want it to be
right, the exact right moment."

Then, tonight came.

I expected it to be—I don't know.

Splendid. Every nerve ending a sparkler.

Once, at the end of seventh grade, I took
a school trip to Puerto Rico, and on the
last night, we swam in a bioluminescent bay.
I thought sex would be like that: all our
movements splashing radiance, blue-green light
pouring off our bodies, the bristling white
stars overhead.

Desire, even the word has its roots in
starlight. It really does. De + sidus. Of the
stars. I looked it up, the way I do. Words are

like people; the more you know about them the more interesting they are.

I expected us to have sex and change into something bigger and brighter and to rise up and be triumphant and jubilant forever.

It was over so fast. And, in the few minutes it was happening: oh, but Gray's face, how it looked in the skim milk light coming through his bedroom window. Pale and scared and like he might cry.

Afterward, he was my Gray again. He buried his face in my hair and laughed his rumbling, car-driving-over-a-wooden-bridge laugh. He ran his finger down the length of my arm and kissed the inside of my elbow. He said, "My beautiful, beautiful Zinny."

And I thought, "Thank you for trying so hard," which was the wrong thing to think at such a moment. I know that.

But maybe my expectations were just too high. I was unrealistic. Overly romantic. Way too hopeful. Silly. Maybe the sky never cracks open the first time; maybe angels never sing. Maybe it was only disappointing because I was so sure it would be splendid. Maybe my mother is right that having faith that splendor and magnificence will come through for you is just stupid.

I'll make it up to Gray. Even though he doesn't know what I've been thinking, all these silent, traitorous thoughts, I'll make it up to him. I'll write him a sonnet, one with fifteen lines, so he knows that I love him too much for just fourteen.

Because I do.

September 15, 1997

My friends and I have always said we'd go to Hell and back for each other, and today, at the start of the second week of senior year, we did.

We call it Hell. Kirsten's mother, who went to our school way back when, says they called it Hades and before that, she thinks it was the Underworld. All fine enough names for the basement of our school, which, when you're in it, feels about a million miles straight down and as cut off from the regular, sunlit world as, well, Hell. I prefer the name Hell since it's the most direct and least pretentious,

although as you can see from the Tantalus bit
in my last entry, I'm not above a mythical
allusion. Plus, as CJ says, if you can't show
off what you know when you're a kid and have
basically *just learned* everything you know,
when it's all still shiny and new and you
should be proud of it, there is something
wrong with the world. Of course, CJ has a
large personal investment in believing this
is true, since showing off what he knows—and
knowing more than everyone else—is arguably
the foundation of CJ's entire personality. But
since it's exactly this quality in CJ that led
us to Hell, we can't begrudge him it. Actually,
we don't anyway. CJ might be a know-it-all, but
he's our know-it-all.

Not everyone feels this way. In fact, apart
from a few teachers, the ones especially
comfortable with themselves and their own
brains, most people give CJ a pretty hard
time. He's a flimsy little guy, almost
translucently pale, with the kind of corn silk
hair only toddlers and Finnish people usually
have. Before he started hanging out with us in
ninth grade, some of the meaner kids called
him Al. When CJ found out that this was short

for "albino," he delivered a tutorial on the genetics and physical traits of albinism to any would-be bully within earshot, which, unshockingly, did not do him a bit of good.

Luckily for CJ, Lucretia Mott School isn't exactly a bully stronghold, and even luckier for CJ, in September of ninth grade, he found himself assigned to a group history project with me, Kirsten, and Gray. At fourteen, Gray was already the starting varsity quarterback, something people claimed had not happened since the school was founded in 1870, which basically granted Gray a spot in the high school pantheon for all eternity.

Kirsten's family is one of the wealthiest in town, and they've gone to Lucretia Mott for a bazillion generations, and she's blond and tan and dimpled and was already curvy as a swimsuit model in ninth grade; in fact, she has all the makings of a queen bee except that she was somehow born not giving even the tiniest crap about stuff like that. Even so, people at LM who don't openly worship her at least stay out of her way, maybe in case she decides to exercise her natural-born queen bee rights and sting them.

And then there's me. I'm not sure how
anyone else sees me, but I know how I see
myself: fiery and funny Zinny, a rare bird, a
wildflower, a comet. I love my friends the way
I do everything: entirely.

Gray, Kirsten, and I—we are CJ's circle of
fire. We keep CJ safe.

The worst anyone does nowadays is steal
his clothes, usually his gym clothes, but
sometimes his regular ones. Not permanently.
They always show up. Flapping on a flagpole or
pinned to a bulletin board or stuck inside the
school's big front entrance display case with
the trophies. Betsy, the big-hearted woman who
has worked at the front desk of the school
forever, keeps a set of CJ-size clothing in
a filing cabinet drawer for when the thieves
strike, which happens at least once a month.

Everyone knows the kids who are doing it:
Tommy Fleming, Quincy Jarvis, Bryan Coe, a
good-natured group who are just one slight
remove from CJ-level nerdiness themselves.
Coming from them, the clothes-stealing might
even be a compliment, and it's definitely
turned CJ into kind of a celebrity. CJ, who
has a seemingly bottomless capacity for

worrying, doesn't really even stress about it
anymore.

But then last year, for his seventeenth
birthday, his grandfather bought him the
saxophone of his dreams, an outrageously
pricey piece of brass curvaceousness the sound
of which I once recklessly joked rivaled the
music of the spheres, which prompted CJ to
go on a long diatribe about Pythagoras and
celestial harmonies and the length of an
instrument's air column and musical notes and
Aristotle, too, I think, along with a bouquet
of pretty Latin phrases, and the upshot seemed
to be that the music of the spheres was not in
fact real and if it were real, it would not in
fact be actual music, just math. But CJ does
not dispute the fact that his saxophone makes
a pure, gold, awesome sound.

The trouble is that because he cherishes
it so much, he is terrified of ever not
owning it. Which means, by extension, that
he's terrified someone will steal it. We
have pointed out to CJ that people who have
been happy as clams stealing gym shorts for
the past six years are unlikely to suddenly
graduate to expensive musical instruments,

but CJ still worries. When the saxophone is at school, the band teacher Mr. Oliver keeps it locked in the band room closet to which he swears he owns the only key, but CJ still worries. Honestly, CJ is downright paranoid about it.

So last January, when we had to submit our proposals for our individual senior projects, CJ chose to research and write a paper on the architectural history of the school.

"It started off as a house built in the early 1800s, and then it was built onto, and onto, and built onto again. And in between, old parts were torn down and the inside was reconfigured over and over, and air-conditioning was put in."

We were outside in one of the courtyards, eating lunch. CJ had just started researching his project and was doing the thing he did when he got excited, which was jitter his legs under the table and flutter his hands frantically around in the air like two white moths.

Kirsten leaned her chin on her fist. "Air-conditioning vents and drywall. Fascinating."

Gray laughed. "It is, though," he said. "It's like the whole story of the school is folded up inside its walls."

"Exactly!" said CJ, jittering and fluttering faster. "And the history of the school is folded up inside the history of the city and the state and the country. For instance, there used to be a full kitchen back near the gym so that girls could learn home ec, while the boys had gym class. Mr. Foulkes the old librarian told me that."

"What's home ec?" asked Kirsten.

"Exactly!" said CJ, practically screeching. "And also there was a room full of typewriters."

"What's a typewriter?" I asked, scratching my head.

"See what I mean? So cool. And that's not all."

"How could there be more?" I asked, smiling at him. To me, an excited, moth-handed CJ is one of the sweetest sights on the planet.

"I know, but there is!" He leaned forward and lowered his voice to a whisper. "Hiding places."

"Who do you need to hide from, honey?" asked Kirsten, frowning.

"Not for me," whispered CJ.

"Oh!" I whispered. "For your sax!"

"Which no one is ever going to attempt to steal. Ever," said Kirsten, rolling her eyes. "Ever."

"Hey," said Gray. "Maybe not. But if a really good hiding place gives CJ peace of mind, that's worth a lot, right?"

It was a Gray thing to say. I picked up his hand with its hills-and-valleys landscape of tendons and kissed it.

And now, months later, when we were supposed to be at lunch, here we were in the basement. Which, as it turns out, isn't just one basement, but three or at least two and a half: one that the custodial staff still use occasionally, then a deeper one you get to through a door, and then another, very small one a few stone steps down from the second one, also behind a door.

Levels! Like Hell!

For some reason, I'd expected dankness. Damp floors and sweating walls, but the place was dry and dusty and crumbly and musty-smelling.

Since CJ had spent the last six months exploring the building and studying old

blueprints and building plans and photographs
from the school archives, he had a lot—and
I mean a *lot*—of information to share, which
he did in a nonstop stream of chatter that
resounded off the basement walls. In addition,
he wore, on his little blond head, a pith
helmet with a headlamp, like a spelunker, so
that every time he turned toward someone,
he blinded them. *And,* for reasons known only
to himself, he carried a baseball bat, which
he occasionally used to pound on something,
usually a wall, in order to demonstrate either
its solidity or its hollowness.

CJ in Hell was something to behold.

The third-level basement was really just a
large room containing a big metal tank-looking
thing with a few little doors in it. CJ said
it was a coal-burning gravity furnace.

"Defunct now, of course," he said.

"Of course," said Kirsten. Kirsten wasn't a
fan of the basement. She kept pulling (mostly)
imaginary cobwebs from her hair.

"But you know what the furnace is now?" CJ
said, grinning.

"I know you'll tell us," said Kirsten.

"What?" asked Gray.

CJ bonked the side of the furnace with his bat, and the clang made us jump.

"The hiding place!" he said.

"You're going to come all the way down here every day to hide your sax?" I asked. "CJ. Honey. Is that not a little crazy? And how will you not get caught?"

CJ thumped his chest with his child-size fist, then raised the fist to the ceiling. "This is my domain!"

"Ooh boy," said Kirsten, pinching the bridge of her nose and squeezing her eyes shut.

"Down here, I feel like we're in a whole different world. And the longer we're here, the more I realize I'm forgetting the real world," I said.

"What real world?" said CJ.

"Maybe it doesn't exist anymore!" I said. "You never know."

Kirsten shivered. "It'd better exist."

For a few seconds, no one said anything. CJ swung his head around, surveying his domain, and we watched his beam of light slide around the walls and ceiling. Then, Gray said, "Maybe we should just stay down here. Never go back up."

He wasn't joking. His voice was as dusty as the room we stood in. And something else. Dispirited. Hopeless. Sad.

Gray has been sad for weeks. Not crying-sad. And not all the time. But even when he's laughing or kissing me or making jokes, the sadness is there, dulling the colors, muting the sounds. Every time I ask him about it, he teases me or kisses me or puts me off. Gray is so good. People with hearts like his should never be sad. It is a cosmic wrong.

"I'll stay down here with you any day," I said, winking at him. But the smile he gave me was just his lips moving.

Later, on the phone tonight, in a colorless voice, he told me that now that he was eighteen, he's decided to go from being a junior firefighter to an actual full-fledged volunteer. Gray's father is a career firefighter, but Gray always says he doesn't like it, that he only does it because he thinks his dad wants him to.

"You have one more year of high school," I said. "Why not stop? Life's too short to spend so much time on something you don't like."

"I guess I just want to get close to my dad," said Gray.

"But you *are* close to your dad."

It's true. Gray's dad is crazy about him, goes to all his games, tells him all the time how proud he is of his football, his grades. He's crazy about me, too. He pulls my ponytail and laughs at my jokes and says he can't wait till I'm officially his daughter-in-law.

There was a long hesitation, and I heard Gray start to say something a couple of times. I could feel his nervousness, a nervousness I couldn't understand, thrumming through the phone line.

Finally, he said, "*Stay* close. I want to make sure I stay close to him. No matter what."

I am going to write Gray a story about a boy so nice he gets elected King of Everything. I'll give him a chapter every day, complete with illustrations. I'll leave the chapters in his car, his locker, his backpack, his football bag to surprise him, and I'll keep writing, the story won't end, until Gray is happy again.

I'm starting it now.

Chapter Eight

GINNY

I found out that my mother was dead on the precise morning—if not at the precise moment—that fall gave way to winter. I was walking to the dog park in the just-before-dawn dark. Little creatures of light that they were, Dobbsey and Walt didn't love darkness; they were moving in the straight-ahead, sandpiper-legs way they did when they were unnerved and just wanted to get wherever they were going. And then, as I was stepping from the curb to the street, as my foot dropped, I swear the temperature did, too. The crystalline air went from brisk to cold. I shivered inside my too-light quilted jacket and thought about the dogs, the chill seizing their tiny shiver-prone bodies, and I was about to turn around to go home and get us all coats when my phone rang, scaring me nearly out of my skin.

It was Agnes, our long-suffering nurse. Lately, since my mother's decline had begun, precipitously, to gather speed, Agnes or another nurse, a new one named Lomy, whom my mother viewed with keen disapproval the way she did most things she hadn't handpicked, had been spending nights at my mother's house. I had a meeting scheduled for the following day with Agnes and our family doctor, Godwin DeGray, who was overseeing my mother's palliative care, to discuss increasing her pain medication. Goddy was my mother's childhood friend, a man so kind he was my best evidence—maybe my only evidence—that my mother had once been something other than the woman I'd known. My mother was not particularly nice to Goddy and seemed to regard him from the same cool distance that she did the rest of us. But Goddy never stopped being nice to her, nice and unfailingly loyal. He was—had been for a long time—as he liked to say, "on the blessed verge of retirement," and I wasn't sure, but it seemed possible that my mother was his only remaining patient. When she was finished, he would be, too.

I stood very still and stared at Agnes's name on my phone screen, the notes of my ringtone pinballing into the darkness. I filled my lungs with cold air and said, "Hi, Agnes."

"Ginny," she said, her voice tinny and strained. "Last night, she sent me home. She said you were staying with her. Are you in there?"

"What? No. I mean I offer to stay overnight all the time, but she flat out refuses. I'm walking to the dog park."

I heard Agnes groan. "Oh God."

"What?"

"I shouldn't have left last night. And she locked the dead bolt. I don't have a key to that. I can't get in."

"Agnes? It's okay. Maybe Lomy is with her."

"She said that you were spending the night, that you'd be there within fifteen minutes. I didn't want to leave before you got there, but she insisted. You know how she insists."

"Hold on just a second," I said.

I sat down on the curb and dropped my head between my knees. I could feel Dobbsey and Walt butting their noses against the top of my head.

"Ginny—"

"Maybe she just wanted to be alone?" I said. "That would be like her, to want a night alone."

"Maybe. I'm standing on your mom's front porch," said Agnes. "You'd better come."

She'd left an envelope taped to her front door. On the envelope, she'd written: *Agnes, Give this Envelope to*

Virginia Before You Open this Door. Call Her Right Now. I Mean It. Inside was a note to me.

Dear Virginia,

I request that you not enter my house. Call 911
and have them send an ambulance, although you can
tell the dispatcher that there is no need for sirens and
lights or for exceeding the speed limit. Insist upon
this. We don't need a circus.

I would prefer that you not see me in what
will be my current state at the time you read this
(although I assure you that I am well turned out and
perfectly presentable), but I anticipate that you will
be tempted to not honor that preference because of
some misguided and ridiculous goal of achieving
"closure." Trust me: I am dead.

I chose this. I made a plan and executed it, the
way I always do. I was entirely sane and clearheaded
at every stage of the process. No one helped. My
death was not the result of foul play, although I
know that if it had been, there would be a long list
of viable suspects, a fact I view as evidence of a well-
lived life.

Do not be foolish enough to assume that I did this
because I was despondent. I have never in my life
been despondent. And for God's sake, don't blame

yourself or anyone else. That would be arrogant and presumptuous. No one but I had anything to do with this.

My attorney Henry Hill has all of my instructions. I will be cremated. No funeral.

I died the way I lived, on my own terms. You might try living that way, as well, Virginia.

Your mother,
Adela Sartin Beale

Shoulder to shoulder, Agnes and I sat together on my mother's front steps as I read this. Around and above us was full-blown morning. Clear blue, cantaloupe orange. A comma of moon, vanishing. From somewhere inside the house, I could hear singing, two women's voices, silver and gold, rippling into and out of each other like tributaries. When I finished the letter, I handed it to Agnes to read and tugged my jacket sleeves over my hands to warm them.

When Agnes finished reading, very soon, I would call 911. The ambulance would come, a tumult of violent red and whirling lights but no siren, a police car, too. There would be chatter and people, neighbors materializing silently on the front walk. I would see my mother's face, sunken above the carefully buttoned collar of her gray silk blouse, her skin like paper that had been crumpled and then smoothed out, her eyes shut.

Soon, I would have to perform an accounting of my feelings, to measure the dimensions of the new Adela-shaped hole in my life.

But for now, for these seconds, there was peace: a shining sky, sleeping flower beds, voices like water.

"Delibes," I said, remembering. "The 'Flower Duet.'"

Agnes folded the letter, slid it back into the envelope, and pressed it into my hand.

"Your mother was too weak to stand," said Agnes, very quietly.

"I know," I said.

"When I left, she was upstairs, in bed."

"Yes, I thought she probably was."

"This letter was on the front door."

"I know."

"She couldn't have done that."

I closed my eyes and imagined Goddy, shutting the front door behind him, taping the letter to it. I think he must have done that. Maybe he did more before then, back in the house: turned on music, administered drugs, kept watch. Maybe he hadn't. But I knew that whatever he'd done he'd done because of a friendship so long-standing it had not mattered when one of the two people in it had ceased, a long time ago, to be a friend.

I put the letter into my pocket and took Agnes's two hands in mine. Her blue eyes were gentle. I looked into them steadily and told her this: "I say she could have. She has always been capable of much more than anyone would ever guess."

For a moment, we sat there, eyes and hands locked. Then, Agnes nodded.

"I'm sure you're right," she said.

I took out my phone and dialed 9-1-1.

When I got home, chilled and dizzy with exhaustion and with so many phone calls to make, a sky-blackening swarm of phone calls hanging directly over my head, I made myself coffee in the French press I'm usually too lazy or impatient to use. And there was a holiness in it. I don't mean in the coffee itself, but in the unhurried act of making it. Pouring hot water into the carafe to warm it, opening the bag of oily, deep brown, clicking beans, breathing in their nutty fragrance, grinding them to a coarse grit. The water tumbling into the kettle made a solemn music. In the intervals of waiting—for the water to boil, for the coffee to brew—I let my mind rest empty as the white coffee bowl Avery had given me last Mother's Day because she knew I liked to warm my hands on my cup. And then the slow downwardness of the plunger, the coffee arcing from the spout. I even frothed milk, and it floated in my bowl like snow. I am not religious, but there is something prayer-like about tasks that you cannot rush through, the steady work of hands, every step imbued with patience.

When I'd drunk, small sip after small sip, and cleaned the press and my bowl, and put everything away, I called Kirsten. Just weeks ago, I would've called Harris, not instinctively, but because he was my husband, the person you call when something happens. But I decided, right then and there, that one of the privileges of having a husband who had lost his mind over a teenager was not calling him when you didn't feel like it. I didn't even know where he was. Although he was technically still camping out in the room above the garage, his car hadn't been in the driveway when I'd gotten home from my mother's. In fact, his car hadn't been in the driveway all that much lately, and my near lack of curiosity about where he'd been spending his days surprised even me.

"Tell me you're calling because you just threw Harris out on his wide ass and you want to celebrate" is how Kirsten answered her phone.

"Could you dial back on the empathy?" I said. "I mean, jeez, compassion is great and all, but this is getting to be too much. And it's not that wide. I'd say wide is the wrong adjective altogether."

"Wrong. Harris has man hips. When those big, muscular Big Foot types age, they get man hips, and Harris is no exception."

"Again with the empathy."

"Your voice sounds weird. What's the story, morning glory?"

I shut my eyes for a moment the way I used to do before I opened them and jumped off the ridge into the quarry. Because my mother's death was about to become real. Even though Agnes and about eight million Fire and Rescue workers and hospital workers and a gaggle of ogling neighbors with coats thrown over their pajamas knew that Adela was dead, it wouldn't become really real until I told someone I loved. Such was the way of my world.

"My mom died this morning. Or maybe last night."

"Oh, honey. That's big."

And as soon as Kirsten spoke those words, I realized that's exactly what it was. Maybe not sad. Or painful. Or a relief. Although it might eventually strike me as all of those things. But it was big because, whatever else she'd been or failed to be, Adela had been *big*.

"Yes."

I heard bumping and rustling on the other end of the line and knew that Kirsten was putting on shoes, tugging on her coat, probably searching for her keys, which she was always losing. Pretty soon, she'd start rooting around in myriad bags and pockets and drawers for her phone before she realized she was talking to me on it.

"First Harris, now Adela. That's a shit-ton of change for you at once. Spectacularly bad timing."

I smiled. "So inconsiderate."

"Okay, okay, so maybe the timing was outside of Adela's control," said Kirsten, in a funny, grudging voice. "Although it's strange to think of anything being outside of Adela's control. You'd think she'd be like, 'Death, bend to my will.'"

"Actually, she *was* like that."

Silence as this sank in, then: "You know what? Go, Adela!" And then: "Wait. I'm sorry. I should be more sensitive."

"Why start now?"

"I actually wasn't being glib, though. For once."

"I know you weren't."

"What did she have? Weeks? Days?"

"Something like that."

"I'm heading out to my car."

"Yeah, but where's your damn phone?"

"Oh crap. Hold on."

"Kirsten."

All the rustling paused. I could picture Kirsten coming to a dead stop in her kitchen, her free hand going instantly to her hair. Kirsten always smoothed her hair when she got serious, as if whatever there was to face, she would face it better without flyaways.

"What?"

"When I went over to my mom's this morning, Avery was still asleep. I left a vague note, giving her permission to ride with a neighbor kid to school. But she'll be home soon."

"I'll help you tell her."

"She wasn't that close to my mom, but this is her first death."

"What about that goldfish?"

"She was four, and I bought a replacement and dropped it into the bowl before she got home from school."

"Can't do that with Adela. She was one of a kind."

"She was."

"Whoever made her broke the mold."

"Probably smashed it to smithereens," I said. "And stomped on the pieces."

"That's my girl! See you in ten, Zin Zin."

When Avery rushed into the house, her cheeks rosy from the cold, she didn't even take off her coat before she plopped down into Kirsten's lap.

"You weigh ten tons and are rupturing my internal organs," said Kirsten, "but, God, you're gorgeous."

"All of your organs?" said Avery.

"Every last one. Except my spleen. That seems to be intact."

Avery bounced. Kirsten yelped.

"Whoop, there it went," she said.

Avery laughed, stood up, then flopped down onto the rug so the dogs could climb on her. Dobbsey and Walt were so small that when they were overjoyed, their bodies became one big wag.

"Seriously," said Kirsten to me. "What do people do who have ugly kids?"

"Hate them," I said.

"Of *course* they do! What if Tex and I have ugly kids?"

Kirsten called her boyfriend Tex because he was the most New England person ever to be born. Sailing. Squash. Harvard. Nantucket red pants. A library with a ladder. His real name was Adams Frost. I adored him.

"You'll hate them," I said.

"Have a baby," said Avery, pointing her finger at Kirsten. "ASAP. I need something to play with."

"Well, in that case," said Kirsten.

There was Avery, still in her down jacket, aglow and sprawled on our rug with easy, face-to-the-sky joy, like a little girl making snow angels, more relaxed than I'd seen her since Harris got fired, and I sat drinking in the sight, wanting the moment to last forever, while all the while I was about to drop death into the room like a bomb. When she was four, riding in her booster seat in the back of the car, she'd spotted a raccoon dead on the shoulder of the road and asked why it was there and if it was okay, and immediately, I said, "He's just taking a nap" ("A nice little nap. On the road. In a pool of his own blood," Kirsten would quip later, when I told her about it), and Harris shot me a reproving look. When we talked about it that night, I argued that she was too young, that even if she weren't too young, a girl who fought off sleep like a demon, who believed, at 3:00 A.M., that there were snakes coiled up in her dresser drawers and scary "ladies made of bones" in her closet, did not need to add death to her night-panic repertoire. The snakes and ladies might be gone, but Avery was still that child grappling with wild fears in the middle of the night.

"Avery, sweetheart," I said, gently.

She sat up fast, causing the dogs to slide off onto the floor. All three of them looked at me with wide quizzical, worried brown eyes.

"Is it Dad again?" she asked, and for the first time that day, I wanted to cry.

After I told her, Avery cried. Not hard. No sobbing. But she cried the way she did sometimes in the car when we went on our insomnia drives. Tears running down her cheeks, but no sound at all. Over in minutes, like a summer rainfall.

"You know what's weird?" she said, afterward, wiping her eyes. "I'm crying because I'm sad that I'm not sadder."

"Don't be, baby," I said. "This is truly a case of whatever you feel is the right thing to feel."

I was sure about this for Avery. For myself, my feelings or lack of feelings? Not so sure.

Avery sat next to me on the living room sofa, both dogs in her lap, their faces turned toward hers, tipped upward like pansies facing the sun. Kirsten sat, cross-legged, on the floor at our feet.

"Your grandmother was just not that good at being a person," I said.

"How did she turn out that way?"

I shook my head. "I didn't know her parents that well, but from what I remember, they seemed nice. A little formal. Her dad seemed to always be reading something, even at Christmastime. A newspaper or a book. My mom had a younger sister who died at the age of maybe ten or eleven. Leukemia, I think. The only reason I know is that there was a photo of the two of them together at my grandparents' house, and I asked about it once. Her name was Frances, and they called her Franzy."

"Franzy," said Avery, thoughtfully. "That seems like a nickname for someone in a happy house, doesn't it?"

"Yes," I said. "I thought the same thing."

"I never knew that," said Kirsten. "About the sister."

"She told me the one time I asked and then never mentioned it again," I said.

"Do you think that's why she is the way she is?" said Avery. "*Was*, I mean."

"I don't know," I said. "Growing up, I wanted to believe that was why, but she had so many chances to change over the years, so many reasons to be different. Trevor, for instance, and me."

"Honestly," said Kirsten, "and I realize I'm biased here because Adela never liked me, not even for five minutes by accident, but for a long time, I thought she was just probably born that way, missing a chip."

"You *thought*?" said Avery. "What changed your mind?"

Kirsten's eyes met mine.

"You," I said to my daughter. "She loved you."

"Oh," said Avery. Her eyes began to well again.

"No, don't feel bad that you didn't know it or didn't love her back," I said, quickly. "I didn't realize it myself for a long time. When you were born, she didn't act interested in you. She came by after I'd brought you home from the hospital, and she didn't even ask to hold you. She just looked you over appraisingly, as if you were a piece of furniture she was thinking of purchasing, and said, 'Well, she got the Sartin ears, thank God. Harris's ears are a travesty.' I was furious."

"She had a point about Harris's ears," said Kirsten.

I shot her a warning look, but Avery laughed.

"One day, when you were about six, our babysitter canceled, and I had to leave you with Adela," I said. "When I went to pick you up, my mother was sitting at one end of the dining room table, working, and you were sitting at the other end cutting out snowflakes, totally absorbed. I used to love to cut out snowflakes."

"Did she teach you?" said Avery. "And then she taught me?"

I looked at her, startled. "You know, I don't know. Maybe. We might have learned in school, but it's possible she taught us. She liked activities that kept children busy."

"Mom," said Avery, reprovingly. "Maybe she taught us because she thought we would like doing it."

I nodded. "You never know. Anyway, months later, I was getting something out of the front hall table in her house, keys or something, and I found a box inside it with three snowflakes in it. You'd written your name on the backs of each one. And that's when I knew she loved you."

"Three snowflakes?" said Avery. "That's it?"

"She kept them," I said. "She never kept anything Trev or I made. And you know what else?"

"What?"

"They were awful. All raggedy and asymmetrical."

"Mom, I was *six*."

"True, but they were some seriously ugly snowflakes. And my mother hates—hated—ugly things. She disdained imperfection, and she kept your snowflakes." I laughed. "I'm sure she chose the three best ones, but they were still some bad, bad snowflakes."

"Keeping three bad snowflakes would not qualify as most people's most loving act," said Kirsten. "But Adela wasn't most people."

"Not even close," I said.

"Not even a little bit," said Kirsten.

"Still, she kept them. *And* she gave you that suitcase full of books," I said to Avery. "What are they, by the way?"

An odd look crossed Avery's face. Guarded, maybe even guilty. "I don't—"

"It's okay if you haven't opened it yet," I said. "Don't worry about it."

"Okay," said Avery.

After a while, she said, "She's just not here anymore. A person can just suddenly—boom—stop *being*."

"It's strange to think about her being gone," I said. "She took up so much space in the world."

Avery tilted her head and rested it on my shoulder for a few seconds. "Are you okay, Mom?"

I fitted my hand to the curve of her face. Was I okay? I felt a bodily tiredness, as if I'd spent a couple of days raking leaves (a task I loved, actually), and the fact that my mother had ended her own life existed beyond me for now, ungraspable. I hadn't spoken aloud or even really thought the word *suicide*, yet. I could sense it waiting for me, a sibilant, slippery presence, part coo, part wail, in the back of my mind. But I was here in my house. Kirsten, Avery, and my little dogs were here. And my love for them was vast and unreserved and elemental.

"Yes, sweetheart. Thank you for asking."

She stood up. "I think I'll go upstairs now."

"Sure. Go do your thing."

She turned to leave and then turned back.

"Thank you for telling me about the snowflakes," she said. "It made me feel much sadder and less sad that I wasn't more sad."

And then, to cheer me up, in case I needed it, my precious, funny girl grinned her cheekiest grin at me, the one that bunches up her nose and makes her eyes turn into crescents.

This is how mothers and daughters are supposed to be, I thought, *this is right and just and good.* Maybe that was where grief would lie: not in my mother's leave-taking, but in all that she had missed out on while she was here.

"Oh, sure," I told her, shrugging. "That's what I'm here for."

Proof that a person can get used to anything is that there were whole weeks when I didn't miss my brother, Trevor, and there were phone calls between us during which the sound of his voice did not make me immediately want to fall on the ground crying and making wild bargains with God to get him back into my life.

Most of the time, though, he was my phantom limb, the pauses between my breaths when I couldn't sleep, the blur caught in my peripheral vision, the voice that came winging at me out of nowhere. I would be in the middle of something—cooking or planting bulbs or watching one of Avery's games—and it would hit me like a punch in the stomach that Trevor and I weren't close anymore and that I would give anything to go back and undo what had come between us.

In the middle of my senior year of high school, Trevor and my mother had had a fight to end all fights, and he had gone away, carried on two waves of rage— hers and his—and had never, in any true way, come home again. And right around the time he left, I—cut loose and falling through my own pitch-black, screech-ing tunnel of depression—pulled away at the exact moment when I should have moved toward, until the space between us got too big to bridge.

He'd gotten married (I'd gone to the wedding; Adela had not), and he and Iris had twin boys, Sam and Paxton. They were almost eight years old and I didn't even know them. I'd visited them two months after they were born, and I'd been in their presence a few times since, but I didn't *know* them. It did not seem to lie within the realm of the possible, not knowing Trev's sons; my up-until-age-eighteen self would've unleashed scorn and fury on anyone who'd suggested such a thing could happen. And yet.

I asked Kirsten to stay while I called him. And right before I did, she gave voice to my own fragile, newborn hope, one I didn't even realize I had before she said it: "Maybe with your mother gone, you and Trevor can find each other again."

"We've seen each other eight times in the past twenty years, never for more than two or three hours at a time, and we've never had a real conversation. If it weren't for Iris, he probably wouldn't see me at all," I said.

"And Avery," said Kirsten. "If it weren't for Avery."

"It's true. They text sometimes, nothing serious, just goofiness and teasing, but it's something."

"Ask him to come," said Kirsten. "I bet it will be different without Adela around."

"I won't ask him to come. I don't want to put him on the spot. If he wants to be here, he will."

Kirsten said, "Oh, Ginny, just *ask him*."

"No."

I asked him.

I didn't just ask him.

I said, "Trev, I know it's been so long since we were close, and it's probably mostly my fault, but I miss you. I wish you would come."

Idiot. Idiot, idiot, idiot.

To be fair to my idiotic self, I didn't lead with that plaintive and pathetic plea. I called and he answered the phone, and I recounted, calmly, clearly, like a news anchor, the events of the day.

Trevor laughed a barbed and bitter laugh and said, cheerfully, "In control till the end, the old despot."

"Yup," I said.

"Let me guess. She planned her own funeral down to the seventeen nauseating, praise-singing eulogies and the exact number of petals on the white lilies."

And there it was: you can hate your mother and leave her and not speak to her for the last twenty years of her life, but you will still, in spite of yourself, remember her favorite flower. What a terrible bind we are in, kids with difficult parents.

I didn't say any of this to Trevor. I said, "I think they always have six petals."

"Yeah, well, if Adela Beale wanted five, someone would probably figure out how to grow them that way."

"Mutant lilies! Now!"

"Exactly."

"I assumed that, too: the big, fancy funeral. Flags at half-staff all over town. But no. She didn't want people to get together and discuss her without her there to edit what they said. No funeral, and she's getting cremated. But she wrote her own obituary."

"I don't want my name in it."

"Who's trying to control the narrative now?"

I meant it to come out teasingly, but Trevor snapped, "Still on her side, I see. Team Adela forever."

After so long, to be still talking about sides. *Don't stoop to defend yourself, Ginny. Don't take the damn bait. Move on like he didn't say it.*

"No," I said. "I can see how you might think it, but that's never been true. Ever."

Silence, during which I silently called myself an idiot and decided—decided *decisively*—to say goodbye and get the hell off the phone immediately.

"Do you think you'll come?" I said.

I said it, then banged myself in the forehead with my fist.

"And what? Sit around eating casseroles and reminiscing about how much she hated me?"

"Oh God, do you think the neighbors will bring casseroles? Because that would make Adela insane," I said.

"White trash food," said Trevor, in a precise imitation of our mother's voice.

"Tuna noodle with cream of mushroom soup! Please, God, let someone bring that."

"With crumbled saltines on top!"

And then my brother, Trevor, laughed. Not the acidic, sneering laugh from the beginning of our conversation, but a true, short-blast Trev laugh that jarred something loose inside of me, a shiny, sharp-edged thing. Love, I guess it was.

"Trev, I know it's been so long since we were close, and it's probably mostly my fault, but I miss you. I wish you would come."

"Gin," said Trevor.

It wasn't "Zin," but it was close enough. I felt like someone had handed me a diamond.

Then, nothing. Then, "Listen, I have to go. Thanks for giving me the news."

"Tell me about *your* mom," I said to Daniel.

It was the kind of winter morning when every leaf is furred with frost. The grass of the dog park crunched underfoot, and the sun floated, a fuzzy white puffball, in the slate sky. The morning felt like a black-and-white photograph colorized here and there: my red gloves; my dogs' jackets, one orange, one yellow; a woman's bright blue knit hat in the distance. In the muffled light, Daniel's eyebrows were two black slashes in a pale face; his eyes shone moonstone gray.

"You want to talk about my mom?" said Daniel.

"All I've done lately is talk about my mom to people. I mean, most of the time, it's because they ask. In the grocery store, in my neighborhood, at her lawyer's office, at Avery's school. But you and Mag have had to hear all the stuff I didn't say to those people, all those thrilling mother-daughter dysfunction stories. No wonder Mag didn't come today."

"Oh yeah," said Daniel. "As soon as you walk away, Mag and I are like 'Can you believe her? Still talking about her mom after four whole days?'"

"So you decided to take shifts," I said, nodding. "Good thinking."

He smiled at me. Daniel's smile involved rampant eye twinkling and several sets of parentheses around his mouth. I'd seen it lots of times before, but for some reason, this time, the sight dazzled me. His smile swept through that gray morning like a lighthouse beam.

"Exactly. Which means I'll have all tomorrow to recover," he said. "So fire away."

"Seriously, I'm sick of the sound of my own voice," I said. "Especially when it's talking about my own life."

"Well, hold on to your hat, then. Because Mary Nash York is a fascinating human being."

"Her maiden name is Nash?"

"Her maiden name is Briggs. Mary Nash is her two-name first name. It's a southern thing."

"I like it."

"I'll tell her. She'll like it that you like it."

"So you grew up in the South?" I said.

When I asked this, Daniel's face turned a shade more serious. He opened his mouth to speak and then hesitated.

"Was that a bad question?" I said.

"No," he said, quickly. "Of course not. There are no bad questions in the dog park, right?"

I'd told Mag and Daniel about how the dog park was my new Quaker burial ground, just blurted that out one morning, mid-conversation, which meant that I then had to explain about my old Quaker burial ground. But despite the topsy-turvy telling, they'd understood instantly.

"It's like there's truth serum in the air," Mag had said. "If serum can actually be in air. Or even if it can't."

"It's like *The Breakfast Club*," Daniel had said. "Except we're nicer to each other and no one has dandruff."

Now, Daniel said, "I guess I just feel a little awkward because I don't think I ever mentioned that I grew up around here. Sort of."

"Oh," I said, startled. "You did? Sort of? You sort of—did?"

He laughed. "Sort of."

"How could I have missed you? Not to embarrass you, but tall? Handsome? Smart enough to become a vet? And you grew up here? Boy, my young self really fell down on the job with that one."

Then, it was as if the invisible person colorizing the black-and-white photo of the morning painted two pink spots, one on each of Daniel's cheeks.

"Well, thanks. But I don't think I was actually any of those things back then."

"You weren't tall?"

"Okay, I was sort of tall. But not this tall. I grew in college."

"Ah. A late bloomer."

"That's a nice way of putting it. The truth is I was kind of a screwup in high school."

"I can't even imagine you being a screwup."

"I started off okay. I was born in Charlottesville, Virginia. My parents met in college there and ended up staying. When I was fifteen, my dad got a new job up here, and we moved, so I spent the last three years of high school at Westville. It was rough, I guess."

Westville was a high school just over the Pennsylvania line. It was big and public, but, probably due to some egregiously strategic school zoning, it drew mostly from an affluent part of the state.

"Rough?" I said. "The mean hallways of Westville?"

"The school wasn't rough. But my transition into it was, so rough that it never fully happened. I hadn't wanted to move. I was shy, and I went from knowing everyone to knowing no one. To get back at my parents, I fell in with some pretty wild kids. We drank too much. Did stupid things. Not terrible things. But stupid."

He dropped his gaze to the frosty grass. "Senior year went completely off the rails. By the time I graduated, I couldn't wait to get out of there."

"My senior year was like that, too," I said, quietly.

"But look at us," said Daniel, brightening. "Back and better than ever."

He pulled off his gloves and got down on one knee to scratch Dobbsey, who was lying, stomach on ground, paws on chin, a position Avery and I called "Flat Dobbsey," at Daniel's feet.

"*You're* better than ever," I said. "I have a would-be philanderer for a husband, a newfound impatience with the directionlessness of my life, and no idea how to grieve for my mother."

Daniel looked up at me, brows lowered, concern in his eyes.

"Do you think there's a right way to do that?" he said. "Could it be that you *are* grieving for her, talking about her, telling stories about what it's been like to be her kid?"

"But all my stories are about how we've never gotten along. Because that's the only kind of stories I've got. The horrible truth is that I don't even know if I miss her. I might not."

Daniel stopped petting Dobbsey, and Dobbsey batted his hand with his paw until he started up again.

"What if—" He paused, and I could see him processing, calling up words. "What if grief isn't only missing people and being sad? That's how we usually think about it. But what if it's just—reckoning with their being gone and with knowing they're never coming back?"

Suddenly, I felt unsteady. All along, all week, I'd been so solid. Now, with what Daniel had just said hovering nearby, without really considering his words or understanding exactly what they meant, I felt my hinges loosening.

"I'll think about that," I said, nodding. "But look! We're talking about me again. I need more info about Mary Nash."

"You can meet her if you want," he said. "She and my dad, Nathan, still live nearby."

"In your old house?"

"Yep. Georgia and I live about a block away."

"Wow," I said. "You didn't just come back, you came back to the same neighborhood."

"Which should have been weird, except that, at the time, I think I just had too many other things to think about."

Daniel stood, but then Dobbsey batted the toe of his sneaker, so Daniel bent down and scooped him up.

"Keep talking," I said, snapping my fingers.

"Bossy," said Daniel.

"Go ahead. Why did you come home?"

"After Libby died, Georgia and I tried going it alone for a while, and I wasn't doing a terrible job. I made dinner, did laundry, got to most of the soccer games before they were over. And my parents would come for a week or so every couple of months to help out."

"That's nice," I said.

"Really nice. But then, after one of their visits, I found Georgia crying. She cried a lot in that first year. So I figured it was that she missed her mom. But when I asked, she said no, that wasn't the reason, not this time. And what she said was 'I miss *you*.' She said, 'When Gram and Grandpop are here to help with stuff, you talk to me. But when they're not, you don't.'"

"Ouch," I said.

"No kidding. She said, 'It's not your fault. I know it's just because you're so busy.' I felt like a jerk."

"So you moved home."

"It feels more like home now than it did when I was in high school, that's for sure."

"If I know Mary Nash and Nathan, they love having you two here."

Daniel smiled. "Nathan's idea of having fun with a twelve-year-old is to just do what he always does but with Georgia. They go birding. And golfing. And out for coffee on Saturday mornings with his buddies. And every Sunday, he brings over sticky buns from his favorite bakery, the *New York Times* crossword puzzle, and two pencils."

"In case you don't have pencils," I said.

"Exactly."

"I'll bet she loves it."

"She does."

"What about my friend Mary Nash? What does she do with Georgia?"

"Well, right now, she's teaching her how to paint."

"Walls?"

"Paintings," said Daniel. "Mary Nash is a painter."

"Really? I used to want to be a painter," I said. "And a writer. I was in love with the idea of making something out of nothing. What are her paintings like?"

"Mary Nash paints portraits of people for a living, mostly children, from life, not photographs. She loves the making something out of nothing, but she loves that part of it, too. The people part."

Impulsively, I reached out and tugged on Daniel's coat sleeve. "You know what you are? You're one of those people who grew up with good parents."

"True."

"Lucky," I said. "That's what you are. Blessed."

And then out of nowhere, I heard my mother saying, *You went full tilt, didn't you? Headlong into everything. You were something to see back then.*

Mose and Walt had ceased adventuring in the gloom and were sitting in the grass nearby, their tails slowly wagging—Mose's golden plume and Walt's thumb-size stub—as if, even with nothing much happening, there was still cause for joy. I wrapped my arms around myself.

"Hey," said Daniel, softly. "You're crying."

I took off my gloves and touched my cheeks with my fingertips and found that he was right. I turned to look at him.

"What if she liked me all that time and I never knew it?" I whispered.

Daniel took a step toward me, handed me Dobbsey, and then he put his arms around us both.

Chapter Nine

November 3, 1997

I can't breathe.

   Or make my brain work.

   I can't write it down.

   I can't write it. I can't write it.

   I can't.

   Nothing is what I thought it was.

   I feel like I got lied to by the entire universe.

   I don't even know who I am now.

   Not Zinny.

   Or even Ginny.

   Not anyone.

I stayed home from school today because maybe
I don't have a fever or a sore throat, but if
anyone was ever sick, I'm sick.

The day before yesterday, he called and said we needed to talk. That's how everything bad begins, isn't it? In movies or stupid TV shows. I should have known. Anyone else would've known that something terrible was about to happen. But us talking has always been good, a completely good thing. So I wasn't ready. I am so stupid.

I trusted him. I believed every single word he has ever said to me.

He picked me up in his car. He didn't kiss me. But I was so happy to see him that I didn't even notice. I hate myself when I remember how happy. I was practically bouncing in my seat like a little kid.

I am so stupid.

I held his hand like I have a thousand times before, his wide, beautiful hand, and said, "Where should we go? The quarry?"

He shook his head, fast and twitchy, like he was shaking off a punch.

"Not there."

That's when I noticed his face. It looked just how it looked the night we'd had sex. Lost and scared and drained of color.

"Hey, baby," I said, "what's wrong?"

"Not now," he said.

He drove and turned into the first really big parking lot we came to and parked in the most faraway spot with no other cars around.

It feels cruel now, that he picked that place. Maybe he didn't want it to be in one of our special places, like the quarry. But there? In the parking lot of the most beat-down grocery store in town? With the dinged-up shopping carts lying around and the giant red ACME letters glaring down at us? The edge of the lot was littered with garbage that looked like it had been there for decades.

No one should have to be staring at fast-food bags snagged in bushes and empty forty-ounce bottles when her life comes crashing down around her.

He wouldn't look me in the eye.

He tried to pull his hand away, but I just held on harder. Because that's what you do when someone you love is sad or afraid. You hold on harder.

Then.

He said.

He said.

How could he?

He said, in this ripped and shredded voice, "I'm so sorry. I'm so sorry. But I'm gay. I'm gay, Zinny."

For a few long seconds, I literally did not comprehend what he'd said. I heard the sounds his mouth made, but I didn't know what they meant.

And then his dark, scared eyes looked into mine and, like a thunderbolt, I understood.

I dropped his hand like it had caught fire and backed up against the car door so hard I banged my head and it hurt.

"You can't mean that," I said, barely getting the words out. "You're lying."

"I wish," he said, dismally.

And then I was screaming at him.

"You say you *love* me, like, every single day! We talk about getting married all the time! How could you do this to me? What the hell is wrong with you?"

He didn't say anything. Just stared out the windshield.

"Was that fun for you?" I screamed. "To lie to me over and over and over, every single day? You're a liar!"

I couldn't stop. I went on and on. Frenzied. Blind. Somewhere in there, I told him I hated

him. He never spoke or looked at me. Only
stared straight ahead with an empty face.

I got out of the car and just started
running.

I can't eat. I feel like throwing up all the
time. I feel like little bits of me are dying.
My mother thinks I have the flu.

I hate him.

How can I hate him?

I loved him so much.

He let me love him.

I wish I could get away from what happened
in that car. Or away from every single day of
the past seven months of my life.

I wish I could go to sleep for the rest of
senior year.

Or forever.

Even now, I don't mean that the way it might
sound. But my heart hurts so much. I wish I
didn't even have one.

November 5, 1997

Kirsten came to see me today. She knows. CJ
knows, too.

I wish I could tell you how it felt to see her face in my house, to see not just someone else who knows this secret that's been weighing me down like rocks but specifically Kirsten, how just the sight of her broke me open and made me cry in a different way from how I'd been crying for days. But I can't make pretty things out of language now. Pretty doesn't have a place here anymore. And anyway, my brain is clumsy and slow and sad. I write this like a three-year-old building something out of blocks. And there's no happiness in it, not a speck. I just need to write these hard things down. I don't even know why.

I let her in the back door, and we went up to my room. The second the door closed behind us, she turned toward me, and her eyes searched my face, and I could see her worry at how bad I look (because I am pasty and stringy-haired and gaunt and a hundred years old), but she reached out, took a scraggly clump of my hair, gently tucked it behind my ear, and said (softly and without any sarcasm), "Leave it to you to still look gorgeous as a movie star even now." And what I realized is that the only thing that had been holding me together for the past three days is that no one had been nice to me. Not my mother because she never is. Not Trevor because I'd been hunkered down in my room, claiming to be sick, and he never had the chance.

She did the hair looping and said that sweet if entirely untrue thing, and my chest started heaving and I burst into croaky sobs so harsh my throat and my whole chest were sore afterward.

Kirsten put her arms around me, and we sat down on my bed, and I cried for what felt like a week.

"I know," she crooned over and over. "I know, Zin Zin."

When I was all emptied of crying, I said, "We had this future all planned out. It was beautiful and exciting and now it's gone. Trashed. Burned. Disappeared."

"I know how much that must hurt," Kirsten said.

"I feel just exactly like someone died."

I heard Kirsten take a deep breath. Then, she said, "But Gray's still alive."

His name said out loud was like someone sticking a pin into me.

"And he's still Gray," she said.

I shook my head. "He's not the Gray I knew."

Kirsten put her hand on the side of my face and swiveled my head to face her. "No. He *is*," she said, firmly.

"What?" I said. "Are you taking his side?"

"There aren't sides, Zinny. This isn't a war with good guys and bad guys."

"So what is it? What is the name for this situation?"

"I don't know. It doesn't matter. The thing is he's still Gray. He's still funny and smart and brave and *nice*. He's our friend. He's all the things he always was. Except now we know this one other thing about him. It doesn't change the other stuff or cancel it out. It's just an addition."

I sat there, my hands pressed together, holding each other tight, like someone praying. But I wasn't praying. I was wrestling with what Kirsten had just said. And I can't tell which I was trying harder to do: understand what she'd said or push it away.

Before I could figure it out, Kirsten said something else: "He's still Gray. And he's scared and sad and hates himself for doing this to you. And—listen to me. Are you listening?"

He's still Gray.

My hands released each other, and I spread them open on my lap, palms down, and I nodded.

Kirsten said, "And he's right on the edge of hating himself in general. Gray, the best guy in the world, who sticks up for everyone, hating who he is. Think about that."

It was like there were automatic garage doors inside my head and as Kirsten said this, they all slid slowly open and light came in. Light and Gray. Grays. One Gray after the next. Laughing. And debating in class. And scraping the cheese off his pizza because he doesn't like cheese but the rest of us do. Gray always laughing with—never at—CJ. And helping Kirsten with math. Gray giving other guys on the team the credit when people congratulate him on a game. Gray listening to me tell a story, giving me his full attention and never interrupting. His face going all thoughtful when he reads something I've written or looks at one of my watercolors. Gray's voice on the phone at night with me, telling me the kind of person he wants to be when he grows up, noble and strong and interesting, telling me I will be extraordinary and brilliant because—*just look at you, Zinny*—I already am.

Gray Marsden had never hurt me on purpose. He never would.

I'd wanted to keep him forever. I'd wanted us to live in our house and share our secrets and raise our astonishing, beautiful children together. And now I can't, ever, ever, and that terrible truth will never stop hurting me.

But what I said next to Kirsten was true, too: "No one is allowed to hate Gray. Especially not Gray. That can't happen."

She gave me a long hug. "My Zinny."

"I wanted to be in love with him forever," I said, so sadly.

Kirsten grabbed my hand and squeezed it. "I know."

"And now I'll have to be just his friend, and he'll go off and be in love with someone else someday."

"I know. But you will, too."

"I can't even imagine it," I said. Tears burned in my eyes again, but I rubbed them away. "But I hope so. I hope it for both of us."

Tonight, I'll sneak out of my house and leave a note for Gray on his windshield, asking if I can come see him tomorrow night.

I am tired and sad and may never be in love with anyone again. But it seems that I am still Zinny.

November 6, 1997

2:22 A.M.

I dreaded seeing Gray. I was scared he would look different to me, like a stranger. I was scared he would look exactly the same to me and I would want him like always and would fall to pieces because I couldn't have him. I was scared that I would look into his eyes and see him seeing me as ugly or repulsive, as someone he couldn't believe he had ever touched. I was so very, very scared that when I heard him coming across his yard to the spot behind his detached garage where we always met, I started shaking and not from cold. My teeth were actually chattering, their clicking sounds so loud in my ears that I was afraid I'd wake up Gray's dad and little brother, Jimmy, and maybe the entire neighborhood.

Then, there he was, tall and broad and moon-stained, a bundle of blankets in his arms, the two Black Watch plaid ones I'd seen a hundred times at least. I waited for pain to run me over, but instead I felt my muscles unknotting, the ones at the base of my scalp and little ones in my temples and forehead that I don't even usually realize I have.

Just being near Gray, even before I fell in love with him, has always made me feel this sense of not calm, exactly (because God knows the guy excites me. Or did. Or does. Does), but something I don't even know the name of. Well-being? Comfort? Or maybe reassurance. You know the song "Let It Be" by the Beatles? Whenever I hear it, instantly, from the opening notes, I'm aware of a solid rightness at the heart of life, and I don't so much think the words "Everything is going to be all right" as feel them in the center of my chest and down the length of my spine.

Gray is "Let It Be" in human form.

But I didn't expect him to still be, not now, after everything, and, really, it wasn't

quite the same. Now, what Gray's presence said
to me was something more like: "Maybe, just
maybe, if we're patient and lucky, everything
is going to be all right." Still, it was
surprising.

"Hey, Zinny," he said.

"Hey, Gray." It came out in a whisper.

Gray handed me one of the blankets, then
billowed out the other to lay it on the
ground, and he'd performed this very same act
in that very same spot so many times that for
a second, the last few days disappeared, and
we were us.

But we didn't lie down, and I didn't
cocoon us both inside the second blanket.
I put the blanket around my shoulders,
and we sat, first me, then Gray, with our
backs against the garage wall and two feet
between us that may as well have been a
mile. For the first time since we'd started
being friends, even including the time I
screamed at him in the ACME parking lot, I
couldn't think of what to say to him, and I
still understood him enough to know he was
feeling the same way.

Finally, I said, "I could never hate you. And I don't think you lied on purpose. I'm sorry I said those things."

Gray let out a long breath. "Thank you. But no way can I let you apologize. Everything is my fault."

"No, I was horrible."

"No," said Gray.

For a long time, we just sat there, our two separate breathings ghosting and vanishing, ghosting and vanishing in the air.

"My dad always told me that if I tried my best, I would succeed. And he was right. About football, about school. I'm not a natural at anything; I have to work hard. But it's always paid off. And I know that makes me lucky," said Gray, in his same exact voice as ever, the voice I loved. Love.

"And I felt for a long time that I might be gay, but I also thought that if I tried my best not to be, it might work," he said. "And then there you were."

"You used me. Is that what you're saying?" It didn't come out angry. I didn't feel angry. But I had to ask the question.

"I guess I did, now that I look back on it. But that's not what I thought then. You've always been gorgeous and fearless. You've always seemed like this magical creature to me."

"Oh!" I pressed my hand over my mouth.

"Zin?"

"It's just—" And I was crying.

"I'm sorry. I just wanted to explain," said Gray, upset. He might be different from a lot of boys in some ways, but he gets just as freaked out by a crying girl as any.

"No," I said, gasping. "Give me a sec."

When I could breathe again, I said, haltingly, "I've just been so worried that you might, all this time, have thought I was—not pretty, or maybe even—disgusting. And you had to force yourself to be with me."

"Zin, no. Never. You're so beautiful. And I love being with you. You're my favorite person. I wasn't lying when I said I loved you. I did. I do."

Those words. From that boy. I knew they didn't mean what I wanted them to mean, but they still made my heart jump. Poor heart.

"It's why I thought maybe I could be different," he said. "There were times when I thought I was almost there."

"But it never happened," I said.

"One night, I realized it was no use. And I knew that if it couldn't happen with you, beautiful, amazing Zinny who I love so much, it wouldn't happen with any girl."

I knew what night he meant.

"I'm sorry it took me so long to tell you," he said. "I couldn't figure out how."

"It's okay."

We talked for a long time, until it was almost morning. Somewhere in there, I told Gray that I loved him, too. And I said that he had to let himself be himself, and everything would be all right. I think that's true. I hope he believed me. I hope that for once, I was his "Let It Be."

I'm making it sound like this conversation tied everything up with a nice bow, but, right now, tonight, everything isn't all right. Almost nothing is. I still want this to all be a bad dream.

Maybe it is. Maybe I'll wake up one day and Gray and I will still be in love.

But in this here and now, this dream or not-dream, I told my friend Gray I would stand by him. And I will. I am.

November 10, 1997

Tonight, Gray told his dad. He called me afterward. He said that his father didn't yell or even get visibly upset.

"He just sat there for a long time. And then he said, 'Are you sure?' And I said yes. Then, he got really quiet."

"Oh," I said.

Gray's dad never got quiet. He was the talkingest man I'd ever met.

"I know," said Gray. "Then, later, right before he went to work, he said, 'Announcing it that way took guts anyway.' I guess it was kind of a compliment, but: *anyway*? He didn't wait for me to answer, just walked out."

"It'll be okay," I said.

"What if he never talks to me—like really *talks* to me—again?"

"He will," I said. "He loves you."

"He loves who he thought I was," said Gray. His voice made me ache for him.

"You are who he thought you were," I said. "You're still you. And he *loves you*. He loves the you in you."

I hope I'm right. I have to be right, don't I? I hope Gray's dad is as kind and decent as I think he is. I hope he's who Gray has always thought he was.

He'd better be.

November 13, 1997

Gray came out in Mr. Whittier's history class today. I wasn't there, but Kirsten said he was magnificent. She also said he gave her a minor heart attack.

"I could've used a heads-up," she said.

"Yeah, I could've, too, actually," said Gray.

We were talking in the third level of Hell, otherwise known as the old basement furnace room, right after school, just before Gray's football practice was about to start. The other fall sports were over, but our football team, led by the great Gray Marsden, was in the semifinals of the state tournament.

CJ had put his headlamp hat down on the cement floor, and we were gathered around it like it was a bonfire.

"So it just popped out?" I said. I thought it must have, since, despite his celebrity, Gray shied away from attention most of the time, and I would have sworn he wasn't the dramatic pronouncement, bombshell-dropping type.

"Not exactly," said Gray. "We were talking about the civil rights movement, and Whittier asked whether it was actually over or still going on today. And Kirsten said it wasn't over because there's still racism and sexism, and plus, now, other groups are fighting for their rights, like gay people."

CJ had been oddly silent since we'd all met in the back hallway before heading down to the basement, but now he said, "You said that? Why would you say that?"

We all stared at him, surprised by his brittle tone.

"Uh, because it's true?" said Kirsten.

"I just mean, why would you bring that up when it's, like, Gray's thing?" said CJ.

"Are we not supposed to bring up homosexuality ever, now? It was relevant, CJ. I was in class," said Kirsten, annoyed.

"But to open the door that way, when maybe Gray wasn't ready to talk about it yet," said CJ.

Kirsten started to retort, but Gray interrupted, saying, "Okay, but it turns out I was. Because it didn't just pop out. I decided to say it. I just didn't give myself much notice about that decision."

Kirsten said, "After I said gay people are fighting for rights, stupid caveman Mongo Pilkington jumped in and said, 'That's different, though. Because black people don't choose to be black. Gay people choose to be gay.' And I said, 'Montgomery—because you know how he hates to be called his real name—"

It's true. What kind of person electively goes by Mongo, when he has choices like Monty? The Mongo kind of person. Total bonehead.

Kirsten went on. "I said, 'Mongo, don't be an idiot. If you are not in fact gay, did you choose to be straight? Or is that just who you are?'" said Kirsten. "And Whittier said, 'No name-calling, please,' but in this manner that suggested he agreed with what I was saying, because Whittier is awesome. And Mongo said, 'Dude, I have a girlfriend. But anyway that's obviously different.'" And I said, 'No, it's not. Gay people are born gay.' And he said,

'You're wrong.' And then, Gray said, 'She's right.' And everyone turned to look at him."

We all looked at him now. Gray said, "Mongo asked how I could possibly know that, and I said, 'Because I'm gay,' and the room went dead silent, and then Mongo said, 'You're shitting me,' and I said, 'Nope,' and then class was over."

I wondered if Mongo had added, "Dude, *you* have a girlfriend," and Kirsten and Gray were just politely leaving it out, but I didn't ask.

Kirsten had jumped up and was across that history classroom in a flash, giving Gray an enormous Kirsten hug. No one else spoke to him, but Kirsten said a few kids slid supportive glances his way.

"Typical," I said. "Gray being brave. Good for you."

Gray smiled at me.

"Okay," said CJ. "But we have less than a year of high school left, and you just opened yourself up to a world of crap from guys like Mongo. I mean, maybe there aren't that many of them at Lucretia Mott, but they are loud and dumb. And mean. You might not know that because they've always left you alone because

you're Gray Marsden. But they can be real
assholes. Wouldn't it have been better, for
everyone's sake, to wait?"

Kirsten and I exchanged a look. *Everyone's
sake.* CJ adored Gray; he was genuinely concerned
about him. But I knew that CJ was also thinking
something along the lines of: If Gray Marsden,
Hero, stops being Gray Marsden, Hero, then CJ
can't be his nerdy sidekick anymore.

Gray said, in a serious voice, "I know the
guys you're talking about. Most of them play
football. I should probably be worried about
what I'm in for. But the weird thing is that
I'm not. I've been carrying around this load of
worry for a long time, but right now, it's gone."

"Good," I said.

CJ sat thinking and, after a minute, said,
"I'm going to be forced to kick major ass now.
You know that, right?"

Gray smiled and said, "Yeah, I do know."

"Same," I said.

"Me, too," said Kirsten.

"Know this, Gray Marsden: we will smite
anyone who comes after you," said CJ, pounding
his heart with a fist. "We will rain fire down
upon them."

Gray laughed, a rumbling, real laugh, one I hadn't heard in a long time.

"Thanks, but you know what I think we should do?" he said. "Rise above. Let 'em know they're not even a blip on our radar screens."

"They're ants," I said. "Gnats. Amoebas."

"Pond scum," said Kirsten.

"*Mycoplasma genitalium*!" said CJ.

"What's that?" I asked.

"A parasitic bacterium that lives in the bladders, waste disposal organs, and genitalia of primates," said CJ.

Kirsten reached over and gave CJ a giant, Kirsten hug that almost knocked him over.

"Perfect," she said.

November 14, 1997

This morning, when Kirsten and I got to my locker, there was a paper pamphlet about AIDS testing taped to it.

"What the hell?" said Kirsten. She reached out to rip it off, but I caught her wrist.

"Leave it," I said. "It's not even a blip on our radar screen."

When I got back from my second class, there was a condom taped next to the flyer. I left that, too.

November 18, 1997

Gray says that at practice today, Mongo and his friends, Pat and Kenny, started calling him Gay instead of Gray.

"Honestly, though, how could they resist?" I said.

"True," said Gray. "They would have been remiss not to."

"Almost too easy," said Kirsten.

"And yet, they've probably been spending every waking minute of the past four days coming up with it," said CJ.

We laughed. But then tonight, Gray called me to tell me how, after practice, Coach Tremblay had pulled him aside to say, "You couldn't have waited till after the playoffs, son? We didn't need this distraction."

Gray had said, "I guess I thought the team would stand by me. Brothers, right?"

It's what Coach always told them: that football is thicker than blood; that they're more brothers than brothers.

"There's a reason 'Don't Ask, Don't Tell' exists," said Coach Tremblay. "To uphold morale, not to discriminate against gays."

"I'll have to respectfully disagree with you on that," said my brave friend Gray.

"Anyhow. A few guys have approached me with the request that you not shower with the team anymore. It makes them uncomfortable."

"Oh," said Gray.

"They're shitheads."

"Thanks, Coach," said Gray.

"But, Gray, I think it's best for the team if you wait till you get home to shower, just until this thing blows over."

Gray said he stood there for a few seconds, staring at the floor, before he looked Coach Tremblay in the eye and said, "Right."

Neither Gray nor I laughed at that.

November 20, 1997

Game day. I wore Gray's football sweatshirt to school just like I had all season.

Someone taped a piece of paper to my locker. In Magic Marker, whoever they

were had scrawled "FAG HAG." I let it
stay.

To the game, CJ, Kirsten, and I brought
signs that said, "Go Get 'Em, Gray!" and "#10
is #1!"

As we walked in, I saw Gray's dad. He
wasn't sitting in the thick of it all in
the stands the way he usually did, talking
a mile a minute and getting ready to cheer
his head off. Instead, he'd brought a folding
chair to the little bluff at the far end of
the field and was sitting by himself, while
Gray's little brother, Jimmy, ran around with
all the other elementary school kids. Gray's
biological mother died and his father and
stepmother are divorced, like my parents, but
they're still friends, unlike my parents. His
stepmom lives nearby and comes to all his
games, too. But I didn't see her anywhere.

Early in the first quarter, I made my way
to where his dad sat.

"Hey, Chief Marsden," I said.

I was still in Gray's sweatshirt and was
carrying my sign. Gray's dad looked me over,
and I think I saw his expression soften.

"Hey, Zinny. How are you holding up?"

"I'm fine," I said. "How about you?"

He didn't answer. Instead, his gaze moved beyond me, to the field.

"They're not really taking care of him out there," he said. "Pilkington and Broward."

"Screw Pilkington and Broward," I said. "Gray doesn't need them."

And even though he never took his eyes off the field, I'm not positive, but I'm pretty sure Gray's father smiled.

I was right about Pilkington and Broward, too. Gray played brilliantly. Laser-beam passes and quick-as-lightning feet. No one could touch him.

Lucretia Mott won, 21-3. The guys didn't lift Gray onto their shoulders, but I saw some of the non-caveman types high-five him or slap him on the back, and I could have kissed them, each one, right on the mouth.

Still, a few minutes later, there was Gray, walking into the school behind the pack of guys, alone, his helmet dangling from his fingers. And it occurred to me for the first time that, even before all this, while the guys on the team respected and even worshipped Gray, they weren't really friends with him

like they were with each other. He'd go out to
dinner with them after practice sometimes, but
mostly, he hung out with us: the artsy girl,
the bombshell, and the geek.

I wondered if Gray had created that
distance between them or if they'd done it.
Maybe it had just happened, without anyone
meaning for it to. Either way, now, when Gray
could use a real, true blue ally on the team,
someone to go out on a limb for him, tell
Mongo and his henchman to go straight to hell,
there's no one there.

Even so, next Saturday, Lucretia Mott is
going to the football finals for the first
time in thirty years. And it's all because of
Gray.

November 24, 1997

We were sitting at lunch, when Coach came up
and asked Gray if he could have a minute in
his office. When Gray came back, for the first
time since he'd come out, he looked shaky,
unsure of himself.

"Whose ass do I need to beat now?" asked CJ.

Gray swallowed. "The parents of a couple of the guys on the team are demanding that I be kicked off."

"You?" I said. "You're the only reason we're in the finals."

"Not the only reason," said Gray. "But thank you. I guess they think I'm a health hazard."

"If this is about HIV, I will start screaming," I said.

Gray shrugged. "Coach asked if I'd consider getting tested before the game."

"Are you *serious*?" said Kirsten. "So he can share your personal medical information with moron Mongo's and moron Kenny's moronic parents? Hell, no."

"Actually, I saw Mongo's parents here this morning. I got here early to fine-tune my bio experiment. But it wasn't Kenny's parents they were with," said CJ.

"Who were they with?" asked Kirsten.

"Robby Fulton's."

"Robby's?" said Kirsten. "He's kind of a decent guy. I don't think he's friends with Mongo."

"He's the backup quarterback," said Gray.

"Oh shit," said CJ.

"But he's nowhere near as good as you," I said. "We can't win in finals with Robby out there."

"His parents might not agree with that," said CJ.

"You told Tremblay he was insane even to ask, right?" I said.

Gray's face turned red. "Uh, I said I'd think about it."

"No," said Kirsten. "No way."

"I agree," I said. "Hell, no."

Gray groaned. "Ugh. I know. You're right. But I just want to play."

"Coach said you can't play if you don't take the test?" I said. I wanted to leap up, march straight to Coach's office, pound the living crap out of him with my bare fists, and then slap him with a lawsuit until he screamed for mercy.

Gray shook his head. "No. But he wanted me to take it. He said, 'Let's prove 'em all wrong, son.'"

"I hate him," said Kirsten. "I hope he drops dead."

"Don't do it, Gray," I said. "Rise above, remember?"

"I won't," said Gray. "I won't do it."

I wanted to grab his hand and squeeze it, but, instead, I rested my hand on his wrist. "I'm sorry this is happening. It sucks."

"It'll be okay," said Gray.

But then tonight, he quit the team.

Not because of the HIV test. Or not only because of that.

When he opened his gym bag after practice, it was full of women's underwear and fishnet stockings.

And when he opened his football locker, it was full of maxi pads and tampons dangling from the hooks, damp and dripping with ketchup.

I will be forever glad I wasn't there to witness his face when he opened that locker door.

Gray took out the underwear, removed his ketchup-stained clothes and equipment from the locker, and walked out, never, ever, ever to return.

I hope one day those boys look back at what they did to Gray and are eaten up with remorse. But I'm not betting on it.

Sometimes, it's hard, it's all I can do, not to lose faith in humanity.

November 29, 1997

Kirsten, CJ, and I were going to boycott
tonight's game, but Gray asked us to go and
then report back to him tomorrow. He's going
to be working at the fire station with his dad
all night. He says his father is talking to
him more now, although they're still not back
to what they were.

What's crazy is that I think Gray still
wants LM to win tonight, which I'd say is
carrying the nice guy thing a bit far. But
we're playing the Cole School, our archrivals
since the beginning of time, and old habits
die hard, especially, it seems, when it comes
to high school football.

So we agreed to go, on the condition that
we could all wear sweatshirts with Gray's name
and number. When he handed them over to us, he
said, "Keep them. I don't need them anymore."
But he sounded so downcast that I said, "I
won't hold you to that," and he smiled and
said, "Thanks, Zin."

I hope that, whatever else happens to me
in the future, I find a way to get over Gray

Marsden. I hope I move on and fall dazzlingly in love with someone else. I can even believe— just barely—that I will someday.

But here, now, just the sound of his voice saying my name makes me want to run out into the wilderness and cry for days.

I won't though. I'll stay here and put on Gray's sweatshirt, and go to a football game like I promised.

Go, Owls! I guess . . .

November 29, 1997

11:30 P.M.

I can't write it. I can't. If I don't write it, maybe it never happened.

I will never stop smelling smoke.

I will never stop seeing the school on fire, as if it were being eaten from the inside out, orange light staining the sky.

Everyone, the players in their pads and jerseys, the parents and students, kids from all the schools in town, holding on to one another, every face turned up.

And then, later, Gray. My Gray.

I can't write it.

But I will never stop seeing him, big Gray
somehow shrunken to childlike smallness
inside his firefighter's jacket, his arms
dangling, ash in his hair, soot striping his
face, his eyes dark and wild with shock and
fear and disbelief.

And his father stretched before him,
strapped to a board. Motionless. Slack-faced.
Looking—no matter what we all hope or pray is
true—like a person broken beyond repair.

Chapter Ten

GINNY

I was trying to capture Walt's right ear, the one that folds over instead of standing up like a sailboat sail as it's supposed to, when Harris told me that he was moving out. Or that he had been moving out, little by little, for weeks, slowly shifting his belongings—the bare essentials anyway, since it could be argued (although it seemed Harris had no intention of arguing) that almost every item in our house at least half belonged to him—from our house to the room above the garage to his rented furnished apartment not five miles away, an ebbing away so subtle and slow that I hadn't even realized it was happening.

Still, I should not have been as surprised as I was, rendered temporarily speechless, my sketching hand frozen midstroke, when he came into the sunroom, a cardboard box in his arms, and said, "This is the last of it, Ginny."

I sat cross-legged on the rug at eye level with Walt, who had, at that very moment, revealed a previously undiscovered talent for modeling, sitting regal as a New York Public Library lion, paws evenly spaced, head nobly lifted. When Harris and his box made their entrance, Walt didn't jump up or change position, just opened his bright root beer–brown eyes wider and smiled his incomparable gap-toothed, guileless smile.

"You mean you're leaving?" I finally managed to say.

"You didn't know?" he said.

"I— I—" I shook my head. "No."

Should I have known? We'd been sleeping apart for weeks—no, months—addressing each other cordially whenever one of us slipped into the other's orbit, which wasn't even daily. Christmas had been an almost jolly holiday, with Harris coming into the house for gift opening followed by breakfast: Avery's homemade cinnamon buns—warm, redolent, yeasty, golden, palm-size galaxies—and French press coffee lashed with cream. Harris and I never touched once, not even by accident, but Christmas performed its sleight of hand, nonetheless, magicking us into a happy family and Avery into a dancing-eyed, carol-humming, care-free child.

Mostly, Avery kept her guard up around Harris, and their relationship seemed reduced to homework talk and wooden hugs. I'd watch her face, though, whenever he left, her eyes following him, her gaze staying on the kitchen door, even after he'd shut it behind him.

"You want to set that box down and stay for a minute?" I said.

Harris tensed and then said, "Sure."

He sat in the blue armchair; I stood up and sat down on the sofa, grateful when Walt settled into my lap, curling himself up like the warm cinnamon bun he was.

"You have an apartment, I guess," I said.

"I rented it six weeks ago," said Harris. "I bring boxes over every so often, spend the night there now and then."

"I didn't know," I said. "I knew you went somewhere, but I didn't know where."

"I didn't want to tell you and Avery until I was sure. As you know"—he smiled ruefully—"I'm not really a guy who makes bold moves or quick decisions. More of a go-slow, test-the-waters type. Cautious."

"Mostly cautious," I said, but I smiled back at him.

"And look where that got me," said Harris.

"Here we two are," I said. "Joking about what happened. It's about time."

Harris said, "I'm so sorry, Ginny. I'd give anything to change what I did."

"I believe you," I said.

"Thank you for finding my therapist. He's helping me see."

"See what?"

"Myself," said Harris. "I never did that before, stepped back and really saw myself."

"What do you see?"

Harris sighed and said, "I am a man who things happen to. School, my job, even you."

I was tempted to disagree. Maybe it would've been kinder. But I said, "Yes."

"I met you and you were young and gorgeous and interested in me, for reasons that I could not fathom. And I should have tried to fathom them. But instead, I went with it, with you, without stopping to ask questions about where we were going or whether or not you were actually in love with me."

"Or whether or not you were actually in love with me."

Harris nodded. "That, too. I knew you were beautiful, and back then, you seemed so fragile. I wanted to take care of you."

"And I let you. I *was* fragile. I hadn't always been. Before you knew me, I was brave, an adventurer. Everyone said so, and it was true. But by the time you met me, I was bruised and searching for a safe haven. You happened to me, too."

"But none of that is quite the same as being in love, is it?" said Harris. "Maybe we would have figured that out, but then suddenly, so quickly, there was Avery. Avery happened to me, and I could not believe my luck."

"Our miraculous girl," I said.

For a moment, we just basked in the exquisite light of our daughter, bound by shared luck and shared cherishing. Harris and I needed to end, should have ended long ago, but in ending we were each losing the person—the only person—who had shared in the private moments of being parents to Avery. The moments when our eyes met over Avery's head. The foods and books and toys she'd loved. Her sleeplessness at four in the morning. The time she came home from school with her pockets full of marbles and beads and pebbles, "manipulatives" from her kindergarten classroom that she'd stolen because they were "so pretty, like stars that wanted to come down from the sky to live in my house." The small, precious, shiny daily stories of her childhood. Losing that—more than betrayal or anger or incompatibility—was the tragedy at the heart of our story. Briefly, I wondered what I could've done to save us from this loss. But I did *not* wonder what I could *do* to save us. That horse, I remained well aware, had left the barn.

"What else did you figure out with your therapist?" I asked.

"That I've been depressed. Not myself. For a long time."

"Really?" I said, genuinely surprised.

"And it's no excuse, but before I—" Harris broke off and rubbed the spot between his eyes with his finger. "Before last summer—"

"Before Cressida came to work for your company."

"Yes. Before all that began, it had been months, a year maybe, since I'd felt—"

"Felt what?"

"That's it," Harris said. "Just felt."

"A year," I said, evenly.

"Don't blame yourself for not noticing," he said. "I did everything I could to hide it."

I knew firsthand what depression was, the light-lessness and bone-deep weariness. The gray, spiraling misery. The hope jumping ship.

"No, don't let me off the hook," I said. "I should have paid closer attention to you, Harris. Not only during that year."

I paid attention now. In the sunroom with winter surrounding us on three sides, the lace of trees, the stone-gray sky, sun like a pearl, I took in the man before me, Harris McCue. I saw that in the months since he'd been fired, he'd lost weight, his sweatshirt loose around his middle, his square-jawed face catching shadows. But if these changes were the aftermath of depression, he didn't look depressed now. There was—I don't know—an animation to him that I realized I hadn't seen in a long time, a receptiveness to his features, a new sharpness in his movements and his gaze and his edges. As I observed him in the here and now, I also tried to summon the Harrises of the year before and the one before that. Harris after Harris after Harris. It wasn't easy. But even my blurred and patchy recollections of my husband, from past to present, coalesced into a vision of a man walking, slowly and at long last, out of the fog and into the open.

"What a disservice I've done you," I said. "Not paying attention. I'm sorry."

The defeated, hangdog Harris of a few weeks ago would've waved off or protested my apology. This one said, "Thank you. And I'm sorry, too, from the bottom of my heart."

"Thank you," I said.

We remained for a few more seconds in the new, well-lit clearing we'd made for each other, and then

Harris leaned over, picked up his box, the last one, said, "Okay, then," and stood up.

As he turned to go, I said, "It hurts to see you leave. I know it's what's best, and I know we'll both be okay, but it stings. I just wanted to say that."

Harris didn't turn around, but he stopped in his tracks. His shoulders rose and fell, hard inhale, slow exhale, before he said, "Thanks, Ginny," and kept walking.

"You're creepy, okay?" I told Kirsten. "What do you have? Spies? Camped out in my front yard? Harris just left, left-left, left for good not—no exaggeration— forty-five seconds before you called me. I may actually still be able to hear his car engine."

"I know, but don't worry. I don't think he saw me. I parked a little way down your street; plus, I may have, you know, ducked when I saw him backing out of your driveway. And even if he saw my car, it's Harris. He could've seen it a million times before without it making even the tiniest imprint on his memory. Harris is oblivious. Hold on. There's probably a word to be created there. *Oblivharris*?"

"What? You're here? *You're* the spy you have camped out on my front lawn?"

"Is that a problem for you?"

"Get in here. No, wait, meet me at the garage. You can help me clean the garage guest suite."

"Being your friend is so fun, Gin. It's like one long party, really."

"Come on. It'll be cathartic."

"Drinking wine is also cathartic."

"Fine. I'll bring wine."

"Yay! And not to be insensitive, but did you inherit those super-huge Waterford goblets from your mom? Because you know how I like heavy stemware."

"I did. And I do. But I think they're for red wine, and all I've got is white."

"Awesome. What better way to get revenge on Adela than use her glasses for the wrong wine?"

"Not to be insensitive."

"God, of course not."

My friend Kirsten has the reputation of being fundamentally unable to keep a secret, but that's only partly true. She's kept every secret I've ever told her since we were twelve years old, which is every secret I've ever had (minus one that I barely shared with myself before I erased it from my personal history forever and so doesn't really count).

What she's terrible—wretched, abysmal—at is keeping her own secrets. In high school, she cheated on every boyfriend she ever had, would tell me about it practically while her lips were still locked on the mouth of the forbidden guy, and swear me to secrecy. But within twenty-four (or four or two) hours, she would have spilled the story to everyone we knew, from her mother to her math tutor to Mr. Jones, the head maintenance worker at Lucretia Mott (who almost didn't count because he was the most trustworthy human on the planet and the best listener and ended up on the receiving end of everyone's secrets), to the poor, dumb, cuckolded boyfriend himself.

So it was not a surprise that we weren't even halfway up the steep stairs to the garage apartment when Kirsten, two steps ahead of me, spun around, flung the back of her left hand in front of my face, just inches from my eyes, and screamed. I screamed, too, and grabbed her hand, and we performed a heartfelt, if highly, possibly life-threateningly precarious, dance for joy right there on the staircase.

"Isn't it shiny?" she said, when we were settled on the couch in the garage apartment. She flipped her hand around in the air in the manner of a very enthusiastic conductor so that the emerald-cut diamond that used to belong to Tex's grandmother scattered prisms all over the room.

"It almost blinded me. Literally almost put out my eye," I said, and then I leaned over and kissed Kirsten's cheek. "I'm deliriously happy for you, sugarplum."

"There was a time, like twenty years, when I thought I'd have to ask you to be my matron of honor, which sounds so, you know, thick-waisted and dowdy, but now you can be my maid of honor, and *I* can be *your* matron of honor!"

"What about thick-waisted and dowdy?"

"I'll be your newly married matron of honor, which is obviously totally different. Although if you don't move fast, I might be sporting a baby bump under my matron of honor dress because the wedding's in June, and we're launching Operation Baby ASAP."

"This June? Doesn't it take forever to plan a wedding?"

Kirsten shrugged. "It's possible that I got a jump on the planning a few months ago. Or six."

"You started planning your wedding six months before you got engaged."

"Only the location. And the caterer. And the florist. Anemones. Don't you love anemones?"

"So you decided to hold off on choosing the napkins."

"Pale pink damask, and I'm talking very pale, like the tights I wore for ballet when I was six. And don't worry, I'll share all my information with you for your next wedding. I've got a file as thick as a five-tiered Victoria sponge wedding cake decorated with sugared berries and floribunda roses."

"That's so nice of you," I said. "But here's a thought: Harris carried off his last box of stuff ten minutes ago."

"Exactly. Times a-wastin'. Start dating, honey!"

"If by dating you mean going on dates, I'd rather poke needles—or three-carat diamonds—into my eyes."

"You've always been a boy magnet. You'll meet someone."

"A boy magnet. My first boyfriend was gay and my second was Harris."

"Third time's a charm! Come on, there must be men you've been attracted to since the Harris blowup. UPS deliverymen. Or those cute newly divorced guys in the grocery store who are paralyzed in front of the peanut butter selection or stand there reading the labels of the egg cartons."

To my horror, my face got hot, and I dropped my head before Kirsten could notice me blushing.

"Holy shit," she said. "Who is he?"

"There's no he, idiot."

Kirsten folded her arms and looked at me, waiting. Kirsten, with her silver-dollar-size blue eyes, could win a staring contest with a dead person. I groaned.

"Shut up," I said. "It's not a big deal. My dog park friend, Daniel the vet."

"The one you said you could say anything to?"

"Yes."

"Is he good-looking?"

I pictured Daniel, backed by the green grass of the dog park, his gray eyes and dark hair and smile as heavenly as my dog Walt's.

"He is. Very, actually. But it's more that he's so *nice.*"

Kirsten's eyes widened. "Oh Lord. You're sunk. It's what they never tell you when you're younger, how when you grow up, nothing on God's green earth will be sexier than nice."

"True. But let's stop this nonsense and talk about your upcoming nuptials."

Kirsten got a funny look on her face. "Yes. Right. Okay. Here's the thing."

"Uh-oh."

"I want you to throw me an engagement party. Soon. Really soon. Like in a couple of weeks, so it doesn't seem like we just got engaged and—boom— we're getting married."

"Oh! Is that all? Well, of course I will! We can do it at my house, unless you think we'll need a bigger space?"

"Your house is perfect."

"Perfect."

Kirsten grimaced. She had an adorable nose-wrinkled grimace and knew it. I had seen that grimace in action more times than I could count.

"What?"

"I want everyone there. Everyone I love best."

This seemingly reasonable request knocked the wind out of me. I knew what she meant: everyone she loved best, who, not coincidentally, happened to represent the bulk of the people (minus Harris) I'd failed most miserably in this world.

"Kirsten. I haven't seen them in seventeen years, and that was at a party while we were in college, and as soon as I got there, they left. They hate me. Not that I blame them," I said.

"I don't think they do," said Kirsten. "I mean, I don't know because we have this unspoken agreement never to talk about you, which I break fairly often, but still, and actually, CJ might still hate you just because he is so loyal to Gray, but, come *on*, it was all so long ago."

"Gray's dad died, and I abandoned him. That's the only word for it. I failed him. At the time, I could barely figure out how to get up in the morning and get dressed, but that's no excuse for letting Gray down like that."

"We never talk about this, you and I," said Kirsten, quietly. "Not really. All those things that happened senior year; it's the only thing we never talk about."

"I know. I try not to even think about it, but I've thought about it a hundred times by accident over the years. What's the point, though? I'd give anything to go back and be a better friend to Gray—or even a not hideously awful friend—and I can't do that. I can't fix anything."

Kirsten absorbed this, and then, slowly, said, "I think— Okay. I think we were so used to you being the strongest and bravest of all of us that we didn't see the toll everything took on you. When Gray came out, you were his champion. You were amazing, like Joan of Arc going into battle. But that must've been so hard for you."

"I was heartbroken. I thought I would marry him," I said.

"Yes. And then his dad died. And then whatever happened between Trevor and your mom happened, and he transferred to Emory midyear and basically disappeared from your life. When I think about it now, when I envision the person you were that whole second half of senior year, I think you must have been depressed. Like, very."

I nodded. "I was."

"So, yeah, maybe you should've been a better friend to Gray. But we three should've been better friends to you. We should've seen that you needed taking care of, too."

My friend Kirsten and I sat inside a haze of regret and remembering, before Kirsten said, "At least, after the fire, things got better for Gray at school."

"Well, yeah," I said, wryly. "It only took running into a burning building to save his best friend and losing his father in the same night for those assholes to stop holding his sexuality against him."

"He's in a good place now," said Kirsten.

"I'm glad he found Evan. I'm glad they got married." I smiled. "I'm dead jealous of course, but I'm glad."

"They're having a baby."

Tears filled my eyes, hot and sudden. "Oh, that's wonderful."

"They used a surrogate. Gray's sperm, and Evan's sister donated the egg, so it'll have both their genes."

"Those are some good genes," I said, remembering Gray.

"Hell, yes, they are," said Kirsten.

"Will you prepare them, Gray and CJ? Tell them I'll be getting in touch about the engagement party?"

"Yes! And, um, one more thing? Or one more person, actually?"

I sighed. "Trevor. You two always did love each other."

"Please?"

"If I die of awkwardness, you'll look after Avery?"

"I love you, I love you, I love you," sang Kirsten, and then she slid over and wrapped me up in the Kirstenest of Kirsten hugs.

Chapter Eleven

December 1, 1997

People say "bear witness" and now I know why.
It's that seeing the terrible, the unstoppable
terrible, the unerasable, it-can't-be-
happening-it-*is*-happening terrible not so much
unfold as inflict itself upon the world in
front of you is heavy, a lead-heavy burden you
bear and bear until you are bent double under
its weight and can barely breathe.

I want to unsee it. I want to undo it,
to reel in that hour—ugly minute after ugly
minute—and hurl it into a bottomless pit.

I'd give anything. But I can't. No one can.

Now, two days after it happened, it feels
like time to piece that night together, all
those impressions that aren't just scattered

but whirling and screeching and flapping
like giant black birds of prey. I will try to
put the night into sentences, to patch those
sentences into an order. It won't change what
happened. It won't fix a thing. But that's what
I do. That's how I bear witness.

During the football game, with nearly two
thousand in attendance, not just from Lucretia
Mott or Cole but from all over, our school
began to burn, the wing that holds the theater
and, beneath that, a floor down, the gym where
the ninth graders have P.E. I don't know how
long it took, whether it smoldered for a long
time first and then crept over the floors and
theater seats or whether it arrived in a burst
and tore through the place, scrambling up the
stage curtains and walls to eat away the roof
in chunks.

It was during the third quarter. I don't
remember the score, but I know we were losing
by enough to have the LM side scared. At
halftime, the marching band had lacked its
usual high-stepping zest, all except for CJ,
who, despite Gray telling us to go ahead and
cheer on our team, hoped with every fiber
of his fierce and scrawny being that the LM

Owls would get pulverized. CJ was practically
dancing across that field, his sax bright as
the sun under the stadium lights.

Later, when he walked up to rejoin us in
the stands, I saw that he had his arm stuck
straight up over his head and was brandishing
his giant "#10 Is the Man!" sign like a sword.
I also saw that, while he wore his hooded
sweatshirt and winter jacket on top, he still
had on his band pants.

"It's kind of nice to know that some things
never change," I said to Kirsten.

"Sorry about the pants there, Seege," said
Kirsten.

"Thieving bastards," said CJ. "But at least
we're still losing."

I don't know how much time passed—not much—
before CJ got a weird look on his face, lifted
his nose in the air like a bloodhound, and
said, "Do you smell smoke?"

I didn't really, but then a few minutes
later, I did. And right then, the refs stopped
the game and the announcer's voice came on
telling us to please walk, not run, in a calm,
orderly manner through the west exit of the
stadium and down the hill to the lower playing

field, even though the announcer himself
sounded anything but calm. He sounded like a
guy who'd expected his biggest challenge of
the evening to be pronouncing the players'
names correctly and who was teetering right
on the edge of freaking out. But some people,
including CJ, Kirsten, and me, followed his
instructions, even as chaos was breaking out
on every side.

We'd had fire drills a lot over the years,
but those were based on the premise that the
fire would take place during the school day
and that students, guided by teachers and
administrators who all knew the drill, would
be evacuated from the building. But this was
totally different: nighttime; the stadium; the
place full of little kids and old people and
people who had never been to LM before the
night of the game; too few people in charge.
And there were so many people there, lots of
them pretty riled up because of the game,
so nothing went the way it was supposed to.
It wasn't a stampede; no one trampled anyone
underfoot, but it also wasn't calm or orderly.
People blurred by, some of them pulling kids
by the hand. Some of them were laughing. Some

of them were running. Crowds bustled and
jostled out both gates of the stadium, and,
once out of the gates, people flew off in
different directions, some of them running,
probably thinking they'd get into their cars
and go before the fire trucks arrived.

My heart was beating fast, and I took hold
of Kirsten's gloved hand, but I wasn't really
scared, not yet. I wasn't even that scared when
we began to see the smoke, pale gray, billowing
in roiling clouds against the dark sky, because
the building had to be empty. It was Saturday,
and everyone who was there was watching the
game, even Mr. Jones and his staff. I'd seen
them standing at the fence near the snack bar.
Still, as I walked between Kirsten and CJ, near
the back of the crowd pouring down the hill
to the field, the cold stinging my cheeks, I
sent up a tiny prayer—even though I'm not sure
there's even a God up there—that said, "Please
let the building be empty."

Then, suddenly, like a high whining wind, I
heard the sirens and, layered over them, CJ's
voice saying, "Oh shit! I'll be right back!"
Before Kirsten and I knew what was happening,
he wheeled around and took off like a shot.

"Meet us at the lower field!" I shouted, and CJ, still running, raised his hand into the air in a thumbs-up.

"Typical CJ," said Kirsten.

"Probably going back for his sign," I said. "Because it's important to have your pep sign when the school is burning down."

"Someone will stop him and make him turn around, and CJ will give that lucky person a long lecture about free will or freedom of speech or some such thing, till they're ready to throw him into the burning building and lock the door," said Kirsten.

When we joined the shivering, noisy, energy-buzzing throng at the lower playing field, we had a clear view of the theater wing in the distance, the entire top of it shrouded in storm-cloud smoke. That's when things got fragmented in my mind. I remember kids running around, dodging through the thick crowd, laughing and screeching with glee like they were at a Fourth of July picnic. I remember sirens charging the air with wildness, the fire trucks passing close enough to splash us with red and white light. I didn't see Gray's face, but in a moment of clarity, I saw the number on one of the trucks—98, our graduation year, that's how I remember it—and I remembered that Gray was working with his dad that night.

"Gray's truck!" I said to Kirsten.

The red trucks strung themselves along the curb like a train, throwing light brighter than day onto the burning roof. From a distance we could see water blasts, ladders telescoping into the sky, firefighters moving around in what, from that distance, looked like, and maybe was, a calm, purposeful, almost choreographed manner. The crowd we stood at the edge of got not quiet, but quieter, watching. I don't know how long Kirsten and I stood that way, mesmerized by the movements of the firefighters, but suddenly, a thought struck me, and I grabbed Kirsten's arm.

"CJ," I said. "He never came back."

Kirsten looked at me, dazed, and then snapped to with a gasp.

We searched, hand in hand, spinning through the crowd, calling his name. When I remember it now, it's like we were on a merry-go-round, a scary one. Faces lurching in and out

of focus, big then small. Dizziness. My own
voice banging around inside my head. No one
seeming to hear us. No CJ. No police officers
to tell. I don't know why. They must've been
there by then. No help coming from anywhere.
And then a screeching-halt moment, when I said
to Kirsten, horror hollowing my voice, "Oh my
God, his sax!"

Her eyes widened.

"That part of the building isn't on fire, is
it?" she said. "It isn't, is it? Is it?"

But we didn't know, did we? How fire moves?
Does it rush around inside walls? Stampede
down hallways? Could it have been stealing
through the interior of the school all this
time without our knowing?

There were other things we could have done.
Other courses of action we could have taken.
But we were the fearsome foursome—CJ, Kirsten,
Gray, and Zinny—a complete set, and all we
could think was to get to Gray to get to CJ,
and then we were running headlong through
the darkness—pound, pound, pound—toward the
trucks and the glow and the smoke. It makes no
sense that no one caught us, but no one did.
It makes no sense that we found Gray almost

right away, at the side of a truck, unfolding
a great ribbon of hose. Under his helmet, his
face looked older, slashed with shadow.

"What are you doing here?" he said. "You
shouldn't be here."

Winded, we panted out our story and saw our
worst fears reflected in Gray's eyes.

"I'll go," he said.

"You?" I said. "What? No. Tell your dad."

"He's on the roof," said Gray, talking fast.
"I'm going. No one else will be able to find
the furnace room, and it will take too long
to tell them where it is. And if I tell them,
they won't let me go. I'm going."

He reached someplace inside the truck and
there was a long-handled ax in his hand.

"Go back to the field," he said. "I mean it."

And he sidled his way along the side of the
truck, then broke into a run, his head down.

Kirsten and I didn't go back to the field.

"I want to stay," said Kirsten, starting to
cry. "Until CJ's back."

I nodded, and we made a break for a row of
trees maybe fifty yards away, on the edge of
the parking lot, and sat against the trunks,
inside the shadows of the branches.

"Let them be safe, let them be safe, let them be safe," said Kirsten, hoarsely, over and over and over, like a chant.

I scooted close and put my arm around her shoulders.

"Let them be safe, let them be safe, let them be safe." She beat out the words to the rhythm of her sobs.

"Let them be safe, let them be safe, let them be safe . . ."

She was still saying it when Gray's father fell off the roof.

December 4, 1997

2:00 A.M.
Gray's father has been dead for five days.

Gray's stepmother told us Gray won't see anyone. He won't speak. He hasn't said a word since it happened.

Gray's father is dead, and Gray is unreachable and shattered by sorrow maybe forever, and nothing could get worse, nothing could happen to make things worse, and then, tonight, something did.

```
I will write this down once. I will write
it down and rip out the pages and take them
to the woods and burn them. Like a rite.
Like magic. Like witchcraft. I will burn
the pages and the thing that happened will
be gone, erased from history. It takes up so
little space. Not a night. Not even an hour.
Fifteen minutes. Fifteen minutes weighs almost
nothing, a tiny wedge of time I can pinch
between my thumb and forefinger and scatter
like ash. Fifteen minutes can only ruin
everything if you let it.
     And I won't I won't I won't I won't
```

And I won't I won't I won't

Avery whispered into the open book in her hands, whispered to Zinny and Kirsten and CJ and Gray, "*What?* What happened?"

In a rush, she flipped through the rest of the pages in the journal. Then, again, just to be sure. All empty, blank as snow. Not a sentence. Not a wisp of pencil sketch.

She read the final written-on page again, then ran a finger down the ragged edge where the next page had been torn out.

She imagined Zinny, the trees towering over her, the smell of the match, a corner of the page catching fire, the orange flame eating the page, turning the white black, turning it to nothing.

Zinny, working magic.

The journal had been in the suitcase Avery's grandmother had left her, hidden underneath the rest of the books so that she'd only found it this morning. Found it and read it straight through.

Zinny. That ferocious, courageous, liquid, shimmering girl who wrote and drew and strung snowflakes on fishing line and jumped off cliffs and invented words and loved her brother and stood by her friends.

Zinny was her *mother.*

Was? Is?

Did you stop being your old selves? Did they fall away? Were you always only the self you were in the present?

Or were you, every second of your life, all the selves you'd ever been? Avery hoped it was this. She wanted to meet Zinny, to meet her and to sit with her and listen to her tell the rest of the story. She wanted it so much.

Avery loved her mother. But she took care of their house and gardened and walked the dogs and worried about Avery. And she had married Avery's father. Had there been a moment with him, too, with kites overhead and the sun straight above, a moment when love arrived whole and perfect and true? Avery could not imagine it.

She found her mother in the sunroom, sitting on the floor, her back to Avery, a sketch pad (a sketch pad!) open on the coffee table in front of her, her hair in a ponytail, her head bent. Avery saw her mother drawing, and she could not remember having seen her draw like that before, and for one flashing, dizzy second, she believed Zinny had come back, flown out of the past and alighted in Avery's present.

Then, her mother looked over her shoulder and smiled at Avery, and she wasn't Zinny.

But maybe she was.

"Hey, love," said her mother.

Avery took the journal from behind her back and held it out to her mother, and her mother stretched out her hands to take it and stopped, her two hands just hovering in the air. Then, she pressed her hands to her mouth.

"Oh my God," she said. "Oh my God."

"It was in the suitcase," said Avery.

"I don't understand."

"From Grandmother."

Avery's mother stood, her face full of confusion, and she walked to the sofa and sat. As Avery went to sit next to her, she glanced down at the sketch pad. Walt looking just like Walt. Noble and cute at the same time. One ear up, one ear down.

"Oh my God, Mom, that's so good," said Avery.

Her mother reached out and took the journal and opened it, turning pages with her pretty, long-fingered hands.

"I can't believe she saved this," she said. She looked at Avery, and Avery saw something in her mother's face that broke her heart a little: surprise. Her mother hadn't realized her own mother had cared enough to save an old journal all these years. This didn't seem to Avery such an unusual thing for a parent to do (her own mother saved everything Avery had ever written or made), but the fact seemed to leave her mother positively awestruck. Her expression dissipated slowly, and she said, "You read it?"

Avery nodded.

"Wow," said her mother. "Oh my."

Her mother pressed a hand to her own cheek and then to her chest.

"So what happened?" demanded Avery, eagerly. "What happened on the missing page? What was the bad thing that happened after Gray's dad died in the fire?"

Avery's mother seemed to snap out of a daze. "What?"

"The torn-out pages, the ones you burned. What was on them?"

And then, before her eyes, Avery's mother deflated, her shoulders sagging. "Oh, honey."

"Come on, Mom, hurry up! I need to know. Just tell me."

"I can't."

Stunned, Avery said, "What? Why not?"

Her mother set the journal in her lap and shut her eyes and rubbed the delicate skin under her eyes with her fingertips. When she opened her eyes again, they were sad.

"I just—can't," said her mother. "I'm sorry."

Avery felt a surge of anger. "But you have to, Mom! I need to know. I can't explain why exactly, but I *need* to."

Her mother shook her head, an almost slow-motion swiveling that made Avery want to take her shoulders and shake her, snap her out of it.

"I would if I could, honey, but I can't. And trust me, it wouldn't do you any good to know."

Suddenly, Avery felt angry. And as much as she wanted to know—was *dying* to know—the rest of the story, she understood that her anger was much bigger than that.

"You don't get to decide that," she said. "Why are you always trying to protect me from stuff? I'm not a baby, and I'm not stupid."

"I—I'm not always trying to protect you," said her mother.

"Are you kidding me? That's all you do. Everything with dad? How you won't even answer my questions about what he did? Or how you act like it wasn't that bad?"

Her mother opened her mouth as if to speak but then shut it again.

"You threw him out of your room. Do you think I don't know what that means? And guess what? He's gone. If it wasn't that bad, why are you getting a divorce, Mom?"

Her mother looked stunned.

"Avery! We haven't even talked about divorce."

"Stop lying. Obviously, you're going to get a divorce!"

Her mother took a deep breath. "Oh. Well. Okay, yes. We will. We just haven't said that word to each other yet, but we will get a divorce."

"Finally." Avery spit out the word; she felt ablaze with anger. "Finally, you tell me the truth."

"But, listen, it's more complicated than what he did or didn't do and—"

"Oh, is it too complicated? Am I too stupid to understand? Am I too *fragile* to handle it? You always treat me like that. But I'm not, Mom. I'm way stronger than you think."

After a long pause, her mother said, "You're right. You and I should sit down and have an honest conversation about what happened with your dad. I should've done that a long time ago," and the stark tenderness with which her mother looked at her when she said this would've softened Avery at any other time. But now it just made her furious.

"Yeah, well, you didn't. And it's not because I'm not brave enough to hear it. It's because you weren't brave enough to say it."

Her mother winced.

"So tell me," said Avery, in a hard voice. "Tell me about what was on the torn-out page."

"Please stop asking that," said her mother. "I can't tell you."

"What the hell? I can't believe you."

Avery yanked the journal, Zinny's journal, hers now, off her mother's lap. She crossed the room in three strides, but before she left, she shouted at her mother, "You know what? If Zinny met you now, she would hate you. She would think you were pathetic."

Without waiting for a reaction, Avery stormed out of the room.

And storming felt very good to her.

Chapter Twelve

GINNY

P eople say fire is cleansing.

Sterilizing needles. Clearing underbrush from forests. Setting meadows ablaze so that they can be reborn. Smelting. Refining. Burning off impurities to find the gold inside.

Applying fire to steel makes it stronger.

People also say: fight fire with fire. And I've learned that this is more than a metaphor for revenge. A controlled burn can stop a wildfire in its tracks.

When I was eighteen and fire entered my life, all it did was ruin things.

Gray wanted his father to see him and accept him and love him for who he was, and I think his father would have, I really do, but some human monster set a fire that killed him before he had the chance, and could anything be sadder than that?

Fire is thievery and heartbreak and lost love and unleashed rage and falling and broken necks and unfinished stories.

And still, there came a bleak and desperate night when I stood in the woods behind my neighborhood and lit a match and put my faith in the cleansing properties of fire, and when I walked away from those woods, my hands empty, I tried hard to believe that it had worked, that the bad had been burned away. But the bad remained. And nothing, not one thing, was cleaner.

The fire at Lucretia Mott School would be ruled an arson, but the night I burned the journal page, not even the fire marshal knew that yet. Rumors were already flying, of course. A drunk public school boy—a known troublemaker—had been seen hanging out behind the groundskeeper's shed, where the rakes, hedge trimmers, lawn mowers, and gasoline were stored. Rumor had it that the boy was overheard making threatening remarks about Lucretia Mott; when CJ was standing in line for the snack bar, he had heard him say that all the spoiled rich LM kids made him sick. Rumor had it that there was gasoline missing from the shed, although later, the groundskeeper couldn't declare for an absolute fact that this was true.

When we heard about the drunk boy, CJ remembered that when he was on his way back after stowing his sax in the hiding place, he'd seen what might have been that same kid run right past him toward the back door to the school, the one CJ had just come out of. As soon as he remembered, CJ went to the police and told them. But even though he was almost positive it was the same kid, CJ hadn't been paying enough attention to make an absolutely positive identification or to recall if the boy had been carrying anything, like a can of gasoline, and even though no one could blame CJ for not remembering (it was dark; he was sneaking around himself, stowing his sax; he was eager to get back to the game to relish LM's defeat; there was no reason at that point to be suspicious), CJ blamed himself, terribly.

Although there would never be enough evidence to arrest the drunk boy, a lot of people were sure he had done it.

But there were people in our city who knew, weeks before the fire marshal's ruling, that the fire had been deliberately set, and who knew, too, that the drunk public school boy had not been the one to set it, and, even though I would've given anything—*anything*—to not have been one of those people, I was.

I couldn't sleep that night.

I hadn't seen or spoken to Gray in the five days since his father's death. His stepmother and brother, Jimmy, had moved back into the house with him, and when Kirsten, CJ, and I knocked on the door, his stepmother hugged us and thanked us for coming and told us that Gray had barely spoken a word since that night. She told us he'd refused to see anyone.

"I know he misses you, though," she said. "And appreciates how much you care about him. I think he's just focused on getting through the funeral tomorrow morning. After that, I'm sure he'll want to be with you."

But that night, I worried—I was consumed with worry—that we had lost him forever.

On top of that, that evening, Trevor and our mother had had a fight about Trevor's girlfriend, Melanie. Her father owned a hardware store, and Melanie had taken a year off before college to work in it, two facts that rankled my snobbish mother. She had thought they'd broken up, and then a friend of hers had seen them out together.

"Leave it to you to bypass the college girls for that piece of cheap goods," she'd said. "That girl is beneath you."

"Almost every night!" said Trevor, winking.

And it got worse from there. Ever since my mother had refused to pay Trevor's tuition at the state university unless he agreed to live at home for his first year of college, Trevor had been a volcano, molten rage—maybe even hatred, although I didn't want to believe that—seething under his surface, ready to blow at the smallest provocation. The fight about Melanie had ended as so many of their fights did: Trevor cursing and hurling threats before storming out, either slamming the door hard enough to shake the house or leaving it wide open, so that my mother had to shut it herself. By then, I was mostly taking their fights in stride, but on top of everything else that had happened, on top of my heartsick worry for Gray, the fight was one thing too many.

As I usually did when I couldn't sleep, I left my bed and crept downstairs in the dark to the family room couch, to see if a change of scene would help, but the full moon beamed like a spotlight through the window, so I left and went to my mother's office, a room just off the kitchen, and tried to settle in on the velvet divan, which, having been purchased purely for its decorative qualities, had cushions hard enough to bounce a penny off. Somehow, though, I fell asleep, so that I was still there when Trevor came home.

The sound of our kitchen door opening must've woken me. It took me a few seconds to remember where I was, and once I did, I was about to get up to see Trev, when I heard my mother's voice say, "Trevor," and I felt the hair on my arms stand on end. My mother could be like that scene in a movie wherein everything seems normal until you notice the moonlight glancing off the butcher's knife in someone's hand. She must have been waiting at the kitchen table for Trevor.

I expected Trevor to be loud and stumbling, but when he answered her, his voice was as cool, as even as hers.

"Sitting in the dark waiting to pounce," he said. "Very dramatic."

"It was not for your benefit. I was enjoying the quiet."

"Well, don't let me interrupt."

"Wait. I have something to say to you."

"What?"

"If you insist on having sex with that girl, I will not pay for an abortion when she gets pregnant."

Trevor laughed. "There's this invention called the birth control pill, Adela. Too bad you weren't using it nine months before you had me."

"Melanie's father runs a hardware store, Trevor."

"Owns. Owns a hardware store."

"Girls like that will do whatever it takes to escape their little lives."

"Melanie's family's life is ten thousand times happier than ours, and she knows it. She's not interested in escaping."

"We'll see," said my mother. "If you're wrong, I will not acknowledge that child in any way, much less support it financially."

"I'm going to bed."

"Furthermore, I am putting you on notice that I am finished cleaning up your messes. From now on, I won't lift a finger."

"Yeah, right." I could envision the sneer on Trevor's face, clear as day. "Like you'd ever let my 'messes' dirty up your sterling reputation. I'll do what I want and you'll make it go away, just like always."

"I hope, for your sake, you don't try to test that theory. Because I am finished."

There was a long pause, and though I wasn't even in the room, I could feel Trevor's anger roiling, getting ready to erupt.

But when he spoke, again, his voice was as clear and steady as before. "Well, that's a shame, for both of us. Because it's too late."

"What is that supposed to mean?"

"It means I've already done something way worse than I've ever done before, and any day now, everyone will know."

"What did you do?" When my mother said this, I could hear something that I'd almost never heard before: a ruffle in her usual implacability.

And in the awful, airless, dark red, pulse-banging, silent-scream silence that followed, I knew what my brother was going to say before I heard him say it, before he dropped that ugliness right into the center of my life.

"I set the fire."

I wrote it down. I tore it out. I burned it.

But it stayed and became a secret.

And the secret ate like acid into everything I loved and dulled my senses and devoured my joy and dragged me into darkness and broke me off like an ice floe from my brother and my friends.

After his father died, Gray went back to school, went to classes, walked down the hallways, but really he was curling in on himself, pushing us away with all his strength, and the only right and decent thing to do was to not let him, was to be relentless, dogged, vigilant, to keep our arms around him no matter what.

And I tried. But Trevor had killed Gray's father. How could I be Gray's friend, knowing and not telling him that my brother had killed his father? And even though Trevor's having committed that impossible, wretched, brutal act meant that he was not the Trevor I had loved for every second of my entire life, I still couldn't, wouldn't, would never rat him out.

So I abandoned Gray, my beautiful friend, when he needed me most. I pretended to be sick for all of winter break, and I was sick, but not with pneumonia. For two weeks, I barely left my room, only showered when my mother stood over me in my dark room and refused to leave. I remember standing, empty-hearted, limp, swaying a little on my feet like an underwater plant, letting the water fall on me until it went cold.

In the end, it was my mother's anger that yanked me out of that stupor. On New Year's Day, two days before school was scheduled to restart, I told her I wasn't going. And she said, "This melodramatic display of grief for a man who wasn't even related to you is making you ridiculous, Virginia. If you refuse to go back to school, if your grades drop at all, you can forget about your fancy private college in North Carolina. You will go to school here and live at home, and Trevor won't even be here to keep you company."

Because Trevor was gone. I don't know if my mother had cleaned up Trevor's mess once again or if the arson had simply gone unsolved, but no one ever came to arrest him. And within a month, Trevor had been admitted as a transfer student to a college in Atlanta that was far too prestigious for him to have gotten into without my mother's help. When winter break ended, he was gone, and for the first time in my life, my brother's absence was a relief.

I needed to go, too, to get as far away from home as I could. Living in that house was impossible. So I went back to school and took notes in class and did my homework. Kirsten tried to talk me back into my circle of friends more than once, and then screamed and called me a traitor and a bitch and left me alone. CJ just hated me in silence. And at the end of January, Gray, his heartbreak still so fresh, came to my house to see me. We stood on my front porch, and he said, "Where are you, Zin? Where did you go? The real you, I mean. I don't understand what's happening."

Oh, but that boy, edged in sunlight, being my friend, standing there and being my friend. I ached for a life in which I deserved him.

Years later, when I remembered that sad, unmoored girl on the porch, I wanted to will her to suck it up, to step forward instead of back, to, yes, keep her secret, but to find a way to reach around it and take hold of that boy.

"I can't tell you," I said. "I'm sorry."

"You can't or you won't?"

"I don't know. I just know I need to be alone. I'm sorry."

For a moment, I saw the old flash of kind concern in his eyes, and then he shut like a box and walked off my porch, and he never came back.

In one night, one night, I lost all of them.

After Gray left, I called a summer camp in Vermont I'd gone to when I was eleven and asked them to send me a job application. I trudged through the last months of school—numb even to my own loneliness—graduated, spent all summer with kids, little strangers, taking them on hikes and canoe trips, teaching them the names of trees, tending their minor wounds. By the time I got to college, I wasn't cracked in a thousand places. I wasn't hopeless. But I wasn't Zinny anymore either, Zinny fierce and true, night-jumper, rule-breaker, maker of things never before seen on planet Earth, Zinny who Adela had thought was something to see. I'd learned the beauty of treading the safest path, a path that led me straight to Harris.

But now, Zinny was back, alive inside the pages of my old journal and inside the head of my daughter.

And the old secret was back, too, here, in my house, throwing up a wall between me and Avery, reminding me that I was a fool—the worst kind of fool—to believe it had ever left.

Chapter Thirteen

AVERY

A very didn't find Zinny at the quarry. She didn't find deep insights in the distance between the quarry's edge and the water or great truths among the dead leaves she scuffed free and sent flying with her boots.

But it was late morning; the day was the bright kind of cold, and the air bore the spicy scent of rotting wood and clean dirt and pennies. When Avery had stepped off the bus at the entrance to the state park, she'd felt as if she were planting her boot soles on the soil of a foreign country, a new world.

That morning, after a silent car ride, Avery's mother had dropped her off at the entrance to the school, and Avery had walked in, stowed her backpack in her locker, and then, a few minutes later, walked out. No one had stopped her. If anyone—any teacher or parent, or even any other student—had noticed, they probably thought she had been given permission to leave because that's who Avery was, or had been, a girl who got permission.

She had never taken the bus before because kids like Avery did not take buses, not even school buses, except to away games or field trips. The bus smelled like diesel fuel, sun-warmed plastic, and air freshener. The driver wore a blue jacket and matching pants and said "Morning," to everyone who got on the bus, including Avery. Avery focused. She tried to take everything in. A little girl's plastic hair clips shaped like bees. A woman wearing duck boots just like Avery's own. A guy listening to music on his earbuds so loudly that Avery could hear it: a beat like a pulse and a tinny voice rising above it. Across the aisle from Avery was a baby who kicked off its tiny sneaker twice and a mother who sighed and picked it up from the floor of the bus and put it back on his foot. Looking out the window, Avery saw a chickadee sitting on top of a mailbox, people running in black running clothes and neon-colored shoes, a couple kissing goodbye on a street corner and going their separate ways.

Just before her stop, Avery got a text from her mother: I got a call from the dean that you missed homeroom. She said one of the other students said he saw you getting on a bus. What's going on? Are you okay? Please text me back right this minute.

Avery considered not answering, but then she sighed and typed in, I'm fine. I needed some time alone. Don't worry. I'll go back to school soon.

Avery could imagine her mother staring at her phone in disbelief at the mind-blowing news that perfect little rule-following Avery was skipping school. She braced herself, waiting for her mother to freak out, explode, demand that Avery tell her *right this minute* where she was so that she could come pick her up.

"I won't," Avery whispered. "I won't."

Her mother's text popped up, and it took Avery a moment to fully absorb what it said: That makes sense. I'll let the dean know you're fine. See you at 3:00. I love you.

Avery felt a rush of wonder at this answer, but then she regrouped. *We are not in this together, Mom,* she thought, *and I am still mad at you.*

At the quarry, Avery thought to herself that this was the place in the story where you take on a side-kick or meet a cute boy. But she found she liked being alone, filling her own hours in her own way, letting her thoughts loose to wander and loop. Maybe as adventures went, hers was tame. But it didn't feel tame. She walked around and sat on the cold ground and then walked some more. Once, she lay on her back in the stiff grass and watched a buzzard—huge, with fringed black wings—circling, circling.

She let her mind circle, too, lightly spiraling inward and inward, until she found, in the center of the circles, her father and Cressida Wall.

How simple it would have been to believe the rumors, the ones that claimed Cressida had preyed on her father to get money or fancy stuff—a Gucci purse, a dark green Mini Cooper, a new phone—that her own father couldn't afford because he was a loser or a meth head or bipolar. Or the rumors that said Avery's dad had paid attention to Cressida only because he was nice and felt sorry for her. But what Avery knew was that her dad had changed. He smiled at her and talked to her tentatively now, like a person who thought he might not deserve to smile at her or talk to her. And he'd lost weight. And he'd gotten fired. And her parents were splitting up. She doubted that those things happened because a man had just been a little too nice to someone.

How much did the truth matter? Did it actually set everyone free? What if finding out the truth about her father and Cressida meant she couldn't love him anymore?

Avery got out the journal and sat in a patch of sun, with her back against a tree, and read it all again. She thought about Zinny, CJ, Kirsten, Gray, and Trevor. Closed her eyes and populated the brown grass at the quarry's rim with the people from the journal, but when she opened her eyes, they weren't there.

Zinny had been a truth-teller, writing down even the saddest, hardest stories, and then, in fifteen minutes, so fast, she'd turned into a person who tore out the truth and burned it and was still tearing it out and burning it twenty years later.

You didn't tell someone part of a story and leave off the ending. It just wasn't right.

So Avery decided to throw her lot in with the old Zinny. In a scary, exhilarating instant, like Zinny on the edge of the quarry in the black of night, Avery took a breath and jumped. *Let the truth come*, she thought, *no matter what.*

When she got back to school, even though Avery felt as if she'd been gone for hours and hours, lunch was still in progress. Some of the high school kids were sitting on the school lawn, eating outdoors in spite of the cold, and Avery could've joined them, but she wasn't quite ready to be with people. Instead, she slipped among the branches of the row of trees at the edge of the parking lot, the place where Zinny and Kirsten had waited for Gray and CJ to come out of the burning school. The theater wing had been replaced a long time ago, right after the fire, but Avery looked up at its roof and invited sadness in, and sadness came.

A man died here, she told herself, *and his son stood over his body, and a friendship died, too, a special one that should have lasted forever, and people walk by here every day and don't even know because there is no sign, there is nothing marking the spot.*

But that wasn't true. She was marking it, Avery Beale McCue, Zinny's daughter.

When Avery's mother picked her up, she said, "Do you want to tell me where you went?"

Avery shrugged. "I went to the quarry. I wanted to see it."

Her mother said, "Oh! I loved that place so much. But I haven't been there in twenty years."

Twenty years ago, when her mom had turned from Zinny to Ginny.

"Mom, why did people call you Zinny back then?"

"Oh," said her mother, flushing. "Trevor called me that when we were little—I think that's just how he pronounced 'Ginny'—and it stuck. But not everyone used that name on a regular basis, mostly just close friends. Other people called me Ginny. And, of course, my mother called me Virginia, always." She smiled. "How I loved the name Zinny, even though it was weird. *Because* it was weird."

"It was original," said Avery.

"Thank you. But 'weird' was a compliment to me back then. I loved everything oddball. *Z* was my favorite letter, probably because hardly anything begins with it."

"What's your favorite letter now?"

"Oh. Huh." Her mother frowned. "I guess I haven't thought about that in a long time. I used to have a favorite everything. For some reason, it seemed very important to keep track of all the things in the world that I loved best."

"Don't you still have favorite things?"

Avery wasn't used to feeling sorry for her mother. It was unsettling. Her mother was protective of her, not the other way around. But suddenly the idea of her mother no longer singling out and labeling the letters, colors, foods, places that were her favorites, the idea that she'd lost interest or that she'd come to feel that one thing was just as good as another, made Avery inexplicably sad.

"Oh, I don't know. Maybe if I thought about it I would realize that I do." She smiled at Avery. "But the only favorite thing that springs immediately to mind is you."

"Well, I think you should think about it."

"Okay. If you want me to, I will."

"Good."

Maybe because Avery had planned on staying mad at her mother for much longer than a day and because she felt her anger slipping away, she said, "Mom, can you please tell me what was on the journal page that you tore out and burned? I won't talk about it to you or to anyone if you don't want me to, but I need to know. I can't even explain why."

The light in her mother's face dimmed.

"Avery, I'm sorry, but I can't."

"So that's it? I can never know? What do you think will happen if you tell me? Will life as we know it end? Will the universe explode?"

"I can't tell you because it's not my secret."

"Like only one person owns a secret," scoffed Avery. "What about Dad's secret? Was that just his?"

Her mother sighed. "I see your point. And I hate that I can't tell you, but I can't."

"The truth will set you free. What about that, Mom?"

Her mother shook her head. "Not this time. Not this truth."

———

Avery had waited until the lights went down in the auditorium of St. Michael's School, before she'd gone in to find her seat. She'd told the woman sitting at a table in the school's atrium selling tickets that she had to leave early, so she needed a seat at the very back, preferably on the aisle. The woman had said, "Well, that's good because those are the only seats left. Next time, if you want a good spot, honey, you should get here earlier. They've probably already dimmed the lights, so you won't be able to find your friends, either. The curtain's going up at any second!"

Not finding friends—or people Avery might know—was the whole point, but she hadn't told the woman this.

Avery had begun to investigate Cressida Wall. An outsider might have branded what she'd been doing as "stalking," but Avery wasn't obsessed and she wasn't just idly curious about Cressida, either. She was seeking truth at all costs, and she knew the costs could be big.

As she had scrolled through Cressida's social media accounts, Avery wondered at the ways hers and Cressida's lives had almost certainly brushed up against each other without either of them realizing it. Friends of friends. Sporting events. Academic competitions. There had been that one debate competition, but there had to have been other moments when they'd been at the same places at the same times. In one photo, Cressida had her long, thin, graceful arm slung around the shoulders of a girl Avery recognized as the field hockey goalie for St. Michael's. Avery wondered if Cressida had been there when Lucretia Mott played at St. Michael's last November, if she'd sat in the stands with her blond hair tumbling down her back, her makeup light but perfect, wearing tall boots and a scarf, while Avery ran around, red-faced and sweating in her goggles and mouth guard.

In another photo, Cressida was wearing an apron and grinning behind the counter of a coffee bar. The caption read: "Having a latte fun at my new job!" Avery recognized the coffee bar, although it wasn't the one she and her friends did homework in on Sunday afternoons. It was a few miles away, and one day about a week after her trip to the quarry, Avery told her mother she was staying after school to make up a test, and instead, she took a bus to Cressida's coffee shop. On the way, Avery rehearsed nonchalance and sophistication, how her eyes would barely flit over Cressida's face before she ordered a whole-milk cappuccino, instead of the coffee loaded with chocolate syrup and capped with whipped cream that was her usual choice. She'd brought a thick leather-bound copy of *Jane Eyre*, one of the books from her grandmother's suitcase, to read while she sipped her drink and surreptitiously watched Cressida do her job.

Avery could not have said exactly what insights she thought she'd glean from watching a girl take and ring up people's orders. Smiling at customers, writing names on paper cups, making change: Was there a method of performing these tasks that would belie—or not—a capacity for manipulation and blackmail, that might betray—or not—the conniving homewrecker lurking within the bright-eyed high school girl? Avery wasn't sure. Maybe it would be more a gut feeling; Avery would see Cressida and just know whether the rumors about her were true.

But Cressida wasn't working behind the register. She wasn't making drinks in the intricate multistep way that always made Avery long to be a barista (the tamping down of the espresso powder was her favorite part) or bringing out food or busing tables, either. For well over an hour, Avery sat with her book open on the table in front of her, automatically decoding the words in the densely packed sentences of *Jane Eyre* without comprehending them and sipping her bitter, cooling drink, hoping that Cressida might breeze in with her scarf trailing and her golden hair clouding around her face. But she never did. When she took stock, Avery was happy to find that she was at least a tiny bit more disappointed than she was relieved at this.

On the way out, she stopped to look at the flyers pinned to the bulletin board by the door, and there, gazing out from one of them, was Cressida, her face smudged and mournful-eyed under the brim of a big, soft mushroom cap of a hat: an ad for St. Michael's School's upcoming production of *Les Misérables*. In eighth grade, Avery had gone on a school trip to see a performance in Philadelphia, so she knew that Cressida was Éponine, brave and hopelessly lovelorn, who got to sing the prettiest song in the show.

Despite the fact that riding the bus—every aspect of it, beginning with checking the online timetables— made Avery feel daring and capable as few things ever had (and she had enough self-awareness to see the humor in this: *Sheltered Private School Girl Rides City Bus!*), she had trouble envisioning herself doing it after dark. For a minute or two, she actually considered telling her mother about the play and Cressida and about her own quest for truth, no matter how ugly the truth might be. Weirdly, she believed her mother would probably be understanding and supportive, even though she'd worry, the way she always worried, that Avery might get hurt. It would be just like her to even offer to drop Avery off and pick her up. But then Avery reminded herself that she might never, as long as she lived, learn the story of the torn-out journal page, and she resolved to leave her mother out of her quest for truth entirely. So Avery had gotten out the cash she'd saved from babysitting and had taken a taxi.

There in the last row of the too-warm auditorium, a funny thing happened while Avery watched Cressida perform: she forgot why she'd come to watch her in the first place. She forgot to imagine Cressida talking to Avery's father at work or in a restaurant; she forgot to wonder exactly who pursued whom and why. All she could think about was Éponine and her wild courage and her lost-cause love for Marius. Her voice— Cressida's voice—was pure and water clear and heart piercing and suffused with sorrow. When Éponine died, in Marius's arms, tears slid down Avery's cheeks for the girl dying in the soft rain, all her devotion and valor come to nothing.

While the actors were still taking their bows, Avery slipped out of the auditorium, went to the restroom, and stood in the last stall for a long time, waiting for the bathroom to empty out and for the clamor in the hallway outside to dwindle. When the school seemed quiet enough, Avery started to open the door of the stall, but three girls came in, talking.

"She's so full of herself it's honestly kind of sickening," said one.

"Sarah was way better," said another.

"Even if she can sing, she's still a slut who goes after old men."

Avery had heard other people malign Cressida like this, and even though her mom had taught her that the word *slut* was a weapon in a mean game to hurt girls and keep them from getting too strong and powerful, had taught her to never, ever use it, hearing the word applied to Cressida had mostly brought her relief. Better that Cressida be called a slut than that her dad be called a pedophile. But now, with Éponine's voice still resonating inside her head, Avery could not reconcile the incandescent girl on the stage with those ugly rumors and that ugly label. She felt the urge to step out of the stall and confront those girls, call them jealous and petty, but she knew how little sense that made: Avery defending Cressida. So she kept quiet and waited until the bathroom door had swung shut behind the girls, then she called the taxi dispatcher, asked that she be picked up a block from the school, and she pushed open the school's atrium doors and stepped out into the cold air.

As she hurried down the sidewalk, she saw, ahead of her, a man with a cane moving painstakingly toward what seemed to be a back entrance to the school, and Avery paused, concerned about his unsteadiness, thinking she should help him but not knowing how. And while she stood unsure of what to do, the door opened, and there was Cressida, wearing sweatpants and carrying a backpack. A light hung over the doorway, and its yellowish glow fell onto Cressida's face, which still held traces of stage makeup and which blossomed into a sunburst, child-sweet smile at the sight of the man.

The man said, "Look at my superstar girl! You were amazing, sweetheart!"

Cressida laughed and said, "Thanks, Dad."

And the man used both arms to wrap her in a hug.

"Careful, Dad," said Cressida, pulling back and kissing his cheek. "You need to keep that cane on the ground."

Her father said, "You worry too much, Cressie."

"Here," said Cressida. She slung her backpack over both shoulders, took hold of her father's arm, the one not holding on to the cane, and the two of them— father and daughter—walked down the sidewalk to the parking lot.

Chapter Fourteen

GINNY

"My friend Nancy is crazy about Mose *and* she's a dog therapist, and she says that your painting captured Mose's inner dog perfectly, down to the smallest whisker," said Daniel.

It was evening at the dog park, almost dusk. A few low shreds of pansy-purple cloud and a ribbon of orange edging the field were all that remained of the sunset. One morning, a few weeks ago, Daniel had mentioned that, in addition to mornings, he and Mose sometimes came for a walk after he got off work.

"Oh, so you've been holding out on me and Mag," I'd said. "I see how it is."

"He's probably got a whole different set of friends at night who think *they're* his only dog park people," Mag had said.

"Okay, I'm actually feeling jealous that Daniel might have other dog park people," I'd said, truthfully. "It's like the cool kids' lunch table all over again."

"Who could be cooler than you two?" Daniel had said.

"So invite us!" I'd said.

"Not me," Mag had said. "I'm old. One dog park trip a day is all the excitement I can take. Besides, now that Ginny's officially getting divorced, isn't it time you two got this show on the road?"

For a second, Daniel and I had just stared at her, and I'd waited for the two of us to be engulfed by embarrassment. But it hadn't happened. Instead, Daniel had laughed.

"That's our Mag," he'd said. "Always the subtle one."

"She kind of has a point," I'd said to Daniel. "You're not exactly moving at lightning speed here."

Daniel had thrown his hands in the air. "Hey, I thought there might be rules about these things. Like a waiting period, maybe."

"You're starting a relationship, not buying a gun," Mag had observed, dryly. "Look, you should call Ginny when you're leaving work in the evenings, and, if she's free, she should meet you at the dog park."

"Fine," Daniel had said.

"Fine," I'd said.

And so it was.

"**Inner dogs** have whiskers?" I asked.

"Are you doubting Nancy?"

"I didn't even know dog therapists existed."

"Are you doubting the existence of Nancy?" said Daniel.

"She thinks I captured Mose's inner dog?"

"Yes. She also thinks that you should paint dog portraits for a living. She says that most dog portrait artists fail to capture the unique soul of a dog. She thinks you could make a mint."

"Really?"

"I think she's right. Ever since I hung Mose's portrait in my waiting room, I've had about eight million people ask if you'd be willing to paint their pet."

"You hung that portrait two days ago. That's four million people per day."

"Exactly."

"Just how much prettier than me is this Nancy the dog therapist person?"

Daniel's smile flashed in the dusk. "She's seventy, and she's been married to Elliott for forty-seven years."

"That doesn't answer my question."

Instead of answering my question, Daniel picked up my hand and kissed my palm, then set my hand on his shoulder. He did it again with my other hand, and I slid my hands around to the back of his neck and locked my fingers. He put his hands in the same spot on my neck and drew me in and kissed me on the mouth. It wasn't a long kiss; we didn't stand in the dog park making out. But it was perfect.

"Well, that set the bar high," I whispered. "For all our future kisses."

"I'm not worried," he whispered back. "I have confidence in us."

I smiled and rested my chin on Daniel's shoulder and saw Mose, Walt, and Dobbsey sitting in a row, their heads cocked, staring at us.

"The dogs are puzzled," I said.

Daniel turned to look. "They're wondering why we just hang out in the dog park," he said.

"They think we should go on a proper date."

"How about Saturday?" said Daniel. "Oh, wait, that's the night of doom; I mean the night of the engagement party."

I'd told him about the party, how I was nervous to see my high school friends. I hadn't told him why, not yet.

Before I knew what was happening, I found myself blurting out, "Why don't you come?"

"To the party?"

I took a step back and blinked in surprise. "Wow. I did not plan to say that to you. But you know what? It's brilliant. I'm brilliant. Will you come?"

Daniel narrowed his eyes at me. "I sense a plot afoot."

"How can there be a plot when that was a completely spontaneous invitation?"

"A subconscious plot, then. A spontaneous, subconscious plot."

"Oh, one of those. Okay, let's pretend for a moment that that's not an oxymoron, that a spontaneous, subconscious plot could exist, what would I be plotting to do?"

"Provide a distraction at the party. So that you don't have to interact with your old friends as much," he said.

"You being the distraction, you mean." I considered this and shrugged. "You're right. Please come. And then you can stay after and help me and Avery clean up."

"I'm not so sure that crashing an engagement party is polite."

"Suddenly, you're Emily Post?"

"I'm always Emily Post," he said.

"Well, yes, I guess you probably are," I said. I looked up at the sloping planes of Daniel's face and at his thoughtful gray eyes. It was true dusk now, but I could see Daniel as clear as day.

"Ugh," I said. "Shit. You're so *nice*."

"I'm sorry about that," he said.

"Ordinarily, I don't care if someone likes me under false pretenses. But you're too nice for that."

"False pretenses? Wait. Are you a spy?"

"I'm not a spy." I sighed. "Can we sit down?"

"This doesn't worry me at all. Not at all."

I laughed, and we sat, and the dogs came over and sat with us.

"When I was a senior in high school, my friend Gray's dad died," I said.

Daniel drew in his breath sharply and then opened his mouth, as if to say something, but I lifted my hand to stop him. I needed to tell my story. I reached for Dobbsey and twined my fingers in his soft fur.

"Someone set our school on fire, and Gray's dad was a firefighter. He died trying to put the fire out."

In a voice that seemed to come from far away, Daniel said, "I remember that fire."

I nodded. "It was awful. Anyway, at the time, there was a lot going on in my life, family stuff, and I tumbled into a depression, a bad one. And I wasn't there for Gray. I abandoned him. I was a terrible friend. And he and Kirsten and our other friend CJ, they were so mad at me for that, and I can't blame them. I completely failed Gray."

I considered adding: *And my brother and myself and the husband I hadn't met yet and should never have married.* But obviously, this was too much to confess to Daniel all at once. Or maybe ever. So a silence fell, through which Daniel waited patiently, as if he sensed there was more, as if he knew to leave it space to go unsaid. Daniel was turning out to be disconcertingly adept at reading me. I picked up Dobbsey and kissed him on the top of his head.

"It ended our friendship," I said, at last.

"But Kirsten's your friend now," said Daniel.

"Yes, Christmas break our first year of college, I couldn't stand not seeing her. I went over to her house and she opened the door and we looked at each other, and she nodded and said, 'Okay. Okay,' and we cried and hugged, and after that we were friends again. But she was my friend for years before we got to know the other two. She was more mine than she was theirs, and we just couldn't stand not to be friends. But Gray and CJ probably still hate me."

"It was a long, long, long time ago," said Daniel. "And now they're coming to your party."

"Kirsten's party."

"At your house. Maybe this is you opening the door and Gray and CJ walking through it," said Daniel.

"Maybe. I hope so."

Daniel said, "Listen, what time will the party be over?"

"Nine thirty. Ten at the latest."

"I don't think it's my place to show up at that party. But how about if I come over after and help you clean up?"

"Clean up the house or the pieces of my shattered heart and self-esteem?"

"I bet it's going to be much better than you think. But both, if necessary."

"Does this mean you still like me?"

"Yes. You are extremely likable."

"What if I die of awkwardness at the party, though? If that happens and you're not coming until after the party, then I won't get to see you."

"If you die of awkwardness, I'll kiss you and you'll wake up," said Daniel.

"And if I don't die, you'll kiss me anyway."

"I'll kiss you no matter what," said Daniel.

I would not have predicted that a party would be a good place to meet old friends who now possibly, understandably, despise you, much less a party you are hosting, much less one celebrating the engagement of your dearest friend (which obviously ups the joy and lightheartedness stakes a thousandfold), much less one at which your fifteen-year-old daughter is in attendance, a leggy, vivid presence, so grown-up-looking in her short dress and as avid and hyper-tuned-in as a rabbit, awaiting the arrival of your old friends—the kids from my journal—the way she once awaited the materialization of her favorite boy band at the stage door after the show. Hosting a party is nerve-racking, period, and I'm no party-planning expert, but I'm guessing that tossing twenty-year-old grief and betrayal and regret into the evening is not what the experts recommend.

But it actually turned out to be okay. I felt like throwing up for the entire four hours. I almost broke down crying at least three times. But it's hard to fear retribution or to hope for a grand reconciliation or even to be completely aware of the past casting its long, raggedy shadow when you're worried that the caramel cementing your profiterole mountain together is insufficiently sticky or that the light under one of your chafing dishes keeps going out or that the supposedly unscented candles you have burning all over the downstairs actually smell like pink rubber erasers.

And the thing about a party is that it goes on. It gathers its own momentum and just goes, carrying you and your guests along like a tide. A party stops for no one and nothing. Not even for the instant when you are standing at your dining room table, pouring cabernet into a decanter, and you hear the laugh of your first love break not over the music and chatter but beneath it, a rumble of thunder in summer, a low guitar strum that you would recognize anywhere.

When I walked out into the living room, Gray's back was to me. He was talking to Avery, who stood starry-eyed, bouncing a little on her toes the way she did when she was four, and holding his coat to her chest as if she were embracing a person. Gray was narrower than I remembered, but the set of his shoulders—ever so slightly bowed—matched exactly the image I'd been carrying around in my head for twenty years. Not his nearly black hair, not the sound of his voice or the way he moved, but the mere slope and angle of him threatened to undo me. I forced the tears back just in time. He turned around, our eyes met, and he lifted his hand to wave. Time didn't stop; the rest of the guests did not blur or recede; the music playing did not cre- scendo. But there was Gray Marsden, waving at me from across my living room, a half smile on his face. I waved back, and then, Kirsten appeared with Tex by her side, and Gray swooped her up in a hug. Before the party enfolded them entirely and I turned to go back to the dining room, I glimpsed a shortish man with a tan face and a head of black curls giving me a look of cool appraisal and knew it must be Evan.

Well, that was easy, I said to myself. And I almost believed it, until I noticed that my hands were trembling. I pressed my palms against the top of the dining room table until they were steady again. Then, suddenly, coming toward me was CJ, in a slightly too large suit, looking so exactly the same as I remembered— pale, little-boy face; corn silk hair, same slightly herky-jerky way of moving—that I blurted out, "CJ, you look exactly the same!"

And right away, a second after I'd said this, CJ showed me how wrong I was, how he was not the same. He didn't give me a goofy grin or set loose a stream of talk riddled with facts. He didn't even speak my name.

Stiffly, he said, "Thank you for hosting the party. I know Kirsten appreciates it. You have a lovely home."

As if I were anyone. His proprietary mention of Kirsten the only sign that we'd ever known each other. Then he tipped forward in what I supposed was meant to be a formal—if disdainful—bow, turned on his heel, literally digging in the heel of his shiny brown shoe and pivoting, and walked out of the room.

I'd loved him, my geeky, hilarious, pure-souled CJ. And he'd loved me. I wanted to shout after him, "We loved each other!" Not so much to remind him but to imprint those words on the face of eternity: we'd loved each other; that happened; that mattered and will always matter.

The face of eternity? I thought. *Ginny, honey, you need a glass of wine.*

I drank the wine. I circulated. I cleared plates and filled glasses. I smiled and met new people. All the while aware of Gray, his proximity to me, the number of people between us. At the same time that I wanted desperately to have a conversation with him, I wanted, desperately, to avoid a conversation with him. The wave and smile had been good; perhaps it was best to leave it at that.

When I went downstairs to the basement to get more champagne out of our second refrigerator, Kirsten followed me and put her arms around me.

"How are you holding up?" she said.

"This is your party," I said. "No worrying about me allowed."

"If it helps," she said, "they're just as nervous as you are."

"CJ thanked me for the party like he was eleven and his mother made him do it. He actually bowed."

"CJ is dying to be friends with you again."

"He said that?"

Kirsten shrugged. "Not exactly. He said he wouldn't be friends with you again if I paid him a billion dollars."

"Oh, good."

"But I know he didn't mean it. No one—and I mean no one in the history of the world—is as nostalgic as CJ. If he had his way, the four of us would still be in the furnace room at LM, shoulder to shoulder around his headlamp, telling stories forever and ever."

"If you say so," I said.

"Now, where the hell is Trevor? The big bum."

"Iris texted to say they were running late. Their flight in to Philadelphia was a little delayed."

"They'll come, though, right?"

"They'll come soon. Trevor would never miss your party."

I handed Kirsten two bottles of champagne to carry upstairs.

"Listen," she said, kindly. "Before the night ends, you should talk to Gray. Not a dramatic rehashing of the past or anything. But just a few real sentences, face-to-face."

"Do you think Evan will let me? I keep thinking he's shooting daggers at me with his eyes."

"Evan's not the dagger-shooting type. But it's possible he's a tad protective. I think he knows that you and Gray need to talk, though."

"Talk sounds scary. A few sentences. That's what you said."

"Let's shoot for six. Six sentences," said Kirsten. "Or maybe six and a half."

"Still bossy," I grumbled. "But okay. For *you*."

"For all of us."

"You still think we're an us? You, me, CJ, and Gray?" I asked. I kept my tone light, but I found that I really, really wanted her to say yes. How crazy, after two decades, to still need that yes.

"Don't be crazy," said Kirsten. "Yes. Of course. Usses like us don't just go away. Yes."

I caught that *yes* in my hand, then pressed it to my heart and carried it with me back to the party.

When Kirsten and I got upstairs, Trevor and Iris had arrived. Iris was as slender and elegant as her name. She was half-white, half-Filipina, and the sheen coming off her blue-black hair could guide ships to safety. When she saw me, she came straight over, gliding across the room in her emerald-green dress to hug me and say, "We've been here two minutes, and I'm already concocting a plan to kidnap Avery."

"She's probably concocting a plan to kidnap you," I said, laughing.

Iris looked like a person who would be cool and distant, but she was exactly the opposite. She wrapped one of her iris-delicate hands around my wrist and squeezed.

"I'm sorry about Adela. I tried to make Trevor come here right after she passed, but you know how he is about your mom."

"I do know. It's okay. You know what I think every time I see you, though?"

"What?"

"How much she would've approved of you. I can't say how much she would've liked you because it's unclear that Adela ever actually liked anyone. She wasn't a liker. But your brains. Your taste. My mother would've thought Trevor had married quite a catch."

"Well, I take that as a compliment. Even though, I think Trevor's the one who's the catch."

Together, Iris and I looked at my brother, handsome in his immaculately cut jacket, listening to Avery talk to him in that way that he had, giving her his absolute attention, as if they were the only two people in the room.

"The funny thing is, if he hadn't been her son, if she'd met him anytime in the past fifteen years or so,

Adela would've approved of Trevor, too," I said. "Not that he would have cared."

"He wouldn't have. He shut down the part of himself that cared about Adela a long time ago."

I wanted to ask her if she thought he'd shut down the part of himself that cared about me, too. But I resisted.

"I guess you heard that Harris moved out," I said.

"Kirsten told us. Are you and Avery okay?"

"I am. Avery is playing her feelings about it all very close to the vest. But I don't think she is okay. Not yet."

"She will be, though. Look at her," said Iris. "So self-assured and strong."

Avery stood in the midst of a party full of adults, talking with adamant hands, inhabiting her beauty with ease.

I nodded. "She is. Since the Harris troubles started, she's been pushing boundaries, taking matters into her own hands. It took me off-guard, and I don't think I'm quite used to it yet, but yes. She's stronger than I knew."

"Like her mom," said Iris, with a smile. "You're probably stronger than you knew, too."

After the champagne toasts, when the rhythm of the party had shifted into ending mode, and I was in the kitchen, washing glasses and gearing up to go find Gray, he found me instead.

He stood, gleaming against the gleaming refrigerator door and said, "Hey, Zinny."

I smiled. "Zinny."

"I guess I should've said Ginny. Since we're adults and everything."

"Look at you, coming in here to talk to me. Beating me to it, when I promised Kirsten I'd find you and talk to you."

Gray laughed his one and only laugh. "I promised the same thing. Six sentences?"

"Possibly six and a half."

Shyness overtook us both.

Finally, I said, "I heard you and Evan are having a baby. That's wonderful."

"It is, isn't it? And we found out it's a girl. A daughter."

"*Your* daughter," I said, correcting him.

"My daughter." He shook his head in wonder. "I don't think I really comprehend that yet, that she'll be my daughter."

"I didn't comprehend it until I saw Avery's face," I said. "She squinted at me from under her tiny furrowed forehead, and I said, 'Hey, I know you.' You'll recognize your daughter when you see her."

Gray said, "Thank you. Avery's beautiful."

"Thank you," I said.

The shy silence settled over us again, and my brain began filling it with all the things I wanted to say to him, beginning with "I'm sorry." I wanted to tell him that for every single second of the past twenty years, I would have given anything for another chance at being his friend. I wanted to ask if it was too late. But I was too afraid of the answer. What I finally did say took every scrap of courage I had.

"Gray and Zinny, standing in the same room, talking about our daughters." And then: "I wasn't sure if you'd want to come, and I know you're here because of Kirsten. But still, I'm so glad that you came."

Gray looked down at the floor, and I held my breath, worrying I'd said that wrong thing. Gray looked up and said, "Maybe you can help me stock up on some daughter-raising advice. I'll need it."

It was all I could do not to burst into tears.

"I look forward to it," I said.

When everyone had left and Avery and I were collecting plates and champagne flutes, she said, "I think you should all be friends again."

"I'd like that," I said. "I hope we can."

She put down the plate she was holding. "Mom, I'm really not asking you what happened the night you wrote the torn-out journal entry. But I want to ask something about it."

"Okay. I'll answer if I can."

"Is whatever happened the reason you stopped being friends with Gray and CJ?"

I sat down in a dining room chair. "Sort of. Something happened and I couldn't tell them about it. I couldn't tell anyone. And no matter how hard I tried to pretend it didn't happen, that secret—the fact that I knew and they didn't and I couldn't tell them—came between us."

"Did it have to?"

"Now, I realize it didn't have to. But I couldn't see my way to that back then, when I was eighteen. Back then, it felt hopeless. It felt like the secret poisoned everything, and there was no—no antidote."

My daughter held me in place with her clear gaze. "But that's a metaphor, right? A secret isn't poison. It's just an event that is supposed to turn into a memory like everything else does. It can only have power if you give it power."

"That is very astute," I said. "I don't think I've considered it in quite that light before."

"Don't you think it's time to take that power away?"

She made it sound easy. I wasn't so sure, but I said, "I'll try."

She said, "Good!" And then she yawned enormously.

"Why don't you go to bed?" I said.

"But then you'll have to clean up all by yourself."

"Um. Well, a friend of mine might be coming over for a bit, to help."

Avery sat up straight and raised an eyebrow. "A friend?"

"Stop it with the eyebrow," I said. "You look just like Adela."

Avery just stared at me, eyebrow like St. Louis's Gateway Arch.

I sighed. "Daniel. The vet."

"Your friend from the dog park."

I nodded, trying to read her face. "Except— Except I might like him as a little bit more than a friend."

Avery said, "Oh. Okay," and nothing else.

I dove in with a rush of words. "But it's early days and who knows? And I realize this probably feels really soon to you, since your dad and I aren't even divorced yet. And I am doing my best to take it slow, and I don't want you to worry, but I just—" I stopped.

"You just like him," said Avery.

"Yes."

"Mom, I think that's fine."

"You do?"

She smiled. There was something a tiny bit shadowy in her eyes, but her smile was wide and bright. "I mean, you're not getting any younger."

"Almost time to put this old girl out to pasture," I said.

"Truth."

"Do you want to stay up to meet him?" I said.

She hesitated. "I'm pretty tired. Can I—meet him next time?"

"For sure."

On the stairs, she turned around and said, "Is this going to turn into one of those supposedly cute TV role-reversal situations where you go out on dates and I stay home watching the clock and waiting up for you to get back?"

"Highly possible."

"Okay, but I draw the line at you borrowing my fashionable teenage clothing."

"Got it," I said. "Not even shoes?"

"Fine. Shoes are negotiable," said Avery.

Daniel kissed me again, first thing.

"Wait a minute," he said, looking around in bemusement. "This doesn't look like the dog park."

"Hey, you're right." I eyed him. "Do I know you?"

"Is this a *Twilight Zone* episode?"

"Who watches the *Twilight Zone*?"

"Not me. Obviously."

"Me either," I said. "What's your favorite episode?"

"'The Hitch-Hiker.' It's your favorite, too, of course. It's everyone's favorite," said Daniel.

"Nope. 'Eye of the Beholder.'"

"Uh-oh," said Daniel. "Trouble in paradise. Already."

"Hopelessly incompatible."

And he kissed me again.

We weren't kissing when Trevor showed up, for which I was grateful, especially after what happened next.

I was scrubbing spilled cabernet off my light green velvet chair, and Daniel was in the kitchen washing dishes. Trevor knocked and then just opened the door and came in.

"Hey, Gin. We got all the way to our hotel before Iris realized she was missing an earring. I texted to let you know I was coming back, but you didn't answer."

I could feel myself blush. "I guess I haven't been paying attention to my phone," I said. "I haven't found an earring. What does it look like?"

Trevor pulled out his phone and read from a text: "'Oval-shaped drops with pavé diamonds. Tell Ginny they're good costume but just costume, so no worries if she can't find it.'"

I heard the water turn off in the kitchen.

"You've got Avery in there doing the dishes, huh?" said Trevor. "I hope our boys turn out to be helpful like that."

"Um, actually," I said.

And Daniel came walking into the room. He held a towel in one hand, a glass plate in the other.

"Hey," he said, smiling.

"Daniel, this is my brother, Trevor. Trevor, this is Daniel."

Daniel shifted the plate to his left hand and held his right hand out to Trevor. To my surprise, my usually smooth brother stood as if he were turned to stone— one second, two seconds, three seconds—before he caught himself and held out his hand and shook.

"Daniel," said Trevor, but more to himself than to anyone else.

"Nice to meet you," said Daniel.

Trevor didn't respond, and I was aware of tension zinging back and forth between the two men. Trevor dropped Daniel's hand, and without ever taking his eyes off him, he said, "Ginny, can I talk to you for a second?"

"Uh, sure," I said.

"Alone," said Trevor.

"Trevor? What's up with you?" I said, embarrassed by his rudeness. "We're kind of in the middle of cleaning up here. Why don't we have coffee tomorrow before you and Iris take off?"

When Trevor didn't shift his gaze or say a word, I said, more loudly, "Trevor," willing him to look at me, which he did.

"Ginny—" he began.

"No, it's okay. I should get going anyway." The ice in Daniel's voice stunned me.

"Wait, why?" I said to Daniel. "Don't leave."

But he had set down the plate and towel and was already walking toward the door, grabbing his jacket off the hatstand without slowing down.

"I'll see you at the dog park tomorrow," I said. I could hear the pleading note in my voice.

Daniel gave me a quick, unreadable glance. "I hope so."

As soon as the door closed behind him, I turned on Trevor.

"What the hell is wrong with you?" I said.

"What the hell is wrong with *you*?" he said. "What exactly is your relationship with that guy?"

I kept my voice as steady as I could, but if Avery hadn't been home, I would have been shouting at the top of my lungs. "Oh, what? All of a sudden you're the protective big brother? That's such bullshit, Trevor."

"Well, obviously, you need someone to call you out on your own bad judgment," said Trevor.

I'd never known what people meant when they said "I saw red," but I understood now. Filtered through anger, the world darkened, and I felt the adrenaline pumping through my body.

"You have no right to speak to me like that," I said. "I'm an adult. And my marriage is over. If I want to get involved with someone new, it's none of your business."

"What are you thinking? Of all the people you could've found now that you've finally gotten rid of Harris?"

"I don't know what your problem is, but you need to leave now."

Trevor's eyes widened. "Oh my God," he said. "You don't know."

"Know what?" I said.

Trevor's entire posture changed; his shoulders dropped, and he said, in a quiet voice, "Can we sit down and talk?"

"No," I said, folding my arms across my chest. "I want you to leave."

He sighed. "Ginny. I'm sorry. Please."

Trevor's tone was gentle, but it didn't reassure me. Instead, I felt a pang of fear. Slowly, I lowered myself onto the seat of the light green chair. I could feel the damp spot through the skirt of my dress. Trevor sat down at the end of the couch.

"That guy, Ginny," he said, in the same kind voice. "That's the Daniel who set the fire."

For at least ten seconds, my brain wouldn't work; the gears just froze. When it started up again, I said, slowly, "You can't be talking about the LM school fire."

Trevor ran his hand through his hair. "Yes. I'm sorry, Ginny. But that's him."

I shook my head and kept shaking it. "No."

"Daniel York. That's his name, right?"

"Stop it," I said.

"Did you never see a picture of him? It wasn't in the paper or anything, but I know that once the word got out that he'd been seen hanging around the grounds-keeper's shed, people at LM got his high school year-book photo and made copies and started passing them around. Remember?"

Vaguely, I remembered photos taped up around school, but I couldn't remember the boy's face.

"When it became clear that the cops weren't going to arrest him, some people even posted them around his neighborhood," said Trevor.

Even though he was sitting right in front of me, Trevor's voice in my ears was faint, as if it were coming from a long way away.

"That's horrible," I murmured.

"It's horrible to burn down a school," said Trevor. "That's him. The guy who was here tonight is the same guy, all grown up, who was in that old photo. Ginny, he killed Gray's dad."

With this last sentence, Trevor's voice stopped being far away. That sentence slammed into me with the force of a blow.

"Shut up!" I hissed. "How dare you?"

Trevor fell back against the couch cushions, surprised. "Ginny!"

I stood up, my fists clenched. I had never wanted to hit someone as much as I wanted to hit my brother at that moment.

"You of all people know he didn't do it."

"Why me of all people?" said Trevor. "What are you talking about?"

To my disgust, tears filled my eyes. I bit out the words: "I. Heard. You."

"What?"

"I. Heard. You. Tell. Mom."

I watched as understanding edged out confusion on my brother's face. His jaw dropped.

"Oh my God," he whispered. "Oh my God."

"Get out! Get out of my house."

"All these years," said Trevor. "You thought it was me. You thought I did it."

"Leave."

Trevor stood up and moved toward me. I felt that if he touched me, laid one single hand on me, I would crack right down the middle.

"Get away from me," I said.

Trevor began talking fast, the words tumbling out. "Ginny, listen to me. I didn't do it. I just told Mom that because I hated her so much. I just— I wanted to shove it in her face that she would never be through cleaning up my messes. She thought I was such a bad kid, such a disappointment. I wanted her to be afraid of me, to think I was capable of anything."

"Liar," I said.

"I took that fire, the fire that killed Gray's father, the fire that Daniel set, and, God help me, it became my weapon, too. I used it to hurt Mom, and I ended up using it to hurt you and myself. And that was an atrocious thing to do. But I did not set that fire, Ginny."

Trevor started to pace and to move his hands in the air while he talked.

"Okay, listen," he said. "Are you listening? That night, the night of the game, I left at halftime. And I know that the fire was set at halftime or right after or something. But it wasn't me. I was long gone. I felt weird being at the game, like a loser who hadn't left town with everyone else after graduation, even though I guess that didn't make sense, since a lot of people from my class came back for that game. But I felt out of place a lot back then. Anyway, I went to the hardware store to see Melanie. She was there late, doing inventory. We went down to the quarry and hung out and talked. We were there until morning."

I felt dizzy and sat down in the green chair and held on to the armrests.

"You can ask Melanie, Gin. Or wait! You can ask her dad. He stopped by the store right after I got there. He didn't think much of me. He didn't understand that I really cared about Melanie. He thought I was just using her. We exchanged some pretty harsh words about the game and my snotty rich kid school. I'm sure he'd remember that."

I held my face between my hands.

"You're saying you didn't set the fire," I said. "Is that what you're saying?"

"He still owns that hardware store," said Trevor. "You can ask him. Please go ask him."

But I knew that I didn't need to ask Melanie's father. I sat in that chair, crying, feeling empty and tired and dazed, and I looked at my brother and the years seemed to fall away until I was looking at the person I knew, knew as well as I had ever known anyone, Trevor of the Quaker burial ground and the quarry, my brother, and I understood, beyond any doubt, that he was speaking the truth.

"I believe you," I said, hoarsely. "I do believe you."

Trevor sat down on the rug. He looked as wrung out as I felt.

"That's why you stopped talking to me," said Trevor, sadly. "After Mom sent me away. I thought you were just taking her side. I couldn't believe it."

"That's why," I said.

"Why didn't you ask me about what you overheard?"

I opened up my hands. "I heard you say the words. I *heard* you. I couldn't believe that you would do something like that."

"But you did. You believed it."

"You hated her so much that it scared me sometimes. I thought you hated her enough to do it just to spite her. I couldn't stand that you'd done it, so I tried to erase it. I told myself that it was possible to burn that conversation right out of existence so that it wouldn't ruin everything."

"It ruined everything anyway," said Trevor.

"It came between me and my friends. And you, you left and never came back."

"I needed to get away. From Mom, yes, but not just her. I got stuck being this person who was always reacting to her or trying to drive her insane. When I think about it now, I think I needed to smash it all, my relationship with Mom and my connection to this town. I had to make sure there was nothing to come back to. So I could start over."

"Oh."

"Gin, you thought I set the school on fire? How could you think I was capable of a thing like that? You knew me."

"I'm sorry," I said. "I'm so sorry."

Then, Trevor said, "So you see why I got upset tonight, when I saw him here."

"Him?" I said.

I had been so caught up in the revelation that Trevor hadn't set the fire that I had forgotten all about how our conversation had started. But now I remembered.

Daniel.

Chapter Fifteen

AVERY

A very's mother told her. She told her what those missing, erased (not missing, indelible) fifteen minutes had contained, the fifteen minutes that her mother had tried, when she was eighteen, to tear out and burn. She told her what she had thought was true for so long and what she knew to be true now. Her mother told Avery how she had lived for twenty years in the aftermath of a lie.

"It never happened," said Avery, awed. "The terrible thing that changed your life never happened."

"I know. I can hardly believe it. Trevor *didn't* set the fire that killed Gray's dad. He didn't, didn't, didn't set the fire that killed Gray's dad. I have to keep saying it to myself."

They were sitting in their favorite Sunday break-fast restaurant, a tiny French corner café and bakery that served warm croissants; eggy, fairy-light crullers; savory Pop-Tart-shaped hand pies; and fishbowl-size hot chocolates adrift with whipped cream.

"You were just trying to protect Uncle Trevor. That's why you didn't want to tell."

"That sounds noble, but it isn't the only reason. I believed I was to blame, too."

"How?"

"Trevor and I, we'd struck a deal with each other to be rule breakers. For Trev, a lot of the rule break-ing had to do with showing my mom that she couldn't control him, and he probably thought the same went for me. I might even have thought that, too."

"But that wasn't why?"

"Maybe a little. Mostly, though, I just loved doing exactly what I wanted to do. I liked following through on my impulses. So when I was little, I'd always be the kid who climbed too high in the tree or went out too far in the ocean or got up and danced when I was happy at school. When I got older, I'd skip school or stay up all night writing or sneak out or decorate my boyfriend's house with paper snowflakes."

"Or jump off cliffs in the dark," said Avery.

Avery's mother shut her eyes and tipped back her head and smiled. "I'd stand on the edge of that quarry, with the air on my skin, and I'd feel alive in every cell. And jumping, jumping was like flying." She opened her eyes. "I guess my wildness was actually pretty tame, but it didn't feel that way to me."

"I don't think it was tame. Zinny was awesome."

Her mother reached across the table and squeezed Avery's hand. "I don't know if she was awesome. But I know I loved being myself, even during those years when kids are supposed to be full of self-consciousness and doubt. I reveled in being Zinny Beale."

Her mother's eyes got serious and she shook her head. "Trevor and I dared each other and pushed each other and never, ever, told on each other and always took each other's side. But his hatred for our mother grew and grew, and it spurred him to go further and further, and I knew it was happening. I saw him getting too mad, pushing the boundaries too far, but I never tried to stop him. To even mention it would've been disloyal."

"You did, though. When he stole the stop signs."

"I can't even tell you how many times my mind has gone back to the night of the stop signs. Over and over. How Trevor said he was afraid our mother was turning him into a monster like her. I tortured myself with that night. Because I let him off the hook too easily. So then when he set the fire, I thought it was partly my fault. I'd let it happen."

Avery said, softly, "But remember? He didn't set it."

Her mother gave a startled laugh. "Right! He didn't. Wow."

Avery sensed something coming alive in her mother, and she thought she recognized it, even though she'd seen it only in the pages of an old journal. Not just one thing, either: fierceness, courage. Avery looked at her mother and caught a glimpse of Zinny.

"Someone did," said Avery. "It's weird to think that the whole time you thought Uncle Trevor did, the person who really did it has been walking around with that secret. I hope it wasn't Daniel." Her mother had told her about Daniel, about how a lot of people twenty years ago had thought he'd done it.

"Mom, do you think it could have been him?"

"No," her mother replied after a pause. "My gut tells me that he couldn't have endangered all those people. He's the nicest person I've ever met, like instinctively nice. Nice without trying. But—"

"But what?"

"He was going through a hard time. He was angry about moving in the middle of high school and about not being able to find his place at his new school. Anger can push people. And so can alcohol. He drank too much back then. He told me that."

"You'd have to be really, really angry to set a fire," said Avery.

"I know. I can't imagine the Daniel I know being that angry."

"Are you going to talk to him about it?"

Her mother sighed. "There's part of me that just wants to let it go. I like him so much, and I know whatever he used to be, he's a good man now. I *know* it."

"Mom, can I say something crazy?"

"Sure, baby."

"Maybe there's a reason that you were drawn to Daniel. Like maybe somewhere in your head there was that picture of him you said Uncle Trevor remembered seeing."

"That's possible. I was in a kind of heartsick haze when people were spreading that photo around, but I had to have seen it. Still, you'd think that if my subconscious recognized Daniel, it would also have sent me running straight in the opposite direction."

"Maybe. But maybe you've never completely thought Uncle Trevor did it. Maybe, deep down, you've always wanted to know the truth. Or maybe—"

"What?"

"Maybe it's truth that pushed you two together. Like truth wants to make itself known. Does that sound crazy?"

Her mother laughed. "Maybe just a teensy bit."

"Okay, but it's not crazy to think the truth is better, right? Better than lies or secrets. Even when it's scary or super hard to face or when it doesn't set anyone free—because maybe it doesn't always—the true story should still win."

"I think it's taken me my entire life up to this moment to learn that," said Avery's mother. "And here you are with it already figured out."

Her mother raised her water glass. "Here's to the true story forever and ever!"

And, after a couple of seconds, Avery clinked her glass against her mother's, and they both drank.

That night, Avery wrote a note and sealed it inside an envelope, and the very next day, after school, before she could chicken out, Avery took the bus to the coffee shop where Cressida worked. When it was her turn in line, she asked the twenty-something-year-old woman working behind the counter if Cressida was coming in that day.

"She's down to just weekends now that track is starting up," said the woman. "But she might stop in after practice this evening."

"I can't stay," said Avery, "but can you give her a note from me?"

"Sure thing, honey," said the woman.

That night, when Avery was brushing her teeth, she got a text from Cressida: I got your note. Sure, I'll meet you. Would it be weird for me to pick you up? We could get coffee and just sit in my car and talk. I'm finished with track at 5:00 tomorrow. If that works for you, send me your address, and if you want to meet somewhere else, that's cool, too. Thanks for asking to hear my side of the story.

Avery thought that the text seemed nice enough, but anyone could sound nice in a text. She thought about her house, how it had always been a completely safe place. Even on the really bad sleep nights when she had felt the need to get away, be anywhere else, leaving was really just a way to hit the reset button on her spinning carousel of a brain. She was always happy when her mom pulled onto their street and the house stood waiting, yellow light glowing in the windows. The sight always filled her with peace. Maybe that was why she left in the first place, not to get away, but so that she could come back and be home.

She finished brushing her teeth and wrote: Thanks for texting back. I actually have to stay at school tomorrow to do group work, so you could pick me up there. I go to Lucretia Mott. If that's okay, you can come to the front entrance, and text when you're there, and I'll come out.

When Avery first got into Cressida's car, she could barely look at her. Her palms were sweating and her stomach hurt and it felt like bells were clanging inside her head. Usually, Avery was good at managing her own exterior, at making sure that, however exhausted or unfocused or anxious she felt on the inside, she could keep the outside smoothed down and confident and glossy. But now, when she would've given anything to come across as mature and calm, she believed she might, at any moment, collapse into a thousand stupid, fidgety, fluttery pieces.

"Hey," said Cressida.

"Hey," said Avery.

"Should we get coffee?"

At the play, Avery had really only heard Cressida sing. Her speaking voice was different from what Avery had expected, higher, younger. Right then, Avery decided that if she was having this conversation in the name of getting to the truth, she might as well start by telling it.

"Honestly, I'm pretty nervous. Caffeine is probably the last thing I need."

"Ugh, same here," said Cressida, making a face.

"Really?"

"The entire way over here, I was wishing I hadn't answered your text. I mean not really. I want us to talk, but I—don't know. I can't even imagine what you've heard about me."

"Well—" said Avery.

"No, actually, I *can* imagine it because I've heard it about me, too."

"Rumors suck," said Avery. "It's like people think if they just put 'I heard' in front of it, they can say anything. No one really cares about the truth."

"I know."

"But I do."

Cressida didn't answer, and Avery gathered her courage and glanced over at her, bracing herself to take one look and get completely intimidated. But it didn't happen. Yes, Cressida was pretty, even in sweats, even with her hair in a high, messy knot and her mascara slightly smudged under her eyes. Her profile was lovely and long-necked with a clear-cut swoop of jawline and a delicate slope of nose. But she wasn't the movie-star-polished, glossy, light-emitting princess from her social media photos; she didn't look like she had just stepped off an airplane from a trip to Paris. She looked like what she was: a genetically blessed but normal human girl, not so different from Avery herself. Avery would have supposed that this discovery would've made things easier. But somehow it shook her.

Oh, Dad, she thought.

They parked in a shopping center parking lot, one with a different coffee shop in it, not Cressida's, not Avery's. After Cressida turned off the engine, no one said anything. Avery watched a family—a man, a woman, and a boy of four or five—walking out of the coffee shop. The parents had white paper cups, and the boy between them held a big muffin in both hands as carefully as if it were a kitten curled up in his palms.

"I didn't do any of those things people are saying about me. I wouldn't. I'm not like that," said Cressida.

"Okay," said Avery. "But something happened that shouldn't have. Because my dad got fired."

Cressida turned to her. "Are you sure you want to hear about this?"

"Yes. I'm scared to hear about it, but it's better to know the truth."

"Okay. Well, I don't know where to start."

"How about at the beginning?" said Avery.

Cressida nodded. "All right, well, so my teacher, Ms. Holt, told me to apply for the internship. The thing about me is that I'm smart. But a lot of people don't see me that way. They look at me and make assumptions about who I am. Probably that happens at your school, too."

"It does," said Avery. "I think people see me as smart but also as—I don't know. Boring. Predictable. Like little boring, good-girl Avery."

"So you know what I mean. And the thing is you start to believe your own hype. So it took me a long time to think of myself as smart, even though I knew I always got good grades. But Ms. Holt is one of the people who thought I was intelligent. And, like, capable. So when she recommended me for the internship, I was surprised but also happy. And when I started last summer, it was awesome to walk into a new place, where no one knew me. I could be who I wanted to be."

"I can see how that would be nice," said Avery.

"I worked super hard and tried to represent myself as mature and professional with interesting ideas, and it worked. I'd feel so good walking into that building every morning in the summer. I didn't even care that I didn't have time for parties or the beach or whatever."

Cressida stopped and looked down at her hands in her lap. Avery noticed that Cressida's nails were bitten, and she felt the shakiness again and something else, like protectiveness. For Cressida. For the girl who had wrecked Avery's family.

"Your dad saw me the way I wanted people to see me. Or I thought so. He was nice. He asked my opinion about important issues. He told me I had exceptional talent and potential. And then he arranged for my internship to extend past the summer."

"Oh," said Avery. She wanted to say more, to tell Cressida that her dad *was* nice. He was just what Cressida had described: a person who saw the good in people, who lifted them up and made them see the good in themselves. But she could tell by Cressida's face that she was getting to the hard part of the story.

"And he arranged for me to be paid." Cressida lifted her chin, defiantly. "But that's it; that's the only money I ever took from him, and I didn't even ask for it. I would've worked weekends for free, just because I liked it and because it would look good on my college applications."

"Okay," said Avery.

"It wasn't like things got weird overnight. It happened gradually. He started to send me these really long emails and not just during work hours. I'd get to school and check, and he would've sent one at like three in the morning. He never said anything obviously inappropriate."

"That's good," said Avery, in a small voice.

Cressida shook her head. "But they got weird. Just the tone of them. And he'd go on and on and on about how gifted I was, but also about a connection he felt with me."

Avery felt sick. She felt like shouting at Cressida to stop. But she'd come seeking truth, and even though Cressida might not be telling the truth, Avery needed to hear her story, all of it.

"He'd say it was uncanny how in tune with each other we were. He said I understood him better than anyone else at the company. Once, he said it was as if I could read his mind. And he'd remember every stupid little thing I'd say. Like once, I said I liked oatmeal raisin better than chocolate chip cookies, and a week later, he brought me some cookies from a bakery. He said he was in a bakery thinking of me and the cookies just called out to him to buy them. Why was he thinking of me at a bakery?"

Cressida sounded like she might cry. Avery sat very, very still and didn't answer.

"You just don't think it could be happening, you know? That a guy older than your dad, and one who's been so nice to you, is paying you the wrong kind of attention. I loved working at that place. I didn't want to believe something bad was happening there. But then he asked me to lunch. I shouldn't have gone. But I'd just sent my application to my early decision school and was really nervous about it, and your dad said he knew someone at the school and could maybe pull some strings. He invited me to lunch to discuss it."

"You should've said no," said Avery.

Cressida threw her hands into the air.

"No kidding! Don't you think I wish I had? Listen, are you sure you want me to keep telling you this stuff?"

No, no, no, no.

"Yes," said Avery.

"Fine. He took me to this fancy vegan place because I had mentioned one time that I was a vegetarian. And he didn't say a word about the college thing."

She paused, and Avery saw that she had tears in her eyes.

"He said he was sure I knew by then that he had feelings for me. He said he'd tried to fight them off because of our age difference, but they were too strong. And he said—"

A sob escaped Cressida's throat, and for a moment she covered her face with her hands.

"He said he knew I probably would not want a full-fledged relationship with him, but that he'd be willing to take anything I could give him, even if it were just an hour or two once in a while. An hour or two. Like I was some kind of—"

She broke off, crying openly.

Finally, she mostly stopped crying and dabbed at her eyes with her fingers.

"I felt so gross and humiliated. And stupid. I felt so fucking stupid because he probably didn't mean any of those things about me being talented and special, and I had believed him. I had felt so good about myself. That's pathetic, isn't it?"

"No," said Avery. "I bet he meant what he said."

Cressida blinked at Avery, her eyes wide and confused, like a little kid's. "You do?"

"But even if he didn't, that doesn't mean you're not talented or special. He doesn't get to decide that."

Later, Avery would be stunned that she'd reassured Cressida in that way and had said things that amounted to defending Cressida against her own father. But she realized that it was because, at that moment, her mind hadn't completely absorbed the fact that the man who had sat at that table and made Cressida feel humiliated actually *was* her father.

"Anyway, then he reached across the table and held my hand, and before I could pull away, I saw your dad's face change and *he* pulled away. He'd seen this guy from work watching us, and that was it. Your dad got fired. I quit.

And people started spreading rumors about me being a blackmailing whore and my dad putting me up to it. And I wouldn't even care what people said about me. But my dad—" Cressida started crying again, quietly this time. "He's the best person and he's had a shitty year. He got diagnosed with multiple sclerosis. And now people are saying terrible things about him. They're all lies."

Avery remembered the man with the cane, how Cressida's face had lit up at the sight of him.

"I'm so sorry that happened," she said.

"It's not your fault. You know what's crazy?"

"What?"

"For a long time, I felt sorry for your dad. I hated what he did, but I felt bad for him. He seemed—lost. Like a person who had lost his way."

"He did. He wasn't always like that. My mom says he got depressed."

"That's awful. But even though I felt sorry for him, when he kept calling me, even after he got fired and it should've been all over, I started to hate him."

Avery froze.

"You're saying he kept calling you, even after my mom found out, after *I* found out?"

Cressida nodded. "Every day, sometimes more than once a day, for a week. I answered the first time be- cause I didn't recognize the number, and he told me he wanted to see me. I told him not to call me ever again. But he didn't stop. He left messages, saying that he loved me and needed to see me. He said he thought he would kill himself if I didn't talk to him. I didn't know what to do. I wanted to block him, but what if he did it? What if he killed himself because I blocked him? But then, after a week, the calls stopped. I thought it was all over, and then, two weeks later, he called again. I didn't even listen to the message. I just deleted it and blocked his number. I deleted all his messages because I couldn't even stand to have them on my phone, but now, I wish I'd saved them, so I could show people that my dad and I didn't do what people are saying, that it was him pursuing me."

Avery wrapped her arms around her stomach.

"No. He wouldn't have done that. I don't believe you."

Cressida's blue eyes regarded Avery with kindness. "Look, maybe he just wanted to see me to apologize."

"Take me back to school."

Cressida started up the car, but before she put it into reverse to back out of the parking space, she said, "It took a lot of guts for you to get in touch with me and for you to sit and listen to all of this. I just want you to know that."

"Take me back," said Avery, squeezing her eyes shut. "Please, please, please just take me back."

Chapter Sixteen

GINNY

"I'd like to tell you something. It's about what happened between us, after the fire. Wait. No. That's not exactly right. It's about how *I* behaved after the fire, when I failed you as a friend. And I want you to know that what I have to say is not an excuse because nothing excuses how I acted. I don't expect you to absolve me. Absolutely not. So maybe it's an explanation, although that also sounds too tidy. But at the very least it's a true story, one that's finally mine to tell, and I hope you'll listen. But you obviously don't owe me that or anything else, and if you don't want to hear it, I'll understand. I really will. But if you do want to hear it, please know that I don't expect you to say anything right away. Or ever, if that's better for you. It's why I called you on the phone instead of seeing you in person.

You should have time to absorb and sort out and think about this story—or to do nothing at all with it. If you want to talk about it, you can call in an hour or a month or a year. Whenever. And if you don't, you shouldn't have to, and I will never, if we see each other again, which I hope with all my heart we will, I will never bring it up again, ever. I promise."

By the time I'd finished saying this to Gray, I was out of breath. It was a mouthful and also, as I was acutely aware, a painfully stilted, qualifier-riddled way to start a conversation. But I was trying to do what I should have done twenty years earlier: put Gray's feelings ahead of my own. Would telling him the story be an unburdening for me? Of course. Would it be the best possible gift if after I told it, he forgave me? Yes, I can't lie. But those could not be the reasons I was telling him. Gray had had a friend who loved him and that friend deserted him at the cruelest possible time and he never knew why. And maybe he'd stopped caring about why, but I didn't think so, because what I knew, as surely as I knew anything, was that Gray had loved me, too. He had loved me and I had let him down and he was a good, kind person, and he deserved to know the story.

Before I'd even caught my breath, Gray was talking.

"I do want to hear," he said. "I'll listen to whatever you have to say."

"Thank you," I said.

I told him. I told him the complete story, from over-hearing Trevor's lie about starting the fire to hearing Trevor's truth about telling the lie. It didn't take long. It struck me as funny: that the story of how I'd mis-judged my brother and betrayed my friends and lost so many of the parts of myself I'd loved best, the story of how Zinny had been frightened right out of her Zinny-ness could be summed up in ten minutes and a handful of sentences.

At the end, I said, "I couldn't have told you or anyone that Trevor set the fire. But I could've worked harder at staying your friend."

After a few long seconds, Gray said, in a quiet voice, "So now I'm supposed to think about this, right?"

"Yes, if you want to think about it. And get back to me soon or later or never, as you choose," I said.

"Okay," said Gray. "Thank you. And thank you for telling me."

"Thank you for hearing me out," I said.

I'd told him he shouldn't respond right away, that he should give himself time to digest what I'd said, and I'd meant it; I had. If I suffered a tiny hypocritical sting of disappointment that he hadn't brushed aside that advice and verbally flung open his arms to forgive me on the spot, I also felt my reservoir of peace get a little fuller.

One thing, I thought, *I did one thing right.*

I would need all the peace I could get because next up was calling Daniel.

I knew Daniel closed his veterinary office early on Fridays, so I thought I'd ask him to meet me at the dog park, but as soon as I called him, while the phone was still ringing, I changed my mind. We don't get many purely safe havens in this life, and even if Daniel and I never entered the sweet bubble of the dog park together again, I wouldn't dilute its magic with a painful conversation. Our phone call comprised three short, flat sentences, one of which was his giving me the address to his house, but afterward, driving there, I felt so flustered that I pulled off the road once, just to breathe and collect myself.

I didn't have a plan. I thought I would see him and intuit what to do and say, but when he opened the door of his little brick, slope-roofed cottage, the sight of him in the doorway—tall and lean in a flannel shirt and khakis, his gray eyes wary and serious and sad—sent such an aching tenderness through me that all I could think to do was wrap him in my arms. But as I stepped forward, he stepped back, opening the door wider, and I walked into his house.

Immediately, Mose, like walking, flowing sunshine, appeared, bumping the palm of my hand with the top of his head. I stroked him and scratched behind his ears, and he regarded me with grateful, infinitely pretty black eyes.

"Do you want some coffee or something?" said Daniel.

"No, thank you. Maybe a glass of water?"

"Sure. Let's go in the kitchen."

The house was scattered with signs of Daniel's daughter, Georgia—a soccer ball and a purple backpack in the hallway, bright hairbands braceleting the coat closet doorknob, and on the stairway, pairs of shoes, one pair per step: orange soccer cleats, black-and-white-checked slip-on Vans, a pair of duck boots just (I noticed with a pang) like Avery's.

"The idea is that she grabs them on her way up the stairs and puts them in her room," said Daniel. "At least, that's *my* idea. Hers seems to be that she ignores them until I yell."

"You yell?" I said, skeptically.

"Uh, no. Not usually. Not literally."

"You yell figuratively?"

"I speak in a manner that suggests yelling but without the loudness."

"I see. I pile things outside Avery's room door, thinking she'll get tired of stepping over them and put them away."

"Do you do it at night when she's asleep, so that when she goes to the bathroom in the middle of the night she trips over them and falls down?" said Daniel.

"No."

"Well, there's your problem."

"Thank you, Dr. Spock," I said.

"Mr. Spock," corrected Daniel.

"You're about to do that V-thing with your fingers, aren't you?" I said.

"I have no idea what you're talking about."

I laughed and Daniel smiled. It was a somewhat dimmer version of his usual star-spangled smile, but still, I felt as if I'd won a prize.

What if I don't bring it up? I thought. *What if we just take this moment, two people being parents of daughters and making each other laugh and smile, what if we just take this and run with it and never look back?*

I might have done it, despite all my tough talk with Avery about truth, just cast the whole subject of the fire overboard and sailed on, but Daniel brought it up first.

"So I take it your brother recognized me," he said.

"Yes."

"I guess I should feel lucky that he's the first person since I moved back." He shook his head. "But I don't."

"Can I tell you what happened after you left?"

"Sure. Why not?"

I told him.

Afterward, in a synchronous moment that would've been funny at another time, we lifted our water glasses and sipped and set our glasses back down onto the table. As if proper hydration might help smooth the road ahead.

"That must've been hard. Thinking he'd done it," said Daniel.

There was Daniel, reaching for compassion first thing.

"Thank you. It was awful. You know, when I first heard him confess it to my mother—or throw it in her face—I didn't believe it. I knew instantly that it wasn't true. As reckless and angry as Trevor could be, he wouldn't be so horribly destructive. He just didn't have it in him. But I'd heard it. I heard his voice saying it. And then I think what I did was, once I'd heard it, without meaning to or wanting to, I constructed a version of Trevor inside my head that matched what he said he'd done. And, honestly, I didn't have to search very hard for memories of Trevor that tipped him from being just an angry, rebellious kid to someone who could be responsible for a man dying. He had a lot of rage toward my mother back then. He would go very, very far, too far, just to try to hurt her."

"But not that far," said Daniel. His face was closed, unreadable.

"No," I said. "Not that far."

Then I said, "Although the person who set the fire probably didn't mean for anyone to get hurt. It was nighttime; the building was empty; everyone was out watching the game. It might have been a prank that got out of control. Teenagers tend not to think things all the way through. All the neuroscience stuff we know now about teenaged brains not being all the way wired together; teenagers don't always foresee consequences."

After a pause, Daniel's eyes met mine, and he said, "That would have been a pretty big fire for a prank."

"Yes, but maybe it started off small. Maybe the theater curtains were exceptionally flammable or something."

"The building might not have been empty," said Daniel. "There could've been a custodian inside. Or a thief trying to jimmy open lockers, or a drunk kid trying to find a bathroom. There were a lot of drunk kids at that game."

"I remember."

Daniel's gray gaze held steady. "Including me."

"Oh."

"When the police questioned me the first time, they said witnesses had seen a person matching my description hanging around behind the groundskeeper's shed, drinking. And I told them that that person matched my description because that person was me."

"I see."

Daniel took another sip of water. "So now I guess you're going to ask me if I did it, aren't you?"

I looked around at Daniel's kitchen, at the specific elements of his specific life: chili-pepper-red enamel tea kettle; thick white diner mugs hanging from hooks beneath his kitchen cabinets; a glass bowl filled with lemons and limes; a white doctor's coat slung over a chair; in the corner, Mose's round bed with Mose sitting in it; and on the wall next to the refrigerator, a bulletin board pinned with postcards and photos. I could see a girl in almost all of the photos. Georgia, in every phase of childhood. I couldn't make out her features, but I could tell, to my surprise, that she was as buttery blond as Mose.

I sat up straight, folded my hands on the tabletop, and shook my head.

"No," I said.

Daniel blinked. "Wait. No? No what?"

"I'm not going to ask you if you set the fire. On my way to your house, in the name of finding and facing the truth, no matter what, I thought I would. I thought it would be a failure of bravery not to ask. But just now I realized that not asking wouldn't be a failure of anything. So, no, I'm not going to ask you if you set the fire."

"You mean not right now?"

"I mean never. I mean I think it's time I trusted my gut."

"And what does your gut say?"

"That you hand me dogs when I'm crying, and, when Mag is sitting on the ground, you help her up every single time. That you have the most open, unguarded smile of anyone I've ever met, except for Avery. That you are an all-in listener. That I can say anything to you, even that I'm not sure whether or not I am sad about the death of my own mother, and you won't judge. That talking to you feels like coming home. That you have a dog bed in every room of your house, and I know I haven't seen every room, but I don't have to have in order to know that you do. That your face fills with easy, graceful, lit-up love when you talk about your mom and dad. That you came back here, to this place that hurt you, that's full of bad memories, the place you had escaped from for what could have been forever, because your daughter missed having conversations with you."

A smile ghosted around the edges of Daniel's mouth. "Your gut says all that?"

"So I don't need to ask because I know you. I know you're a person who grants others the full measure of their humanity. And I know you couldn't set a fire that had the potential to hurt innocent people. Not now, not twenty years ago. Not ever."

Daniel tipped backward in his chair and let out a huge, windy sigh that ended in a hoot.

"Thank God you didn't ask," he said. "You would've been within your rights. No one could've blamed you. Not even I could've really. But I have been asked if I was responsible for that terrible, killing heartbreak of a fire so many times by so many people, and I have said no so many times, and if you had asked me—"

He ran his hands through his hair and smiled at me.

"The thing is I like you," he said. "I'm maybe an inch away from total, point-of-no-return in love with you. But I am finished with that question. And I just don't know if I could be with someone who felt the need to ask it one more time."

"Yikes. Dodged a bullet there, I guess."

Then, he shook his head and laughed. "Okay, I would've wanted to be with you anyway. But I am still glad you didn't ask."

Regarding him across the table, his lean face and his smile lines and his inky eyelashes, I wondered how I'd seen him in the dog park for all those months without realizing he was the handsomest man to ever breathe air.

"So—an inch away? Really?" I said. "Because the word *inch* sounds tiny, but inches are bigger than people think."

"Maybe a centimeter."

"I was right about dog beds in every room of your house, wasn't I?"

"Does a walk-in closet count as a room?"

I laughed.

He said, seriously, "You know it won't be easy. I saw the way your brother looked at me. I'm thinking that some of your friends would look at me the same way."

I considered this. "I'll convince them it wasn't you."

"What if you can't?"

"Then shame on them. Their loss. But I will."

"All these years and no one ever figured out who set that fire," he said.

"I guess probably they never will now."

"Sometimes, I wonder how hard they actually looked," he said.

"What do you mean?"

"Remember what I said about drunk kids looking for a bathroom?"

"Yes."

"It wasn't totally hypothetical. The line for the restroom was crazy long, even after halftime had been over for a while, and I had the brilliant idea that I might go find one inside the school. So I went walking around the perimeter of the building, searching for a way in, when I saw this girl running out of a door at the back of the school."

"A girl? What did she look like?"

"I didn't see her face. She had her hood up, and it was dark. But she was thin and wearing white pants. It spooked me, seeing her. So I went back to the stadium and got in line for the restroom. I told the police about her when they questioned me."

"I never heard about a girl. I was pretty depressed and out of it once I thought Trevor had done it. But I think I would've remembered hearing that the cops were looking for a girl."

"No, you're right. I never heard anything about it, either. My dad even called them a while later to see if they'd found out anything about her, but they blew him off. Said that lead went nowhere. But he didn't get the sense that they'd taken me seriously."

A thought struck me. "Oh no."

"What?"

"After Trevor told my mom, I'm sure she did what she always did: made his problem disappear. I wonder if she heard about that lead and convinced someone to let it go. Trevor's not a girl, obviously, but it would've been like her not to have wanted to take any chances that it might have been Trev you'd seen."

"Well, I guess we'll never know whether she did that or not. But it doesn't matter now."

Before I left, I kissed Daniel and said, "I'll make sure everyone I care about knows you didn't set that fire."

"Even if you can't convince them, it's nice of you to try. Thank you."

I turned around to open the front door, then turned back.

"Oh, listen," I said.

"I'm listening."

"I almost love you, too. In case you were wondering."

"Me? Are you kidding?" he said. "Why would I wonder about that?"

Daniel grinned and I kissed his grin and leaned down and planted a kiss on the warm, blond curve of Mose's head and left.

If it is possible to walk on air while driving a car, that's what I did all the way home from Daniel's house. I'd made light of the task of convincing my friends and family that Daniel had not—could not have, for love or money or rage or sorrow—set the Lucretia Mott school fire or any other, but I knew it wouldn't be easy. Still, I had kept faith with a person who deserved it; I had trusted my own instincts; and I was one slender centimeter away from true love, so it seemed like a good afternoon to give myself over to joy. And then, just as I pulled into my driveway, Gray called. He hadn't waited a week or a year. I'd talked to him at ten that morning, and it was two thirty in the afternoon. I held my phone in my hand and listened to it ring, and for a few trills, I pondered whether it was a good sign or a terrible sign that it had taken Gray less than five hours to absorb all I'd told him and call me back, and then I decided to just answer.

"Hey, Gray," I said.

"It's crazy how your voice sounds just like your voice."

"Yours, too," I said. "Which is also crazy."

"I talked to Kirsten and CJ."

"You did?"

"And we were hoping you would come to my house for dinner tonight."

"Oh!" It came out as a squeak.

"Unless—I know it's last minute, so we can also do it—"

"No, no. Tonight is fine. Wonderful, actually. I need to check in with Avery. She seemed a little quiet last night and then again this morning before school. She'll probably be fine with my going, but I should talk to her first."

"Why don't you bring her?"

"Really?"

"Sure. I'd love that."

"So I guess that means you guys aren't planning to rake me over the coals too hard?"

"What? Like we wouldn't do that in front of your kid?"

"Probably *you* wouldn't."

"Well, Kirsten is pretty miffed that you didn't tell her first."

"It took a lot of self-restraint, to be honest, but I thought you should hear it from me, and Kirsten—"

"Would've had a hard time keeping it to herself."

"Yes. She wouldn't have spilled, but it would have taken a Herculean effort," I said.

"And why put her through that?" said Gray.

Zinny and Gray, talking about our friend Kirsten, finishing each other's sentences. It took my breath away.

"What about CJ?"

"CJ is not quite—there," said Gray.

"I understand. I can't say I blame him. He's always been so loyal to you."

"Yeah, but mostly I think it's that he's gotten used to being mad at you. He never was all that great with change."

"That's true. But oh, how I adored that kid. When he got excited about something? He was, I don't know, the Gulf Stream or el Niño. A force of nature."

"El Niño," said Gray, and I could tell he was smiling. "That fits."

"At Kirsten's party, he looked like an eleven-year-old wearing his dad's suit."

"He may actually be reverse aging. It's eerie. You'll come, then? Tonight? Is seven okay?"

"Yes. Thank you for inviting me. And for not never speaking to me again."

There was a silence.

Gray cleared his throat and said, "Before we're with the others, can I say something?"

"Sure."

"I can't have you thinking you're the only one who wishes you'd handled things differently twenty years ago or that you're the only one who needs forgiving."

"Oh."

Looking out my car window, I noticed for the first time knobs of leaf buds studding the branches of the trees bordering our driveway and emerald spikes bunched in the mulch in our side yard.

"I guess I have been thinking that," I said.

"Well, can you stop? Because the way you were, after the fire, it was a pretty drastic change."

"I know, I know, and I'm sorry."

"No, I don't mean that. We should've realized something was really wrong. Kirsten says that she sees now that you were depressed, and even though we might not have understood that completely back then, we should have reached out. Instead, we just got mad."

"You'd just lost your dad, Gray."

"I know. But still."

"There's no 'but still.' I know your day-to-day must have been so rough. You were just getting through. No one could've expected you to take care of someone else."

"Maybe not. But before then—"

"Before when? Before the fire?"

"I don't know quite how to say this."

"You don't have to," I said. "Whatever it is, it's okay."

"It's not, though. Look, I don't want to say that I regret our being a couple because you were my best friend. Being with you made me smarter and better and happier. In so many ways, I loved you and loved being your boyfriend."

"Thank you."

"But I got into the relationship under false pretenses. I knew I was gay. I didn't want to believe it, and I hoped it would change, but deep down, I knew. You were so good to me. You trusted me. And I hurt you."

"You were in a really hard situation," I said.

"What I did was still wrong. I'm sorry."

"It's okay. I mean it." And I found, as I said it, that I did mean it.

"Thank you. See you tonight?"

"Yes."

Gray's husband, Evan, answered the door. He greeted Avery, whom he'd charmed within an inch of her life at Kirsten's engagement party, with a luminous smile and a hug, but even before he'd fully turned to face me, I could feel it: razor-edged, unyielding, protective. A fierce, fearless, gatekeeper kind of love, a variety I recognized because I loved Avery exactly that way. Once upon a time, it's how I'd loved Gray and Trevor and Kirsten and CJ and everyone.

"Thank you for having us," I said to Evan. "I can only imagine what you must think of me."

If I'd hoped to disarm Evan with my directness, it hadn't worked. Not a muscle in his smooth, high-cheekboned face moved.

"After your vanishing act, he never stopped missing you. Not for two decades. Did you know that?" he said, evenly.

"I missed him, too," I said. "And I regretted what I did. I would have given anything to go back and undo that vanishing act."

Evan was short and compact and dashing, with shiny black curls and blazing black eyes. After a stony second, his expression softened, just a little.

"You know what? If I were judged exclusively by the mistakes I made when I was eighteen, I'd be in real trouble," he said. "At least, you're here now."

"I'll do better from now on," I said. "I promise."

"Let's hope so," said Evan, then he tipped his head sideways, toward the interior of the house, where I could hear Kirsten's crazy crow-caw of a laugh burst through the fabric of conversation and music. "Come on in. And welcome."

After we were seated and had filled our plates from the platters heaped with fragrant shredded chicken, thin ribbons of steak, glossy roasted peppers and onions, crumbled white cheese, and half-moons of sliced avocado, a paralyzing awkwardness fell upon us. We sat and applied salsas and squeezed lime wedges and forked up food and swaddled it in tortillas (folding with great concentration, as if our lives depended on it) and listened to Thelonious Monk beat out wisdom and sorrow on piano keys and tried not to chew too loudly, and just before—seconds before—we all would've crawled under the table or run screaming from the room, Kirsten saved us. She worked her signature brand of miracle: turning—not water into wine—but slow, dull, sucking quicksand into champagne.

She held court, launching into a long, funny, effervescent, starry-gold flood of chatter about her wedding, her dress, the buttons on her dress, the hem of her dress, the exact lowness of the neckline of her dress, her veil, her bouquet, and, at the end, slipped in what had to be the most enchanting description of canapés in the entire history of describing canapés. When we were all laughing and joining in and when the air of the dining room seemed to be filled with inaudible birdsong and invisible iridescent bubbles, she stopped short and said, "Not to be wildly insensitive, but don't you think it's about time we addressed the elephant in the room?"

And maybe because Avery was in a state of bewitchment after all Kirsten's spun-gold talk and believed that anything might be possible or maybe because she was too young to be familiar with the idiom "elephant in the room," she began to look around the dining room, presumably in search of an actual elephant. When her roaming and quizzical gaze finally settled on me, I said, "She means what was on the torn-out journal page and how it wasn't true after all."

"Oh, that," said Avery. "Uncle Trev and the fire."

Kirsten said, "That, yes. And I have a few remarks to make about it, if no one minds."

"Oh boy," mumbled CJ.

"Okay with me," said Gray.

"You'll make them anyway, even if we do mind, right?" I said.

Kirsten raised her pretty shoulders in a conciliatory shrug and said, "Still, it seemed polite to add 'if no one minds.'"

"Go ahead," I said.

"First, Zin, you could have told me. Back then. You could have told me what you overheard Trevor tell Adela. I wouldn't have turned him in to the cops. I wouldn't even have told Gray and CJ, although I would have struggled with that, struggled mightily. You know how I do."

"I do," I said.

"Nevertheless, I wouldn't have breathed a word to anyone. And it might have helped you to tell me. I know it would've helped me to know," said Kirsten.

"Yes, you would've kept it a secret for sure. But it wasn't just that I didn't want to get Trevor in trouble. I wanted it not to have happened at all, and I had this idea that, if I never told a soul, if I tried with all my might to pretend it didn't happen, it would go away."

Avery said, solemnly, "She wrote it down in her journal and tore out the page and went into the woods and burned it."

"Magical thinking," said Gray. "I've done my share of that."

"It didn't work, though, did it, Ginny?" said CJ, caustically.

"No," I said.

Kirsten darted a warning look at CJ. "On to my second remark, which is: this explains a lot. Obviously, it explains how you changed and checked out and retreated into yourself."

"Not really," muttered CJ.

"I couldn't tell you guys," I said. "And I was horrified at how my family, my own brother, had caused so much pain and destruction. I felt guilty that he'd done that and guilty that I had to keep it from you all, and I just ended up living inside that guilt all the time."

"It isolated you," said Gray.

"Yes. And it made me feel hopeless there for a while."

"I'm sorry," said Kirsten, "I wish you hadn't had to go through that alone." She touched her fingers to her lips and blew me a kiss.

"But," she continued, "it explains other things, too. Like Trevor leaving. I just thought he'd had another blowup with your mom about something, but then he never came back. Did she not let him? Or did he not want to?"

"Both," I said.

"Also, it explains Harris," said Kirsten.

I glanced at Avery, who said, "It's okay."

"What happened," said Kirsten. "How everything went crazy and fell apart. I can see how that would lead you to Harris."

I said, "Boundaries can be good. The straight and narrow can be good. Harris was kind and steady and knew the value of boundaries."

"It sounds like he made you feel safe," said Gray.

"He did. We weren't a good match, not really. But by the time I woke up to that fact, we were married and had Avery." I smiled at my daughter. "My gorgeous, smart, sleepless, funny girl."

"Thanks, Mom," said Avery, blushing and fiddling with her napkin.

"Okay," broke in CJ. "But none of that changes the fact that you let Gray down. His dad *died* and you just turned your back on him like you'd never even been friends."

"CJ," said Gray.

"No," I said. "He's right. Somehow, the thing with Trevor just flattened me. I shouldn't have let it. I'd always felt so fearless and strong, and then, I just— sank. But I've thought over and over again for all these years that there had to have been a moment when I could've rallied, turned it around, and I missed it. So, yes, CJ, I should've fought harder to be there for Gray and for all of you. I'll never stop being sorry."

CJ looked taken aback, as if he hadn't expected me to admit I'd done wrong, and then his expression shifted into one I recognized: CJ processing, his eyes narrowed, his lips tucked in, his jaw muscles twitching ever so slightly. I used to love watching CJ process.

"Maybe you should, though," said Gray. "It seems like it could be time for all of us to stop being sorry and move on."

I thought about that, what it would be like to let go of the regret I'd been harboring for all of my adult life. I wasn't sure I knew how, but it seemed like a useful skill to try to learn.

Evan had been quiet all evening, but now he said, "The four of you have been carrying around all this stuff—grief and grievances and secrets—for so many years, and all the time, there's been some person out there carrying around the true story of who set that fire."

"That kid," said CJ. "The public school guy people saw drinking behind the shed. Everyone knew he did it. Well, I guess not you, Ginny, since you thought it was Trevor. But everyone else knew."

"They never arrested him," said Gray.

"Yeah, but he did it," said CJ. "I *saw* him, remember? He ran by me. He must have been on his way to set the fire."

Kirsten looked at CJ with surprise and said, "Back then, you weren't so sure it was him."

CJ flushed. "Not a hundred percent sure. Not sure enough for the cops. But he was a troubled guy. Everyone knew it. He was drunk and making threats against our school. If you want to know what happened go ask Daniel York."

"Oh, that was his name," said Kirsten. "I'd forgotten."

"Mom," said Avery.

"I know," I told her.

"What?" said Kirsten. "No secrets allowed."

"Ha," said CJ. "That's funny."

I cleared my throat. "Here we go," I said to Avery, who gave me her best "you can do this" smile.

"He didn't do it," I said. "I know him. And by that I mean not just that I've met him but that I truly know him. I know his heart, Daniel York's heart. He is the best person I've ever met, and he didn't set that fire."

No one moved, and I heard Kirsten gasp.

"Not the dog park guy?" she said.

"Yes. I didn't know until the night of your engagement party," I said. "He came over after everyone was gone, but then Trevor stopped by unexpectedly and recognized him. But he didn't do it."

"Wait," said CJ. "You're saying you're involved with this guy?"

"I am," I said. "Very."

"Perfect," said CJ. "That's just perfect."

"Listen, all those years ago, I didn't trust my instincts. I heard Trevor tell my mother he'd done this horrific thing, and my first thought was 'No. No way.'

I knew he didn't do it, but then, I wavered and doubted and rationalized and second-guessed, all in the name of facing the truth. And the truth turned out to be a lie. I know Daniel didn't set the fire. Trust me on that."

"We're supposed to exonerate him because you say so?" scoffed CJ. He tossed his napkin onto the table.

In the silence that followed, my heart did a little sinking.

It doesn't matter, I tried to tell myself. *It would be nice if they would accept that Daniel didn't do it, but you don't need their approval. You really, really don't.*

Then, Kirsten said, "I'm in."

"What's that supposed to mean?" said CJ.

"Zinny's say-so is enough for me." Kirsten was answering CJ, but she was looking at me. I felt so grateful I could have climbed across the table to kiss her.

"Plus," said Kirsten. "It was high school. Remember high school?"

"I do," said Avery, wearily.

Kirsten smiled at her. "There were also rumors that I'd had sex with the entire starting lineup of the boys' basketball team."

"Which was ridiculous," I said. "Since all the cutest boys rode the bench."

"Oh my God, Jack Maupin. And Dylan Dyer!" said Kirsten, fanning her face with her napkin.

"It was a travesty that Dylan didn't start," said Gray. "That kid could drive inside like a pro."

"You're telling me," said Kirsten, fanning harder.

Everyone laughed. Even CJ cracked a begrudging smile. But then he said, "That's different. It wasn't just rumors. Daniel York was *questioned* by the *police*. He was a suspect, for God's sake."

"He was questioned, and they didn't arrest him," said Gray. "Presumably because they didn't have a case."

CJ made a disgusted sound and waved off Gray's comment.

"Look. Just as an experiment," I said. "What if we all assume that Daniel didn't set the fire. Can we try that?"

I figured that if anyone could be enticed by the idea of an experiment, it would be CJ.

"He did it!" said CJ. "He got lucky, too, because there was that hidden fire wall between the theater wing and the rest of the school, built back before World War Two. If it weren't for that old wall, the entire school could've gone up."

"And more people could've gotten killed," said Gray. "Thank God for that wall."

"Someone got lucky that wall was there, but it wasn't Daniel," I said. "How do you know there was a fire wall?"

Kirsten rolled her eyes. "His stupid *project*. On the architectural history of the school. Remember how he couldn't stop yammering on about that project?"

"Oh, right," I said.

"That 'stupid project' found a permanent place in the school archives," said CJ, and then added, "Permanent. For posterity."

"I know what *permanent* means," said Kirsten.

Then, in an instant, CJ's moon-pale face went scarlet. "Uh, actually, though," he mumbled, "I didn't learn about the fire wall when I was doing that project. I somehow must have missed it. I read about it in newspaper accounts of the fire."

"Ha! Shoddy research!" said Kirsten, wagging a finger at CJ. "Frankly, I'm stunned."

"Stunned and disappointed," said Gray, shaking his head grimly.

"We expect better, CJ," I said. It just slipped out.

CJ slowly turned his head to look at me. Underneath the table, out of sight, my hands gripped each other for dear life. I knew—probably everyone at the table, even Avery and Evan, knew—that this was a moment of truth.

Finally, CJ said, "Great. I thought I'd have more time before you started giving me crap, too. Ever heard of a grace period, Zinny?"

My hands released each other. It was all I could do not to leap out of my chair and merengue around the room. Instead, I lifted an eyebrow.

"I've been here for well over an hour," I said.

And then my old friend CJ slapped his hands onto the top of his beloved, silver-blond head and laughed.

"So getting back to Zinny's experiment?" said Kirsten. "Assuming someone other than Daniel set the fire?"

"Fine," said CJ. "Whatever."

"Daniel saw someone that night. It was after the second half of the game had started. A girl in white pants and a hooded sweatshirt, and she was running out the back entrance to the building," I said.

"Really?" said Kirsten. "A girl? For some reason, I always assumed whoever set the fire was a guy."

"Um, isn't that kind of sexist, Aunt Kirsten?" said Avery.

"You know what? It absolutely is! My bad," said Kirsten.

"What kind of person would try to burn down a school?" said Evan.

"Someone angry," said Kirsten.

"Someone with a vendetta against the school," said CJ. "Like a student who was failing or suspended a lot or something. Or maybe someone from the Cole

School, although they probably wouldn't disrupt the game since their team was kicking our butts."

"Someone who just liked to set fires, maybe," said Gray. "My dad had stories about people like that. Fire-bugs."

"But if that were the case," I said, "you'd think there would've been a cluster of unexplained fires. I don't think any others happened around here at that time. Or before that time. Or since."

"So someone who hated the school, like CJ said," said Kirsten.

"How could anyone hate school?" said CJ.

"Nerd," said Kirsten.

"Slut," said CJ.

"And, oh Lord, white pants? In November?" Kirsten shuddered. "A person who wears white pants in November is capable of absolutely anything."

"You sound like Adela," I said.

"I do not sound like Adela," said Kirsten.

"White after Labor Day is for people who go to all-you-can-eat buffets and watch afternoon soap operas," said Avery in a devastatingly accurate imitation of my mother.

"Wow," said Gray.

"Holy crap," said CJ.

"Oh my God," said Kirsten to Avery. "It was like you were possessed for a second."

Avery blinked and looked around, confused.

"What do you mean? Wait, did I say something just now?"

Everyone laughed. Gray rumbled like a car going over a bridge. CJ slapped his hands onto the top of his head. Kirsten tossed back her head and set loose a clamor like an entire flock of crows.

And I laughed, too, because my daughter was funny and because she made my old friends Kirsten, Gray, and CJ laugh and because, if only for that one glowing moment, it was exactly as if the twenty-year chasm running down the middle of our friendship had disappeared, closed up, healed.

Chapter Seventeen

AVERY

B ecause, for months, she had been mired in confusion and conflict regarding her father, Avery had
been trying to write her way to clarity. She wasn't a
natural writer like Zinny; she wasn't really a storyteller
like Kirsten, either. But anyone, she told herself, could
make a list. So she listed reasons, at least one every day,
to believe that her father was a good person and/or a
good father. Was it possible to be a good father and a
bad person? Or a better father than you were a person?
Or vice versa? In the before—prior to her father's
getting fired—Avery probably would've said no. A
man was just who he was, whether he was at work or in
a restaurant with an eighteen-year-old girl or at home
cooking French toast in the exactly right way for his
daughter. In the after, she wasn't so sure. It was one of

the issues she hoped the list-making would resolve, but so far, it hadn't.

The French toast was number six on the list. He dusted it with cinnamon sugar.

Number nine was how if a stranger was rude to him or to someone else, he wouldn't be rude back but would tell Avery to remember that sometimes people just had rough days.

Number fourteen was how mad he got when referees made bad calls, at Avery's games, on television, at the Sixers or the Eagles games, anywhere. It was one of the few times he yelled. Maybe some people wouldn't count this as a positive trait, but Avery understood that his anger resulted from knowing the rules inside and out and from his strongly developed sense of justice.

Number thirteen was how, ever since she was six, he'd taken her to Sixers and Eagles games. They'd wear jerseys and would drink soda—which normally she wasn't allowed to have—and eat soft pretzels with mustard, and they'd cheer until they were hoarse.

Number two was how they could sit in a room or at the breakfast table or in a car together and be quiet. Sometimes, the silence could get uncomfortable, but mostly Avery liked it. Her dad didn't bombard her with questions the way her mom sometimes did. There was a generosity in his silences. They invited her to speak or not speak; they gave her the choice.

Number twenty was how, on Sundays, he'd drive to the corner near the entrance to the highway ramp and buy a newspaper from a man named Jake, whose teeth were dark yellow and who didn't look as if he had access to a shower. Her dad did this even though they got a different Sunday paper delivered to their house.

Number twenty-one was how he knew the man's name was Jake.

Number one was how absolutely patient he was when he helped her with her math homework. Even when she cried. Even when she threw her pencil across the room or let her gaze leave the book or the piece of paper and wander to the ceiling. He'd said (how many times over the years? Hundreds? A thousand?), "I get it, Aves. Math is a bear." Who said that: Math is a bear? And in the calmest voice anyone had ever heard? No one in the world but her dad.

The day after the dinner party at Gray and Evan's, Avery called a meeting. In school, they'd been learning about South Africa: apartheid, Mandela, the Truth and Reconciliation Commission. Avery thought that the Truth and Reconciliation Commission was surely one of the most splendid organizations that had ever existed. The victims of injustice got to tell their stories, and so did the perpetrators of injustice. No matter what side a person had fought on, no matter how awful their injuries or horrific their crimes, they could speak their truths, recount their heartbreak and loss, and, if necessary, ask for forgiveness. Amnesty. Even when amnesty was refused, they'd gotten to say they were sorry in front of everyone, to put words to the shapeless, overpowering regret that must have lived inside them. Avery believed that was worth a lot.

While she didn't tell her parents, in Avery's mind the meeting she'd called was a convening of her family's own Truth and Reconciliation Commission. She needed answers. And maybe the truth wouldn't set them free or maybe her father wouldn't be able to tell it and maybe, if he told it, she wouldn't be able to grant him amnesty. But she hoped.

She'd considered having the meeting at her father's apartment instead of at the house. If it went terribly, blew up in her face, at least it wouldn't have happened in her house. Rooms had a way of keeping what had happened in them. But then she'd decided to have it at their house after all. It was the place the three of them had lived and been a family, where they'd eaten meals, opened gifts, done jigsaw puzzles on snowy days, and watched cooking and baking shows (which her father unaccountably loved). Their dining room table was where her father had sat, sometimes until late at night, teaching her math. What had taken place between her father and Cressida was part of all that, part of their family story, however much all of them might wish it weren't, so that house, that table, seemed to Avery the fitting and just location for their family truths and reconciliations to unfold.

Before the meeting, Avery opened her notebook and read her list all the way through, once and then again.

Whatever else he is, she thought, *he is this, too.*

And she tried to believe it.

Avery hadn't seen her father in almost two months. After Christmas, she'd felt more and more uncomfortable around him, until she could barely stand to be in the same room with him for more than a few minutes. In late January, he'd asked her if she thought some time away from him might be good for her, and she'd told him yes. Now, as he walked into the dining room and sat down across the table from her, she noticed he was thinner. Not in a wasting-away way. He looked healthy, younger. Her mother had told her that he'd gotten a new job at a company that manufactured and sold medical technology, including robots that could perform exquisitely delicate surgical procedures. At another time, Avery would have been eager to talk to her dad about the robots, but now, with things as they were, she had Googled them instead.

Her mother offered her father coffee, and he said no, so Avery's mother sat down next to her father and clasped her hands on the tabletop. Avery noticed that neither of them wore their wedding ring anymore. Avery's own hands were in her lap, holding on to the hem of her oversize sweatshirt. She focused on steadying her breath and on not jiggling her legs, and she tried to channel Zinny standing on the lip of the quarry.

Just do this, she instructed herself silently, *just jump*.

"I met Cressida," she said.

Her mother sighed. "Oh, honey."

Her father began turning pink, the flush starting in his neck, the way it did, and traveling upward.

"I—I'm sorry," he said. "I hoped you wouldn't have to run into her."

"I didn't," said Avery. "I got in touch with her. I asked if we could meet. And talk."

Her father slumped, as if he'd had the wind knocked out of him. "Oh" was all he said.

"You did that?" said her mother. Avery had expected her mother to react with worry, because that's so often how she reacted to anything that might be difficult for Avery. But instead she sounded proud.

"There have been a lot of really ugly rumors going around about her," said Avery. "At first, I liked hearing those rumors because if people believed them, they wouldn't believe bad things about Dad. But rumors aren't the same as the truth, no matter how many people believe them."

"No, they're not the same," said her mother.

"So I thought it was only fair to hear her side of the story, Cressida's side."

"I see," said her father, in a tired voice.

"That took courage," said her mother.

"And now that I've heard it, I need to ask you if it's true, Dad."

Her father tensed.

"You shouldn't have to bother with all this," he said. "You're too young. Just please go to school, have fun and live your life, and let us handle it."

"I'm sixteen, now," said Avery. "I'm not a little kid. This *involves* me. It's part of my life, too. And I need to know the truth."

Her father stared stonily down at the table.

"We need to listen to her, Harris, to whatever she has to say." She nodded at Avery. "Go ahead, baby."

Avery took a long, slow breath and then nodded.

"Okay," she said. "Okay."

She said "you," addressing her father directly, the way she'd planned. She took her time, recalling Cressida's exact language, beginning at the beginning with Cressida getting the internship. She told them how Cressida had said that things got weird slowly, how she hadn't wanted to believe what was happening. Avery told her father that Cressida said he'd email her at all hours and bring her little gifts and would tell her that he felt a deep connection with her and seemed to be thinking about her all the time. As she spoke, her father sat completely still, staring at the table. She described the wild rumors about Cressida's dad and the blackmail plot. Her mom put her hand over her mouth and said, "Oh God."

Once Avery got to the part where her dad and Cressida had gone to the vegetarian restaurant, she faltered and almost allowed herself to edit what Cressida had told her. But she knew that if she didn't follow through with her plan to tell the entire story, she would regret it. A truth commission wasn't one if you smoothed the truths over and made them prettier than they were. So she pushed through her embarrassment. She sat at that table across from her father and recounted the story of how he had professed his love for Cressida and of how he—and his proposition that they meet once or twice a week—had humiliated her. Before she'd quite finished, her father pushed his chair away from the table.

"I don't think this is an appropriate conversation to be having," he said.

"Dad, don't leave," said Avery.

"Harris," said her mother, in a warning voice.

Her father left his chair where it was, a few feet from the table, but he stayed in it. When he finally met Avery's eyes, she saw that he'd lost his healthy glow and his new youthfulness. One conversation—Avery's words, her insistence on telling—had taken it away. The sight of him old and weary hurt her heart.

"What do you want me to say?" he said.

"I want to know if Cressida's story is true," said Avery.

Her father leaned forward, rested his elbows on the table, and pressed his palms to his forehead.

"And Dad?"

"What?"

"You need to know that whatever you tell me I will believe. When Cressida told me her story, it sounded true, most of it anyway. I'm sorry to say that but it did. But if you tell me it didn't happen how she said it did, I will believe you because you're my dad. And I need to have faith in my dad. So please, please, whatever you do, don't lie to me."

"Oh, baby," said Avery's mother, her eyes filling with tears.

"Yes," he said. "That story is accurate. I didn't mean for it to happen. I hadn't been feeling like myself for a long time, and even though what I did was very, very wrong, I didn't quite understand that at the time. But that lunch, what I said to her, it was me hitting rock bottom. As soon as I saw Dale Pinckney watching us across that restaurant, it was as if I were seeing myself through his eyes. It hit me like a ton of bricks that what I was doing was terribly wrong. I felt so sick and sorry about how low I'd sunk and how close I'd come to doing something even worse."

Then, he added, "I didn't, though. I didn't get involved with her. I stopped in time."

"Dad," said Avery. "She wouldn't have anyway."

For a moment, her father didn't respond. Then, he said, "I'm sure you're right."

"And after that, you changed," said Avery. "Right? That moment in the restaurant. You said it was rock bottom. So after that you changed."

It came out sounding more plaintive, more pleading than Avery had wanted it to. She saw her mother notice and saw her shift—instantly—into high alert.

"Yes," said her father, lifting his head. "Yes. I've been working with a therapist for months now, and it's helped me beyond what I could have imagined. What happened in that restaurant and the stupid move to try to get Dale not to tell anyone, and then getting fired, letting you and your mother down the way I did—"

"And hurting Cressida," said Avery's mother, interrupting. "Don't forget that."

"Yes, that, too. All of it, as reprehensible as it was, was good for me, in the end. It was a wakeup call that came just in time."

Avery felt the muscles in her chest relax. Despite her father having just admitted to being creepy, even possibly predatory, Avery was filled with relief.

"I knew it," said Avery. "I knew that part of her story couldn't be true."

"What do you mean, honey?" said her mother. "What part?"

"I knew he wouldn't do it. Not after you and I knew, Mom. After we were, like, part of it. I knew he wouldn't do that to us."

"Do what? What did she say?" said her mother, the pitch of her voice rising just a notch.

"She told me that after everyone found out and Dad got fired and she quit, even after it was all supposed to be over, Dad kept calling her, like, every single day for a week and then one more time after that. She said he left messages saying he loved her and saying he felt like killing himself. She said she had to block his number."

"Oh my God," said her mother. "Harris?"

And they both looked at Avery's dad, whose face had gone from scarlet to ashen.

"Dad?" said Avery, her heartbeat quickening. "She made that up, right?"

"I think she must have—" her father began and stopped. "I don't know why she—"

"Harris," said her mother, sharply. "You can't lie to her. You cannot do that."

To Avery's horror, her father's face crumpled, and his breathing got shallow, and he began to cry.

"I'm sorry," he said. "God help me, I am so sorry. I was out of my mind over that woman. But I'm different now. It really is over. I look back and it's like a different person did it, made those calls, all of it."

"Jesus Christ, Harris," said her mother.

Avery began to shake, not out of sadness. It was as if all the fury she'd tamped down, the fury of months, had jumped the fire wall and set her ablaze and roared in her ears.

"*Woman?*" she yelled. "Are you *kidding* me? She's not a woman. I *saw* her! She puts her hair in a messy bun and bites her nails. She's a girl. Like me, Dad!"

She got up out of her chair.

"You are disgusting, do you know that?" she hissed. "You called her? After Mom and I already knew?"

"I'm sorry," said her father. "Please, sweetheart."

"You lied. You sat here and lied to me, and I hate you," shouted Avery. "I never want to see you again. Do you hear me?"

"Yes," said her father, drearily. "I hear you."

"Get out!" she yelled. "Please just get out of here! Leave!"

Avery flung out her arm and pointed toward the door, and her father got up from the table, wiped his face with both hands, and left.

Chapter Eighteen

GINNY

The morning after the day Harris admitted to wrongdoing beyond what his daughter, strong as she was, could bear, Avery appeared in my room at a little past seven, her eyes full of exhaustion and wonder, and said, "The birds are singing."

I got out of bed, and we walked together into her bedroom, tugged open her heavy, room-darkening blinds (once upon a time, I'd had high hopes that those blinds would magically allow Avery to sleep), and looked out into the backyard. The grass, the garage roof, the cable wire, the Adirondack chairs were bedecked with singing robins. Avery opened the window, and their flurry of whistles spilled over us like glitter.

Spring doesn't arrive overnight, not literally, but, in my experience, it seems to. There is a moment every year when spring, however long it's been stealing in, suddenly breaks like the cleanest, brightest wave, drenching the world in newness. That this moment should come on this particular morning felt to me like a personal gift to my girl, a benediction, and I closed my eyes and sent a message of gratitude sailing out into the fresh, song-spangled air.

We sat there for a long time, not speaking. I knew sometime soon we would need to talk about the blackmail rumors and about all the dreadfulness I knew my own mother must have unleashed upon the world, but neither Harris nor Adela had any place in this morning. Finally, I said, "What if we call Kirsten and see if she wants to go for a walk. We could bring lunch."

Avery said, "Would it be disrespectful to eat at the Quaker burial ground?"

I smiled. "A while back, I spent quite a bit of time with those dearly departed Quakers. I think they'd be happy to see us."

While Avery showered, I called Kirsten and filled her in on the events of the night before. I'd expected her to erupt into a profanity-laced tirade against Harris, but Kirsten had always had a lovely way of flaring out into empathy when you least expected it.

She groaned and said, "Oh, Harris, you have made our job of salvaging you in the eyes of your daughter pretty damn hard."

"If anyone can do it, we can," I said.

"Of course we can. We can do anything, especially for Avery."

"Even have a picnic with dead people?"

"You know I have a strict no-eating-on-the-ground policy."

"I do. And I also know that every one of your policies has an Avery exception clause."

"True. Wine would definitely help. How long till Avery can drink wine with us?"

"Five years."

"Fine. I'll bring cake."

We took our time and the scenic route, a path stitching alongside the river, through trees—some bare, some misted over with pale green—past the gorgeous, castle-like ruins of grist and powder mills and under the soaring stone arches of bridges. At Avery's request, Kirsten and I told stories about high school in our jumbled manner, talking over each other, interrupting, correcting, finishing each other's sentences, rambling off on tangents, bouncing from one story to the next. Avery was quieter than usual, but when she laughed at our stories, it was like coins falling from the sky.

By the time we got to the Quaker Meeting House downtown, it was nearly one o'clock, the Meeting House and the yard striped with sun and empty of Sunday worshippers. In a spot between the dotted lines of gravestones we spread our blanket, sat down, and like three sunflowers, lifted our faces toward the sun.

Later, when we'd finished the sandwiches and had started on the cake, Avery said, "This was your place, yours and Uncle Trevor's."

"It was. Holy ground. For the Quakers and for us."

"Do you think you'll be friends again, now?" asked Avery.

"I think so. I hope so. It hurts his feelings that I could have believed he'd set the fire," I said.

"It hurt your feelings to believe it," said Kirsten.

"A lot," I agreed.

"Plus, he left and never came back. He could've tried harder to stay close to you," said Avery.

"We could've both conducted ourselves differently," I said. "But we've wasted twenty years. We probably shouldn't waste more time on regret or might-have-beens."

"I wish Grandmother had known that Trevor didn't really do it. She died thinking he did," said Avery. "That's so sad."

"It is. I'm not sure it would've made much difference in their relationship, though. They may have been beyond help or forgiveness," said Kirsten.

"They were a bad match for sure," I said. "But then Adela was a pretty bad match with everyone, with human beings in general. My mother just never got the hang of loving people. I don't know why."

"Remember how the other night Evan said something about how all of you have been carrying around secrets and stories?" said Avery. "Maybe Grandmother was, too. Maybe there's a story that explains why she was the way she was."

"Maybe," I said. "If there is, I don't think it'll ever see the light of day."

I looked at Avery, sitting eating her cake in the sun, and I was aware that our conversation had moved into dangerous territory: parents and secrets and forgiveness. I wondered where she stood now on truth-seeking, on bringing stories into the light.

Maybe because Kirsten's thoughts were moving along the same lines, she changed the subject. "I wonder if we'll ever find out who really set the fire."

"The girl in white pants might have done it," said Avery. "Whoever she is."

Kirsten grimaced. "White pants in November. Yeesh."

"Most people shouldn't wear white pants ever," I said. "Most people look like the ice cream man in them."

"Or like an Elvis impersonator," said Kirsten, laughing.

"Or like they're in the navy," said Avery. "I think navy guys wear those, right? I can kind of picture them marching around in white pants."

A thought struck me hard, and I put down my cake plate.

"They do," said Kirsten. "Back in college, I dated a guy who went to the Naval Academy. An ensign, they call them. Eric Rogerson. He was swoony in those white pants. Remember Eric, Ginny?"

Inside my head, pieces were falling into place. Pieces I never wanted to find falling into places I never wanted them to go.

"Marching around in white pants," I said to Kirsten. "Oh no."

"What's wrong?" she said. And then her blue eyes widened.

"Oh my God," she said.

When CJ opened the door to his apartment to find Kirsten and me standing there, he was smiling his guileless fourth-grader smile.

"Hey, guys!" he said. "Welcome to my humble abode. Come on in."

CJ's apartment was in a building from the early twentieth century that had once housed an automobile showroom and then became the headquarters of a Philadelphia newspaper. It was lovely, seven stories of windows and terra-cotta, but something about CJ's apartment made me sad. A big oak table serving as a desk took up half his living room, and bookshelves stood against every wall. On the mantelpiece over the gas fireplace there were framed photos of CJ in various famous places (the Grand Canyon, Paris, the steps of the New York Public Library) and one of CJ, Gray, and Kirsten sitting on a park bench in Rittenhouse Square. None of these elements was sad in and of itself, and it was a pretty enough apartment, but somehow, the place seemed overhung with loneliness.

Someone needs to give CJ a dog, I thought.

"I'm glad you guys called. Sundays can be pretty slow around here. What can I get you?" said CJ, waving his hands excitedly. "Wine? Cheese and crackers? I guess Gray is on his way?"

"CJ," said Kirsten. She sounded like what she was: near tears.

The smile faded from his face.

"What's up?" he said.

"Can we sit down?" I said.

"Uh, sure."

CJ gathered up the sections of the Sunday *New York Times* that were scattered across his couch cushions and dropped them onto the coffee table. Kirsten and I sat, and CJ sat across from us, his fingers drumming on his knees, his eyes darting nervously between Kirsten's face and mine. I wanted to hug him. CJ had always been so easy to love.

"I hate to have to ask this, CJ. But on the night of the fire, were you the person Daniel saw running out of the building in white pants?" I said.

CJ's finger-thrumming accelerated until his hands were a blur.

"He said it was a girl," said CJ.

"But he never saw the person's face. I think," I said, gently, "I think he assumed it was a girl because the person was small and slight, but mostly because they were wearing white pants, and boys don't usually do that. Unless they're in marching band."

"They stole your jeans," said Kirsten, in a choked voice. "They were always doing that."

"Wait, wait, wait, wait, wait. Hold on there. You think I set the fire?" said CJ. His voice cracked at the word *fire*.

"We don't want to believe that," said Kirsten. "But we're afraid that you might have."

"That's ridiculous. You said yourselves that it was probably someone who hated school, and I loved school. You guys know that."

"The other night, *you* were the one who said it was someone who hated school, who was failing or who got suspended a lot. I just agreed with you," said Kirsten.

CJ tossed off a sharp laugh. "Well, yeah. You agreed because that's the only explanation that makes sense."

"You told the police about Daniel drinking near the groundskeeper's shed," said Kirsten.

"Hell, yes, I did! He was there! Other people saw him."

"Yes," I said. "But you were also the one—the only one—who said you'd seen someone who fit Daniel's description running toward the back entrance of the school. And who'd overheard him making threats against the school earlier that night. But he never did either of those things."

"You're taking his word over mine?"

"You were late coming out of the building after halftime. We were well into the third quarter, and all the other marching band members had been out for a while," said Kirsten. "I remember seeing some of them."

"I had to stow my sax," said CJ.

"You always stowed your sax after games, and it never took you that long," said Kirsten.

CJ ran his hands through his hair.

"I can't believe this," he said.

"CJ," I said. "Back then, you were afraid of everything. You'd say it yourself that you were a physical coward, remember?"

"I have a strong sense of self-preservation," said CJ. "So what?"

"You ran into a burning building," I said, softly. "I know you loved your sax, but that was so dangerous. Back then, I was reckless, always plunging in without thinking first, but even I wouldn't have run into a burning building. It never made sense to me that you did."

CJ stopped drumming his fingers. His hands stopped moving entirely, along with the rest of him. And I knew; I knew he'd done it. Perpetual motion CJ never sat still. Not a muscle in his face moved as he stared down at his thin white hands resting on his khaki-covered knees. Kirsten let out a sob.

"You did find out about the fire wall when you were researching your project, didn't you?" I said. "You'd never overlook a detail like that. That's why you could so calmly run back into the school to get your sax. At that point, we weren't even sure where the fire was. We saw the smoke in the sky but not the burning. But you knew exactly where it was and knew that it would never spread to the other end of the school. What you couldn't have known was that the door to the furnace room would get stuck."

"Why would I do that?" said CJ in a thin voice. "If I'd set the fire, why didn't I just bring my sax out with me afterward?"

"I don't know. Maybe in your rush you forgot," I said. "Or you might not have had time."

"Can you look at me, Seege?" said Kirsten, tears on her face. "Please look at me."

Slowly, CJ raised his head, and his eyes met Kirsten's.

"You would never have hurt anyone on purpose," said Kirsten. "We know that. We love you."

CJ's chin began to tremble.

With enormous gentleness Kirsten said, "It's time to tell, honey. If you set that fire, it's time to tell."

Tears filled CJ's blue eyes, and very, very slowly, he nodded.

Kirsten covered her mouth with her hands.

"Oh, CJ," I said. "Why?"

CJ swallowed hard. "Because of Gray."

This answer was so unexpected that for a few seconds, I hardly registered his words. And then, all at once, I thought I understood.

"Because you were mad at the football team? For the way they treated him? Were you trying to disrupt the game?" I said.

CJ shook his head.

"I knew about the fire wall. And I also knew that the door to the furnace room would stick. I knew it would stick because I made it stick," said CJ.

Kirsten and I looked at each other in confusion.

CJ wiped his eyes.

"After Gray told people he was gay, the entire school turned on him. Everyone but us. Since ninth grade, he'd been everyone's hero: smart, star quarterback, nice, pretty girlfriend. They'd feel lucky if he even talked to them. And then, boom, they knocked him off the pedestal and loved doing it. Even the ones who weren't openly mean treated him differently. They stopped looking up to him, would whisper behind his back. And then his coach and his stupid fucking teammates ran him off the team. It was so unfair."

"It was," I said. "It was despicable."

CJ lifted his chin. "So I decided to make him a hero again. I planned it all out. And at the beginning of that week, I started bringing small containers of gasoline to school and hiding them in the basement, the part the maintenance staff never went in. I went to the public library and did research on fire. I didn't want a huge conflagration, just a fire big enough so that people would take notice and be scared. So that the guys who put it out would be heroes."

"Oh," I said. "Oh."

"I knew Gray would be working the night of the game. And I knew that, when I ran away and said I'd be right back and then didn't come back, I knew you two would figure out where I was. And I knew that when Gray found out, he would try to save me. I couldn't be absolutely positive that Gray would be the one to run into the school to find me, but I knew he'd want to. He was always brave. And he could be very persuasive when he wanted something. But at the very least, he'd tell them where to find me, and if I had to, I was ready to play that up afterward, how I could've died if it weren't for Gray. He'd be a hero again; I'd make sure of it. And the people who'd treated him like shit would feel horrible about it."

He smiled. Tears were sliding down his face, but he smiled. "It worked, too, didn't it? Everyone liked him again. I saved him. Good old CJ."

He spat out those last words so bitterly, I ached to hear it.

"Oh, CJ, honey," said Kirsten, crying.

"There was no one in the auditorium. I made sure of it."

He dropped his head into his hands. "I was so arrogant. I thought I was so smart that nothing could go wrong. I had it all figured out. But then the fire, it got so big. And Gray's dad—he just slipped. Lost his footing doing something he'd probably done dozens and dozens of times before. I don't know; I just didn't think of the firefighters getting hurt. The fire was supposed to be small and contained, and they were *firefighters*. Gray's dad was this larger-than-life guy to me. I didn't even consider the possibility that he would get hurt. I thought I was so smart, but how stupid was that?"

"If you'd known," I said, "you wouldn't have done it. You would never have hurt Gray or his father on purpose."

Kirsten got up, sat down next to CJ, and put her arms around him. He toppled sideways into her, and she held on harder.

"Nothing could ever make up for what I'd done. But I tried. I have tried to make it up to him for all these years," said CJ.

"By being his friend," I said.

CJ sat up and leaned back against the cushions of the couch.

"And, Zinny, I didn't set out to hurt Daniel, either. But I'd seen him drinking near the shed, and I heard people who also saw him say he was a bad kid, a trouble-maker. And I just went with it. I spread the rumors and lied to the police. But I knew he wouldn't get in any real trouble because I knew they wouldn't find any proof."

"What can we do?" said Kirsten, bleakly. "Just what are we supposed to do now?"

"What do you think, CJ?" I said.

CJ wasn't crying anymore; he seemed drained of tears, of nervous energy, of everything. He looked at me and said, "I think it's time to tell."

Epilogue

Late June

AVERY

The water is too cold to swim in for long, but it's beautiful: maple syrup–colored at the edges where the marble walls throw down their slanted shadows, shining like glass where the sun hits. Avery sits on the rim of the quarry, a sweatshirt over her swimsuit, and watches petals drift sideways across the dark rock face like snow. Behind her are long tables covered in red-and-white-checked cloth and laid with platters of sandwiches, fried chicken, and slabs of tomato pie; bowls of green salad and potato salad; and round plates bearing deviled eggs arranged in concentric circles like chrysanthemum petals and dusted with paprika. Metal buckets hold bottles of water, beer, and wine, and the grass is spread with quilts. On one of the quilts, Dobbsey and Walt sleep in identical curled-up positions like quotation marks, while Mose stands guard, his fur steeped in sunlight. At the center of it all is a small white party tent. Under the tent is a rocking chair (Gray carried it through the park upside down, with the seat resting on his head) and a bassinet for Gray and Evan's month-old baby, Dahlia.

Technically, the party is part of Kirsten and Tex's wedding week, a kind of pre-rehearsal-dinner picnic for their closest friends. But everyone here is paying homage to Dahlia, no one more than Kirsten herself. They rock her and coo over her and feed her bottles and dance around with her in their arms, whispering to her.

Earlier, Avery had sat in the rocker and watched Dahlia make faces—phantom frowns and smiles—in her sleep and thought how wonderful to be so loved by so many people. She'd thought about her grandmother and wondered if, as Avery had seen Gray and Evan do, she had ever sat spellbound, riveted by her baby's— Avery's mother's or her uncle Trevor's—loveliness or held one of them in her arms with an expression on her face that said, "Never, ever, in the history of the world, has anyone been so lucky." *It's how it should be for babies,* thought Avery, *so much love, love every single second, everywhere they are.*

Avery sits on the soft grass at the edge of the quarry and listens to the sweet tangle of voices and laughter behind her and feels the sun drying her hair, and she understands that in this instance, she is completely happy. Her life isn't perfect (she has not seen or spoken to her father since the Truth and Reconciliation night), but this moment is. She remembers what Zinny had written: *You know those times when the person you are and the person you want to be are exactly—down to your smallest fingernail moon and flimsiest eyelash and your left knee and the part in your hair—the same person?*

Avery does know.

Two days after the Truth and Reconciliation night, Avery and her mother had talked for hours. Her mother had told her how, after Avery's father had gotten fired, she had gone to Adela to ask her to do what she did best: take the story of what her father had done to Cressida and clean it up, make her father look better, kinder, more innocent and then send the new story spinning off into the world of their town. She'd gone to Adela because she had wanted to protect Avery.

"Somehow, I got used to imagining that you are fragile. I underestimated your ability to face the truth; I thought you weren't as strong as you are. I swear I will never, if I live to be a hundred and twenty, do that again."

Adela had wanted to go further, to twist Cressida into someone conniving and cruel, but Avery's mother had told her no.

"Even so," she'd said to Avery, "even though she agreed not to tarnish Cressida's reputation, I knew, deep down, that she could be ruthless. I shouldn't have gone to her at all."

Then, Avery and her mother had talked about reparations; when they finished, the sun was coming up, and, sitting in Avery's window seat, they watched its low light stream through the tree branches and gild the lawn.

Afterward, Avery texted her father: Cressida and her father have suffered because of our family, and we need to try to fix it. I want you to write a letter of apology to Cressida that makes it very clear what you did. Send it to me, and I'll give it to her. Please do this. It's the right thing to do.

Nearly a full day passed before her father wrote back, Okay, I will.

When the letter from her father to Cressida arrived, Avery sent another text, this one to Cressida: After track today, could you please meet me at the coffee shop near my school?

They met, and when Cressida walked across the room to Avery's table, Avery watched people watch her. When she sat, Avery felt everyone's eyes on the two of them, saw people—kids from her school, from other schools, even adults—whisper to one another. It was fine. It was what she'd wanted when she'd asked Cressida to meet. If Avery could've arranged for everyone in town to have been there seeing Avery and Cressida drinking coffee together and talking, she would have.

Avery told Cressida that her father had admitted to everything, even to the phone calls he made after it was all supposed to be over.

"I want you to know that my mom and I are going to do whatever we can to make sure people get the real story. We'll spread new rumors, true ones this time," said Avery.

She gave Cressida her father's letter, which contained an apology that made up for in thoroughness what it lacked in heartfelt eloquence. Her father's letter made his own wrongdoing plain; it left nothing ambiguous. At the end, he said he regretted any harm he had brought to Cressida and her family. After Cressida read it, she folded it back into its envelope and regarded Avery with astonishment.

"You asked him to write this?" she said.

"Yes. I wish he'd thought of it on his own, but at least he did it."

"He admits everything," she said, wonderingly. "Anyone who sees this will know that what happened wasn't my fault."

"That's right," said Avery.

Cressida looked down at the letter in her hands and then at Avery. "What should I do with it?"

"Whatever you want," said Avery. "It's yours."

Gray appears and smiles down at Avery. He's tan in his white shirt, and he holds two cupcakes, one in each hand, and Avery thinks, as she's thought before, that it's no wonder Zinny fell in love with him.

"It's not really time for dessert," he says, "but it made me feel like less of a thief if I also stole one for someone else, so chocolate or coconut?"

"Coconut, please," she says. "Want to sit?"

They sit and eat and talk about the baby.

"The day my mom found out you were naming her Dahlia, we went to the garden store and bought some dahlia bulbs and planted them in our yard," says Avery. "So now when they bloom, we'll bring her some."

"She'll love that," says Gray.

He squints, gazing down at the bright water.

"It's a perfect day, isn't it?" says Avery.

He hesitates before he says, "Yes."

Gray starts to talk about CJ, how strange it is to be in this particular place without him. He says the two of them have hardly spoken to each other since the day CJ told him he was turning himself in to the police for setting the fire.

"Do you think he'll go to prison?"

"I hope not," says Gray. "Kirsten got her dad to hire a big deal defense attorney for him. And my family will ask for leniency. I can't even imagine CJ in prison. I'd hate that. But you know what?"

"What?"

"I can't be his friend right now or maybe ever again, and I feel so bad about that."

Avery's impulse is to jump in and tell him that he shouldn't feel bad, but she knows exactly what he means. So she stays quiet, giving Gray time to say what he needs to say.

"All this time, everyone's assumed that whoever set the fire did it out of anger or hatred. I know CJ did it out of friendship. He was trying to help me. And he was my best friend before it happened and for twenty years after it happened. But it was there, all the time: CJ set the fire that killed my dad. Only one of us knew it, but it was there. And I can't figure out how to forgive him for either of those things: for setting the fire and for letting me go along being his friend without telling me."

"Forgiveness is hard," says Avery.

"I still miss him. I can't believe he's never met Dahlia. I picture him holding her, how completely awkward he'd be, and I miss him. You know what I mean? Do you miss your dad?"

Avery nods. "Even though I am so mad at him. Sometimes, I sit at my dining room table doing homework and just wait for him to walk in. He used to tell me 'math is a bear.' I miss that."

"Lately, I've been thinking about it this way," says Gray. "They love us. And they've done something bad that hurt us. You'd think those facts would cancel each other out, but the crazy thing is that they don't."

"You really think they don't?" asks Avery.

"Not only that, but I'm beginning to believe that the bad might not take anything away from the love. I mean, it's possible, isn't it? They might care about us just exactly as much as we always thought."

Gray and Avery sit side by side at the edge of the party on the edge of a cliff on what feels like the sun-struck edge of the world with the conundrum of love between them and the azure sky overhead and the shining water below.

GINNY

In the grass, in the lilac hour just before nightfall, we are dancing.

Kirsten with Gray. Trevor with Iris. Tex with Kirsten's mother. Evan with Tex's mother. Daniel's daughter, Georgia, with Dobbsey and Walt. My nephews, Sam and Paxton, with the implacable Mose. Dahlia with my lovestruck Avery. Me with Daniel. All of Kirsten and Tex's beloveds and their beloveds' beloveds swaying and twirling. No one's arms are empty.

Because Kirsten and Tex will honeymoon in Paris, the music is French, Edith Piaf singing "La Vie en Rose," wistfulness and vibrato threading through the trees, winding upward, hovering over us like the first stars, the cradle of a quarter moon.

I press my cheek against Daniel's.

"You never know," I say to him, savoring the words. "What might happen next. You never know."

I feel him smile.

"Isn't it wonderful?" he says.

When the song ends, we all stand for a moment in the lucent pool of quiet the music has left behind, holding on, before we let go, and the talking, like a joyful engine, starts up again. Avery hands Dahlia to her fathers, and the baby, tiny planet with her own magic gravity, pulls us in.

Avery's voice shouts, "Mom!"

She is mere outline, a sapling-slender silhouette with her arms wide open. And then I am rushing toward her, stripping down to my swimsuit as I move, shrugging off my cardigan, pulling my dress over my head, laughing, leaving a trail of clothes, like husks, behind me. As she sees me coming toward her, my daughter throws her arms above her head, victorious, and says, "*Yes!*"

We turn our bodies away from the light and noise and the people we love and toward the enormous, held-breath, star-scattered darkness. Afterward, Gray and Daniel will meet us down below, will wrap us in quilts and hand us our shoes and we'll travel back together, up the trail, to where everyone is waiting. But for now, it's just the two of us, balanced on the edge, our arms extended, our fingertips as close as they can be without touching.

"I can't believe we're doing this," I say.

"I can," says Avery.

"Don't look down," I say.

"Never!" says Avery, laughing. "Never, ever."

And we jump.

Acknowledgments

I am grateful to:

Jennifer Carlson, for fifteen years of being my agent, my friend, and my North Star;

Jennifer Brehl, my extraordinary editor and friend, whose keen eyes, ears, and guidance distill and sharpen my storytelling and keep my metaphors from running amok;

the wonderful William Morrow team, especially Andrew DiCecco; Jennifer Hart; Tavia Kowalchuk; Nate Lanman; Andy LeCount, Carla Parker, Mary Beth Thomas, and the entire sales team; Virginia

Stanley and the library marketing team; Pamela Barricklow; Jeanie Lee; Elsie Lyons; Fritz Metsch; and Liate Stehlik;

my friends, who lift me up and make my heart happy and with whom I could (and would and might) talk forever and ever, especially Karen Ballotta, Sherry Brilliant, Mark Caughey, Susan Davis, Taiasha Elmore, Dan Fertel, Susan Finizio, Linda Jaworski, Dawn Manley, Ciara O'Connell, Theresa Proud, and Kristina de los Santos;

Jim and Dawn Manley for allowing me to spend many hours and days writing this book in the tranquility of their beautiful shore house;

my father, Arturo de los Santos, for always, always being there for me, and my mother, Mary de los Santos, whose love surrounds me daily, even though she's gone;

my dogs, Finny and Huxley, who sit on my lap while I write and who are, every single time I walk through the door, more thrilled to see me than anyone has ever been in my entire life;

my kids, Charles and Annabel Teague, in the light of whose wit and heart and gorgeousness I am blessed to live;

and, as always, my love and my home, David Teague, to whom I'd give anything.

About the Author

A *New York Times* bestselling author and award-winning poet with a Ph.D. in literature and creative writing, **Marisa de los Santos** lives in Wilmington, Delaware, with her family.

HARPER LARGE PRINT

We hope you enjoyed reading
our new, comfortable print size and found it
an experience you would like to repeat.

Well – you're in luck!

Harper Large Print offers the finest in
fiction and nonfiction books in this same larger
print size and paperback format. Light and easy to read,
Harper Large Print paperbacks are for the book lovers
who want to see what they are reading without strain.

For a full listing of titles and
new releases to come, please visit our website:
www.hc.com

HARPER LARGE PRINT

SEEING IS BELIEVING!